Praise for *USA Today* bestselling author Nina Bocci's
Hopeless Romantics series

Meet Me on Love Lane

"In the feel-good second installment of Bocci's Hopeless Romantics
series . . . the idyllic setting is vividly rendered and Charlotte's personal growth as she builds a home for herself is handled with com-
passion. Readers will enjoy this sweet, fluffy tale that sits squarely at
the intersection of romance and women's fiction."

—*Publishers Weekly*

On the Corner of Love and Hate

A Goodreads "Most Anticipated Romance Novel of 2019"

*A *Hypable* "Most Anticipated Summer Book Releases
for 2019" Pick*

*A *Bustle* "21 New Rom-Com Novels to Spice Up
Your Summer Reading" Pick*

"Romance at its finest with a colorful cast of characters and a couple
to root for."

—*New York Times* and *USA Today*
bestselling author Sylvain Reynard

"Emma's everywoman appeal lends charm to the story, and her
self-deprecating humor is a plus. This is a fun bit of fluffy enter-
tainment."

—*Publishers Weekly*

"Charming. . . . Bocci puts her characters through an emotional wringer, but balances the pining and misunderstandings with humor and an overall uplifting message about community involvement, family and hope. Readers looking for a feel-good romance set in a diverse, quirky small town will be entranced by *On the Corner of Love and Hate*."

—*Shelf Awareness*

"Plenty of wit and feisty characters. . . . If you're looking for one last summer read, something comfortable and warm to help you settle in and get ready for even cozier reading this fall, you most definitely don't want to miss *On the Corner of Love and Hate,* because it's everything you're looking for . . . and probably a little bit more."

—*Hypable* (4 stars)

"With its picturesque cover and super cute (and clueless) hero and heroine, *On the Corner of Love and Hate* was an absolute joy to read. I can't wait to see what entertaining story Nina Bocci has for her readers next."

—*Harlequin Junkie* (4 stars)

"Nina Bocci is a wonderful storyteller. *On the Corner of Love and Hate* is a delight with a cast of characters that you will adore. Brava."

—*Fresh Fiction*

"Slow-burn romance with great banter and plenty of laughs!"

—*Daily Waffle*

Praise for *Roman Crazy*
With Alice Clayton

"A comedic and deliciously whimsical romp only this pair could deliver. Alice Clayton and Nina Bocci have struck gold."
>   —*New York Times* bestselling author Christina Lauren

"There are books that make you laugh out loud, make you teary, make you hot and bothered, make you smile. And then there are books that make you want to crawl inside them and live within their pages. That's what *Roman Crazy* is."
>   —*New York Times* bestselling author Emma Chase

"I went CRAZY over *Roman Crazy*—this is simply a perfect romance!"
>   —*New York Times* bestselling author Jennifer Probst

"A sexy, steamy slow burn that takes you from the cobbled streets of Rome to the bedroom and everywhere in between. Get your fans out! Five stars of smolder."
>   —*New York Times* bestselling author Helena Hunting

Also by Nina Bocci

THE HOPELESS ROMANTICS SERIES
On the Corner of Love and Hate
Meet Me on Love Lane

WITH ALICE CLAYTON
Roman Crazy

the ingredients *of* you *and* me

a novel

Nina Bocci

GALLERY BOOKS

New York   London   Toronto   Sydney   New Delhi

Gallery Books
An Imprint of Simon & Schuster, Inc.
1230 Avenue of the Americas
New York, NY 10020

First Gallery Books trade paperback edition April 2020

GALLERY BOOKS and colophon are registered trademarks of Simon & Schuster, Inc.

For information about special discounts for bulk purchases, please contact Simon & Schuster Special Sales at 1-866-506-1949 or business@simonandschuster.com.

The Simon & Schuster Speakers Bureau can bring authors to your live event. For more information or to book an event, contact the Simon & Schuster Speakers Bureau at 1-866-248-3049 or visit our website at www.simonspeakers.com.

Interior design by Davina Mock-Maniscalco

Manufactured in the United States of America

10 9 8 7 6 5 4 3 2 1

Library of Congress Cataloging-in-Publication Data

Names: Bocci, Nina, author.
Title: The ingredients of you and me / Nina Bocci.
Description: Gallery Books trade paperback edition. | New York :
   Gallery Books, 2020. | Series: The hopeless romantics series ; v. 3
Identifiers: LCCN 2019047916 (print) | LCCN 2019047917 (ebook) |ISBN
   9781501178894 (paperback.) | ISBN 9781501195945 (ebook)
Subjects: GSAFD: Love stories.
Classification: LCC PS3603.L396 I54 2020 (print) | LCC PS3603.L396 (ebook) |
   DDC 813/.6—dc23
LC record available at https://lccn.loc.gov/2019047917
LC ebook record available at https://lccn.loc.gov/2019047917

ISBN 978-1-5011-7889-4
ISBN 978-1-5011-9594-5 (ebook)

To my real Golden Girls:
Mama G, Zias Suzie, Pauline, Dinah, Clara, and Lillian

the ingredients *of* you *and* me

1

"Coffee is on, bagels are artfully arranged on the platter, cream cheese is chilled, and nerves are shot," I said to the blissfully quiet space. Knocking my knuckles nervously on the marble table-top, I proceeded to do one more walk through the bakery.

In five minutes, the place would be teeming with people. *My* people.

Fifty minutes after that, it would be teeming with more people. *Not* my people.

I should have allowed myself more time to break the news to my longtime staff that things were changing.

Drastically.

It was like many of life's great, unexpected changes. One day you were going through the motions of the day-to-day—albeit a bit stressed because of *work*—and the next you were fielding an offer that would take all the stress and the exhaustion away. The trajectory of my life and those in it was about to change profoundly. And not just because I had a newly beefed-up bank account.

But there was no time for worrying about that now. While I was going through a cluster of emotions, I needed to remain focused on delivering the news to my staff that I had sold my business a month ago. The one that I, quite literally, had poured blood, sweat, and tears into over the last six years.

This was the best possible move for me, and I hoped my employees would be happy for me—after the initial shock, of course.

After all, they still had their jobs if they wanted them. I just didn't have mine, or any clue of what I was going to do next.

Thankfully, just as I was about to futz around with the bagel display one more time, the staff began filing in and I took a second to look over the cards I held in my shaky hands. I decided that five more minutes to go over my notes would help.

"Guys, grab some coffee and breakfast. I'll just be a second," I said, stepping behind the curtain that led to the storeroom to compose myself. The nerves and anxiousness I was experiencing weren't feelings that I was used to. I usually fed off the energy, but this was different. Their lives and livelihoods were in for a major upheaval.

Pulling out my notes, I went through the talking points in a whisper while the staff milled about on the other side of the curtain.

"As you know, Delicious and Vicious isn't any run-of-the-mill bakery in New York. While we aren't winning any awards for being the best in the city—creamiest icing, nuttiest of brownies—we are known for something no one else does. The delish part is easy but with you guys by my side, we've made our bakery into a destination. It's the vicious that sets us apart."

I thought about the vicious part. It really was the reason we stood a head above other bakeries of similar size in the city. We sent any, and I do mean any, sort of message to anyone through our desserts. Need to break up with a boyfriend? Order our "I really hate kissing you" special. Want to quit your job with just the right message to your horrible boss? We'd bake you the "Sorry for your loss" cake along with your two weeks' notice letter. Found out that your husband was cheating? You'd get the "P.S. I was always faking it" or the "I hope it falls off."

"We give vicious a whole new definition." I smiled thinking about that line, knowing that while I once loved that aspect, I'd grown weary of it.

"Everyone knows about Magnolia Bakery and Sprinkles, but people also know about D and V, and that's because of this team. In record time, we have become a staple in the city, and I am so proud of what we've built." My voice wavered, just as I knew it would when I delivered this for real.

"But while this has been a run unlike anything else in my life, in a week, D and V will be transformed into a bigger flagship location under new ownership." I was finally clipping these wings.

By the time I walked out, the staff was already seated. My two head bakers and one part-timer sat on one side of the table I'd set up, and the two decorators sat on the other. The company IT master-slash-order-taker was opposite where I stood.

We were a team of misfits that wouldn't cut it in a traditional bakery. Save for me, no one had formal training, and keeping them all on staff was a part of the contract with the new owners that I wouldn't budge on. They couldn't replace them because of their lack of pastry schooling. But my staff had drive, discipline, and a willingness to start from the ground up and learn. It was risky, but thank goodness it was worth it.

I knew they would appreciate that when I finally gave them the news.

I wondered what about the current structure would remain and who, if anyone, would go. Over the next few weeks, this space, my once hole-in-the-wall boutique bakery that I started as a terrified twenty-five-year-old, would be transformed without me at its helm.

But before I ventured off into the sunset, I had to let my people know. Each one was looking up at me expectantly. All it did was make me that much more nervous. Not nervous about the choice I made—I was proud of the decision to sell—but I was nervous about how they'd take it. At the end of the day, these people were, in essence, my family.

Rolling my shoulders back, I took a deep breath and remembered why I'd sold a piece of my heart in the first place. It was time I put myself first, and the bakery would be better off for it.

"I want to thank you all for coming on a Friday afternoon, especially on such short notice. I know it's the last day of our week-long vacation, but I have an announcement to make and I can't wait until Monday," I began, standing at the corner of the table, keeping my hands folded together.

"We know," someone said, their voice interrupting my thought.

"What?" I said, looking up. They were all smiling and nodding. "You know . . . what?"

"Well, we have an idea," someone else said.

"It's about the Food Network again, right?" my lead baker said, getting up from the table and coming over to stand beside me. "We're excited for you to compete again. We saw the casting information sheet on the bulletin board in your office."

"Oh," I mumbled.

I squeezed her hand. "Okay, yes, I was asked to come back to the *Kitchen Sink* baking competition, but I declined." *Kitchen Sink* was about bakers who created masterpieces with totally random items, and I'd been on it a couple of times already.

The nervous rumblings started, "Why?" being the most re-peated question.

"Declining was easy. They didn't ask me to be a baker this time. The only way they wanted me was if I came on to judge. Perhaps if they wanted me to compete again like the last few times, I would have considered."

A few years back when we weren't sure if D&V would make it, I applied for a show on a dare by my best friend, Charlotte. I entered the Food Network's *Next Best Baker* competition after a lot of back-and-forth about it being the wrong time. It was risky to try out, considering D&V was failing at the time, but the prospect of being on national television and getting the business exposure won out. Of course, I never thought in a million years that with all the appli-cants, they'd choose me. But they did, and it had the exact effect I had hoped for D&V: a windfall of business from around the country. Visitors now trekked to my little corner of Brooklyn to snag a cup-cake, and a photo.

It also gave me a bit of an ego boost. Over the last few years, I went on various types of baking shows on the network, not just be-cause I loved competing but because my business flourished thanks to the appearances and to my frequent wins. Funnily enough, many of the shows were sponsored by The Confectionary, the company that I'd just sold my bakery to.

"Well, that's flattering, right?" someone said from the end of the table. "You being a judge is considered a step up, isn't it?"

I laughed, picking at the smudge of melted chocolate chip that was crusted to my knuckles from the cookies I had made earlier that day. I supposed that it *was* a step up, but it didn't feel that way.

"So, you are going to do it? Be a judge on the next show?"

I shook my head. "After a lot of reflection, I turned them down. It feels a bit like the passing of the torch, if that makes sense. I've been on more than a dozen times. Even *I'm* sick of seeing myself on television. It's about time I give someone else a moment in the spotlight."

"That's awfully magnanimous of you."

"Don't get the martyrdom certificate out yet. I tried to finagle something different out of them, but they didn't go for it."

"What?"

I smiled ruefully. "I was looking to start a new online series to piggyback off of what I already did with the videos we made and posted to YouTube from here. Streaming content on their website and social." The excitement I felt about the prospect was only heightened when I did an informal poll on my own accounts to see what people wanted. Just hearing *more videos* was an ego boost enough, but to have folks requesting specifics from me? Well, that solidified that it was a smart move on my part. People wanted back-to-basics, and I would be scratching the teaching itch I had been actively ignoring for ages. Except . . .

"My hope was that the Food Network would be interested, and they were, but their terms were outrageous. I'd be doing all the work, and they'd be reaping all the benefits from sponsored posts and partnerships, with me only getting a slim percentage."

"Yes, but we would have had a windfall here anyway, right? You would have gone on one of the shows again just to parlay it into more D and V business. Not that we need it," one of my newer bakers said, waving his hand toward the towering stack of order slips on my desk.

My recently devoid-of-all-personal-items desk. If they noticed, they didn't comment.

"So, if you're not going back onto the Food Network, what's the announcement?"

This was it. I took a deep breath and made a mental note to savor the signature D&V scent that I would forever associate with this place: vanilla sweetness with the spice of cinnamon.

"I sold D and V," I blurted awkwardly. Maybe I was vanilla drunk from the heady fragrance, or I was sleep deprived, but I had a plan—and notes—and I just hit a foul ball.

"You what!" the group called in unison.

I sighed and pulled out the last stool at the makeshift conference table.

"Parker? What do you mean you sold D and V?"

"Was business bad? Is that why?"

"What about us? Are we out?"

Folding my hands, I kept them locked together on the cool table, and I stared at my friends' shocked and worried expressions. I had every reason to be proud of this moment, but I couldn't ignore the nervousness.

"No, business wasn't bad. The opposite, in fact. And I'll answer every question you have, but don't be nervous. You're all fine."

"Then, Parker, why?"

I took another deep breath. I owed them an explanation and I was going to be as honest as I could be. "Some of you remember the early days when I started D and V out of my apartment kitchen. Borrowing neighbors' ovens, making homemade double boilers because I couldn't afford the real thing, begging people to let me use their KitchenAid mixers and watch my oven while I ran a delivery to Queens? No one was more nervous than I was that my idea was going to flop. That the format of D and V was nothing more than a gimmick, even though I was still willing to sink everything into it." I saw heads nod.

"My willingness to devote everything to it never wavered, but lately my willingness to put myself first is winning out. Months ago, I got an offer. Not to get all *Godfather*-y on you, but it really was one that I couldn't refuse. I went back and forth over whether or not to take it. And after a lot of thought, and a lot of wine, I decided to sell," I explained.

I hated the look of confusion and sadness on their faces as they grasped the hand of the coworker, the friend, beside them.

"I just don't know what to think," said one of my bakers. "Why didn't you tell us? Confide in us—"

I held up my hand. "Before we go any further, I need you to know something truly important first. While it's great, this isn't about the money."

"What is it about, then?" my decorator asked.

"Time," I said honestly. "For the past six years, I've spent twelve hours a day *here*. Taking orders, baking orders, placing orders, delivering orders. I'm thirty-one and my body feels like it's seventy-one. And that's just what I do in the bakery itself. At home I spend a few hours working on recipes every day, plus uploading videos and interacting on social media. It's been a hamster wheel for me."

"But why sell? Why not just take a vacation or work less? You've got all of us to pull the weight," the woman who ran all things ordering and IT asked. She'd been willing to learn more of the business end of things in the past few months because she saw how burned out I was becoming.

The tears that I had hoped wouldn't come plopped on my hands. "That's a valid point, and that was the first thing I considered. You know I've been taking a few weekends off here and there since the summer. And it's helped. I thought about not selling and just taking a step back instead, turning over the reins just enough that I could seek out other avenues—like going back to teaching classes or even just trying my hand at baking for restaurants part-time—while still being involved with the bakery. But in the end, I needed a solid break. You know I'm not a half-in kind of person. It's all or nothing for me. And if I leaned on you guys more, I didn't want you to feel the exhaustion that I've been feeling. Or worse, for D and V to suffer. This is about keeping D and V the best possible bakery that I can while maintaining my own mental health and yours. All of you guys are the best and will do a fantastic job taking over when I'm gone."

My lead baker held on to one line from my speech. "You wanted to teach again? I thought you hated it?"

I laughed. "I'm sure it seemed that way. Believe me, working on opening the business and getting it off the ground, plus teaching classes on the side on the perfect piecrust, was not ideal, but I needed the cash while I was starting D and V. But remember a couple months back when that bridal party came in wanting to learn how to make a crème brûlée? It sparked something. I forgot just how much I loved instructing. I didn't really consider it as an option because I was always here. If they hadn't asked . . ."

"None of this would have happened."

I shook my head. "No, I think it still would have. This wasn't just a spur-of-the-moment decision. I've been feeling the changes coming on for a while. It's sort of been the perfect storm of reasons all leading toward this moment."

"You'll have more time with your new man."

I smiled. "No comment."

I hadn't explicitly told them that I was seeing someone, but when asked why I was so cheery, I didn't deny it, especially when I'd take time off. We'd had some tense moments where my being busy with D&V caused some waves. But I was sure my newly established free time would remove any barriers from us moving forward in our burgeoning relationship. He didn't know about the sale yet, but I was eager to tell him and see where things led.

My team was quiet for a moment, glancing worriedly at each

other before one of them finally broke the silence with the question that I knew would be coming next.

"What about us?"

I smiled, which seemed to put them slightly at ease. "You're all remaining on, with raises—*if* you want to, of course. The Confectionary has big plans for this place. Contractually, everything operationally stays as-is, which, of course, includes all of you."

"Except the face of D and V will be gone," my lead baker said, wiping away her own tears.

Yes, I had become the face of D&V. And now I couldn't wait to get *me* back.

2

Two Months Later

You've made these nine hundred times, and yet here you are forgetting ingredients, measurements, and— Shit, I forgot to wash out the mixing bowl."

It wasn't just that my KitchenAid mixer held a suspect-looking substance, but the same goop was dripping from the bottom of my white cabinet. When I'd plugged the mixer in, I didn't realize I'd left the switch in the on position. Needless to say, everything went flying up and out of the bowl.

Now chocolate, or something formerly resembling chocolate, was oozing down the side of the cabinet, plopping onto the counter and right onto the paper where I was desperately trying to write down the recipe I'd been creating.

It had been like this all morning; nothing was going right. First, I'd tried to open a bag of chocolate chips with one hand. They sky-rocketed out of the top with such force, I was surprised any of them landed in the double boiler. I'd be finding those in all corners of my apartment for the next month.

Then, I forgot to turn on the oven. I didn't have any pie weights for the pie crust I had attempted earlier, not that it looked much like a crust, so I tried to use cans and ended up boiling a can of corn.

My poor oven would never be the same.

I needed to try something else, something foolproof that I knew I would knock out of the park.

"These brownies are one of the easiest things I make and yet, here I am." Frustrated, I paced the small kitchen. Maybe some movement would help the synapses fire on all cylinders. Hell, I'd be happy with just one cylinder working at this point. I shook out my arms, rolled out my neck.

The joys of being unemployed.

Logically, I knew I could do this. Rote memory wasn't supposed to fail.

It didn't seem to matter, though, because for months my baking skills had been floundering. Even before I sold my bakery, I noticed a distinct shift in prowess. Perhaps I should have stuck to something simple right out of the gate. Like truffles, those were easy as pie. Which was ironic because I was trying to make what was once known as my signature.

"Maybe if I take a nap, I'll dream of the answer," I reasoned, but deep down, I knew from the other three naps I'd taken the past week that a nap wouldn't yield anything but a headache and a crick in my neck.

I still took the nap.

When I woke up an hour later, I didn't feel any better, as predicted, so I decided to make a cappuccino to wake myself up. After I poured the ingredients into my fancy cappuccino machine—at least I could still make coffee—I watched the slow drip of the espresso plop into the mug. It was one that my old roommate Charlotte left when she moved out. It had a Temple University owl logo on it, which at one point had two fancy gold gems for eyes. Those were long gone, just like Charlotte.

She had moved out, moved on, I liked to add. Headed to a little touristy town called Hope Lake, about two hours away from our apartment in Brooklyn in the middle of a currently snowy Pennsylvania valley.

She was born in Hope Lake, living there until third grade or so. She only moved to the city around her tenth birthday. That's when we met, and as dorky as it sounds, we'd been best friends and inseparable ever since.

In the time since she'd left, we set aside Tuesdays as our day to catch up—spending an hour gossiping about her small town, her adorkable boyfriend, Henry, and the group of her childhood friends that I grew to love when I visited.

But two months had passed since I officially sold Delicious & Vicious, and while Charlotte and I exchanged texts here and there, we still hadn't spoken. I kept finding reasons why I couldn't talk—I needed to run an errand or check out a new baking supply store—to actively avoid bringing up my lack of plans or direction. These last two months had been the longest, and potentially the most boring, time of my entire life. Which was saying something because I took an entire semester of linear algebra back in college.

Sitting in the chair in my small office space off the living room, I spun around, arms falling to my sides and eyes trained on the ceiling, until I heard my cell phone buzz, skittering across the desk beside me. Siri announced Charlotte, and I debated for a moment whether or not to ignore it *again*. Letting voicemail pick up had been the answer for the past few weeks, so I figured I might as well let it be the thing to do today. After the phone stopped buzzing, I pushed the voicemail notification to hear what Charlotte had to say.

Her normally cheery voice was nowhere to be found. Instead, she sounded disgruntled. Rightfully so. "Listen, you're screening. Don't deny it. You know that I know that you're screening. I get that you're in a funk and weird headspace right now, but it's been like a hundred thousand hours since we last talked, and this is bull. I need to know that you're okay or I'm going to drive into the city, and I still only have a permit so I'm not sure that's allowed. That's probably jail time or something if I get caught. Call me back or I'm going to keep calling—"

It ended because I assumed she was calling again. But there wasn't another call. Just a *ding ding* that signaled I had a text message. Then a swoosh sound signaling an email. Charlotte was being persistently annoying, but I knew it came from a place of love.

"Okay, okay," I said to the empty apartment with a smile. I pushed her name to call her back. It barely rang once before she picked up.

"This is Charlotte Bishop, how can I help you?" she said with a long, exhausted sigh.

"Hey."

"Hey, yourself," she said, followed by a long solid minute of silence.

Charlotte might have been persistently annoying, but one thing that didn't change was her ability to hold a grudge. She wasn't going to make it easy, but I knew that. Hence, the reason I'd been avoiding the conversation in the first place. When you had a friend who knew all of your faults, your secrets, and your fears, it was hard to admit that you were scared, worried, and lonely without them.

"I'm sorry I've been a shitty friend and haven't called you back." She sighed again.

"It's been a really rough couple of weeks," I added.

"And you didn't think I would want to help you with that? What do best friends do, Parker?"

"I know, I know, honestly I do."

There was silence for a bit and I knew that meant Charlotte was contemplating forgiving me for avoiding her and putting back on her best-friend cape.

She sighed. "Talk to me. What is going on? It's been a while."

I thought about her question for a moment and the problem was I didn't really have an answer for her. "I thought all this free time would be amazing, and yet . . . I don't know. I've gotten into my own head so deep that crawling out seems impossible. Have you ever been there? So twisted up over what's next that you're literally incapable of doing *what's next,* and as a result, ignoring people in your life? I'm a shitty friend."

She grunted. "Stop saying that. You're not a shitty friend. You're going through a life transition and I get that. I just wish you'd let me help you sort it out. You don't have to do anything alone—you know that, right?"

What I wanted to say was *but you're not here,* but that would be selfish. She was the happiest I'd seen her in ages. I wasn't about to fill her in and have her rush to New York because I couldn't get my shit together.

I shifted in my seat, scratching a doodle into the scrap pad on my desk. The word I kept tracing read *bored.*

"I don't know how anyone can help. I'm just so stuck. Uninspired and worried that I won't ever get a burst of creativity again. And the problem is I don't even know what I want to do next. How am I supposed to find a new path if I can't see the forest through the trees?"

"Parker Eulalia Adams, you listen to me. You'll never be too far into the hole to get out because you've got people to throw you the world's longest rope."

"While I appreciate the sentiment—" I began, but Charlotte was on a roll. It's what I knew would happen after avoiding her for weeks.

"Maybe you're a little lost because you're forcing yourself to be creative. You're not letting it happen organically. You think Da Vinci beat himself up if he had a day or two where he wasn't feeling the *Mona Lisa*?"

I laughed. "Number one, I can't believe you used Da Vinci as your example for me, and number two, 'feeling the *Mona Lisa*'?"

"Shut up, I'm tired. All I'm saying is that I get that you're not used to relaxing or having free time, but try and enjoy it! Buy a latte, sit in the park and read the paper. Or visit a museum, take a pottery class. You can literally do whatever you want!"

I threw the pencil across the small room. "I'm trying!"

She laughed. "You need a creative outlet. Something that sparks that fire in you. Something that inspires you to say *holy shit* and run back to the kitchen to make a masterpiece. Going back and doing what you love is the answer."

I snorted. "Baking is what I love; I can't seem to do it anymore. It's like I'm you now. I'm broken in the kitchen."

Charlotte switched the call from audio to FaceTime and I was greeted by her lovely, freckled, and frowning face. Her reddish hair was pulled into Princess Leia–style buns and she had a daisy sticking out of the top of one of them.

"I resent that remark." She laughed, and I forgot how much I missed having her around all the time. "You'll never be as bad as me in the kitchen," she continued. "My lack of skills is a once-in-a-lifetime gift and I'm not sharing it.

"Look at you, you're covered in flour. And oh, Parker, is that egg on your face? I can tell that you're working," she said with a pinched expression. She was trying not to judge my wayward appearance. Rolling my shoulders back, I wiped at the smudge of flour that I knew was across my cheek. "I'm digging the bandana, by the way, very farmer friendly."

I gave her the finger and touched my red bandana, which was holding back my long blond hair. "I ran out of hair ties. This worked, and I promise I didn't look quite so shabby pre–baking disaster."

"Enough about how gorgeous you still look even with egg, literally, on your face. What have you baked that failed? I don't believe it. I once saw you create a trifle out of leftovers and people offered to buy it."

The comment gave me a little pick-me-up. My ego needed that bit of a nudge. Actually, my ego needed a swift kick in the ass, but I wasn't complaining about any amount of boost. Pushing off of the chair, I walked into the kitchen, turning the phone toward the trash so she had a bird's-eye view. In the bag were a dozen supposed-to-be chocolate-coffee cupcakes, a dozen chocolate chip cookies, and a couple cinnamon scones that could have doubled as bricks in a fireplace if I needed them. "See those?"

"Are you practicing for Henry's birthday cupcakes?" she asked, trying to lighten my sour mood. "You know we'll eat anything you bake for him, even if it requires a visit to the dentist afterward."

"Thanks for the vote of confidence, but he can't eat these. It's all so bad." I reached into the trash and took out the scone that was on top. Holding it like a softball, I rapped it on the edge of the counter. It made the most glorious *thud*.

"Still want to eat this? I'm not paying your bill from the oral surgeon afterward. You'll need it."

As I turned the phone back toward me, my stomach dipped. Charlotte looked worried. Her gray eyes were missing their usual light and she wasn't smiling, like she almost always was.

"Parks, what's up? Really? This is so unlike you?"

I shrugged. "The last, I don't know, *dozen* things I've made have been awful. Like, Charlotte-awful, no offense."

She shrugged. "None taken. You'll remember I once burned water, and I'm not sure any of your failures beats that. The FDNY hasn't been to the apartment yet, right?"

I laughed. "Nope."

"Good, then there is still hope. Is there something I can do to help? To kick the mojo back into you? What about your idea to start the baking classes? Did you decide against it?"

Did I?

I shrugged. "I can't exactly teach someone how to bake when I seem to be incapable myself."

"Valid point. Then what's next?"

I shook my head, keeping my eyes trained on the swirls in the floor. "I mean I have no idea. I'm stuck."

"When I get overwhelmed, which is often, you know that, I go back to basics. You've been doing some wild and crazy recipes for years now. Maybe you need to Betty Crocker it up. Make basic things that even I could swing. Like, I don't know, pound cake. Is that still a thing?" We both laughed. Even the most pedestrian recipe was out of reach for her. Thank goodness Henry was a great cook, or she would survive only on Pop-Tarts and packaged crackers.

"I've tried almost everything, Char, and I still can't bake anything worth eating," I answered with honesty.

"Okay" was all she said. But by the look on her face I could tell she was trying not to look concerned. Crap, now I was bringing her down.

"Speaking of Henry's birthday," I said, trying to change the subject, "any plans? Anything romantic and exciting?"

Her face lit up. "Nothing crazy, just dinner. Maybe . . ." she started, chewing on her pencil. "You can come? I mean, you don't have much going on."

I threw my head back, laughing. "Wow, harsh much?"

"Am I wrong?" she deadpanned.

"No, but you're right, and subtlety has never been your strong suit."

She waved at the stack of yellow order slips beside her workstation and then at the calendar that hung on the wall. It was color coded and positively filled with scribbles. "As you can see, I don't have much time for subtle these days."

"That's why I love you." I looked around the office she was in. "Busy tonight?"

She wiped her forehead dramatically. "So busy, but it's good. I'm still gathering all the paperwork that I need to get the loan, but Lucille says that everything is looking good and I should be the proud owner of Late Bloomers by summer."

Seeing her face light up at the mention of owning her own floral shop lit me up inside. Charlotte had been so lost for so long and she had finally found true happiness. If I didn't love her so much, I'd be rolling in jealousy. We couldn't be in more opposite positions.

"C, that's amazing. I'm so proud of you. Here you are in the process of getting your own business—your dream business—and I just sold mine."

Just as easily as her face lit up, all that happiness evaporated at my words. "Parks, I'm sorry, that was so insensitive of me. I—"

I cut her off with a wave of my hand. "Stop it. You have every right to be over the moon about buying Late Bloomers. And I know selling D and V was the right decision. I was beginning to feel morally bankrupt with all the divorce and cheating cakes. I still have no idea how they're going to franchise it, but—"

"It isn't your problem now, sister!" she teased, and she was right. It wasn't my problem.

"Have you been good otherwise, though? Shop's good? Friends are good?" I asked, trying not to sound like I was fishing for information.

"The business has been a godsend in terms of dealing with this weather. If I was home, I think I'd lose my mind. I've never seen so much snow and there's nowhere to put it!"

"It's only January, honey. You've got at least two more months of it," I explained, laughing when Charlotte pretended to tug at her hair in frustration. "Where's your delightful professor? Out shoveling?"

Charlotte was dating her childhood BFF, Henry, after reconnecting when she arrived back in Hope Lake last year. It was incredible to see the change in her from being back in her hometown, especially because she fought the relocation tooth and nail.

She smiled, looking dreamily at a framed photo on the corner of her workstation. It was from the Fourth of July last year, when I'd surprised her with a quick visit. Well, sort of quick. The photo included me, Charlotte, Henry, her friends Emma and Cooper, and their friend Nick. I bit back my grin at the sight of Nick.

Something clattered onto the worktable near Charlotte's hand. "Damn it, I'm so clumsy lately. Anyway, where was I? Oh, Henry is back at school after Christmas break, which was lovely because we both got a small reprieve over the holidays. I wish you could have seen this place for Christmas. It looked like a Hallmark movie."

"Too bad I missed it," I said, twirling a pencil between my fingers.

"You should come visit Hope Lake. It's Henry's birthday, plus you miss me, and who knows, maybe a change of scenery will help kick you in the ass a bit."

"That's not a bad idea," I said, and surprisingly, I realized I felt excited about the prospect.

"You can actually veg out, take a break for a minute. I think you deserve some free time." Charlotte winked, knowing damn well I was free *all the time* now.

"Again, I say to you, subtlety is an art you have not mastered."

Charlotte, suddenly serious, faced the phone head-on. She E.T.'d the phone, pushing her index finger onto the screen. I responded by placing mine against hers, causing the image to wobble a moment. "I miss your stupid face. Come visit."

"Well, with an offer like that, how can a girl refuse?"

"I'm serious, Parker. I know you; you're floundering."

"What's the phrase? My new normal? I'm trying to figure out exactly what that is. I spent years building D and V and now it's gone. I mean, I'm glad it is because I was a zombie all the time, but what do I do now? Who am I without it?"

She sighed, and I was pretty sure if we were face-to-face and not screen-to-screen that she would have pulled me into one of her crippling hugs. "Delicious and Vicious was a part of you, but it's not all you are. Selling it was the best decision you made. You saw me last year when I was having a hard time. You didn't let me give up, and I'm not going to let you either. Come visit. Recharge your batteries and enjoy this godforsaken snow," she suggested as I plodded toward my small office area.

"How's the sledding in Hope Lake?" I asked, jumping up from

the chair to skid into my room. It was now or never. If I faltered in the plan, I knew I'd back out. I grabbed a suitcase and began tossing essentials inside. What I didn't bring, I could buy there.

"The best." She glanced at her watch. "If you catch the three o'clock bus, you'll get here in time for dinner."

"I hope you're not cooking," I joked before hitting the red button.

3

"Nice to see you again, Parker," the bus driver said, waving to me. I had just disembarked the bus into Mount Hazel, a town neighboring Hope Lake.

Charlotte, as promised, was waiting at the stop and came careening over, sliding the last few inches thanks to an icy patch. "What did the driver mean, 'see you again'?"

I coughed, delaying my answer. "Oh, you know. Last time I was here. I must have a face to remember."

The lie rolled off of my tongue so effortlessly, I was ashamed of myself. Charlotte, my very best friend in the world, didn't know how many times I had ridden the midnight bus to Mount Hazel, the next town over from Hope Lake.

Charlotte didn't bat an eyelash at the lie. "You're here!" she yelled, pulling me into a tight hug. "Weather is a bit different from last time."

Uh . . . She wasn't wrong, but she wasn't right either. Eventually, Charlotte and I were going to have to discuss the number of times I'd been to Mount Hazel and why I didn't let her know about all the visits—or who picked me up to drive me to Hope Lake. And whom I was visiting.

"Oh my God. You weren't kidding when you said you got a lot of snow here," I said, changing the subject as we trudged through at least eight inches of fresh powder to get to Henry's Jeep, which sat at the very edge of the parking lot.

"This is just from today?"

She nodded, hooking her arm in mine to help us steady each other.

Everything was covered. That wasn't an exaggeration either. The thinnest branches on the tallest trees had a crystal layer of ice and snow. Mounds were plowed off of the streets and wedged along the sidewalks. Besides the snow giving everything a glistening sparkle, the town looked exactly how I remembered it. "It looks like a goddamn storybook."

I let go of Charlotte's arm. "If I throw myself into a pile of snow and make angels, will you pretend like you don't know me?"

Henry, who had been busy helping an elderly woman with her luggage, joined us, laughing when he heard me. He slung his arm over her shoulders as he pulled my wheeled suitcase behind him. "I think you should do it."

"Henry, don't encourage her, she will."

I slapped her arm. "I can't wait to see Gigi. Your text from earlier said we're getting together tonight?"

"Yes, some of us are having birthday cupcakes for this guy," she explained, resting her head on Henry's shoulder.

My stomach did a flip. "Some of us?"

Charlotte nodded. "Yeah. Henry, me and you, Emma and Cooper, Gigi's crew, and Mancini. Don't leave out that crazy old bird."

Out of nowhere, a stout woman with gravity-defying and cosmetically altered jet-black hair popped up from behind Henry's Jeep. She was wearing a beaming smile and a Kelly green tracksuit. "You summoned me?"

The three of us jumped back, me nearly collapsing into the snow pile behind me. She literally appeared as if conjured up from the depths below. Even Henry was startled as he let out the daintiest peep at the sight of her looming by the bumper.

"Mrs. Mancini!" Charlotte sang, going over to the woman and giving her a quick kiss on her plump cheek. "I didn't see you there."

"Of course you didn't, darling. You were too busy with your Henry to notice me eavesdropping," she explained, not seeming the least bit put off that she was listening in. "I'm happy to see you again, Parker. What brings you back to Hope Lake this time?" Mancini was fighting back a grin, and thankfully, Charlotte and Henry didn't pick up on her innuendo. The last time I saw Mancini, it was under much different circumstances, and it looked like she wasn't going to go easy on me. Mancini was another one of Gigi's cohorts, and the woman was a gem. Though I'd only met her twice, I found her delightful.

Mancini appraised me in that motherly, or rather, grandmotherly way. Starting from the top of my head, where she was probably determining that the blond was *too blond* compared with my usual light brown shade. Which was funny, considering her coloring was anything but natural looking. I didn't have any makeup on because I was traveling, but I knew that without mascara I looked more tired than usual with my thin blond lashes. My shirt was wrinkled, and my jeans had a permanent stain on the knee from an accident when I was dyeing fondant for a specialty divorce cake. Overall, though, she gave me a once-over as if she approved.

I rolled my shoulders back and stuffed my hands into my cold pockets. I'd need a warmer coat while I was here. Mancini gazed on expectantly, reminding me of her question. What *exactly* was I doing here?

The first thing that came to mind was the truth, and it tumbled out. "Charlotte suggested I come stay here while I figure out what Parker Phase Two is, and I jumped on it."

Mrs. Mancini smiled. "I like that, Parker Phase Two. I wonder if I can have a new phase for me. Something like Phase Eighty-two but acts Twenty-eight," she said with a titter.

I bit back another grin. What a piece of work. I could tell that Charlotte and Henry loved her as well. She was the type of woman who would give you the absolute honesty that you needed to get your life together.

Her cell phone suddenly rang in her pocket, an unexpected Pit-bull ringtone—one that you'd typically hear on a Pandora dance station and not an eightysomething's cell phone—blasting out.

"Oh, that's Gigi. Stay put, I have lots of questions."

"So do I," I deadpanned, looking to Charlotte and Henry, but Charlotte was also looking at her phone.

"Hey, I hate to do this, but my assistant, Nellie, had an emergency at the shop. She sliced her finger pretty badly. I'm going to have to have Henry take her to my dad for stitches, so I need to go man the shop."

"No problem, give the good doctor my best. I'll see him soon," I said. Charlotte's father ran the small doctor's office in town.

"I'm sorry I have to run after you just got here. Can I get you an Uber?"

"You mean *the* Uber?" I asked, teasing because there was only one of the ride-share cars in town. On more than one occasion in the past, I'd needed to use him to venture back to the bus.

"No, *an* Uber. We've got more than one, you know."

Henry stepped in. "Well, two, but only one has four-wheel drive for all the snow."

Mrs. Mancini came back over just as Charlotte was pulling up the Uber app. "You'll do no such thing," Mrs. Mancini said, pushing the phone down gently. "I'll drive her where she needs to go. We have loads to catch up on."

"Are you sure? You look awfully busy," Henry interrupted. He looked toward Charlotte with wide, worried eyes.

Mrs. Mancini gave him a look. "I'm never too busy for an old friend. Where are you staying, dear? I have lots of rooms, you know. You're more than welcome to stay in my humble abode."

"I've seen your house, Mrs. Mancini, and there's nothing humble about it. It's why I like it," I said honestly. She lived on the outskirts of town next door to where Charlotte's grandmother Gigi lived. Their houses couldn't be more different. One was a bright explosion of color and whimsy and the other was modest and traditional. Both were Victorian-style treasures.

"Go big or stay home, that's my motto." She winked. "Seriously, though, you two skitter off and I'll take care of Parker here. Not to worry. I think for now she needs a snack. You look peckish."

As if on cue, my stomach growled. "You're not wrong."

Henry, still looking nervous, pulled me in for a hug. "She drives like a lunatic when there's no snow . . ." he warned as he passed me to my best friend.

Charlotte stifled a laugh at his admission. "She's from New York. Nothing will faze her," she said, giving me a hug before she and Henry walked away hand in hand.

"I tell you what," Mrs. Mancini said, pulling me toward her. "I have a lasagna ready at home and fixings for a salad right here." She tapped the reusable shopping bag hooked on her arm. "Oh, and wine."

"Sold!" I exclaimed. "Where's your car?"

She pointed to the end of the road where a cherry-red Hummer was parked. "You're kidding, right?" I asked, but she didn't respond with anything other than a beaming smile. "Mrs. Mancini, you're my idol."

She preened, pursing her lips and lifting her eyes up. "You call me Suzanne, or just Mancini. That's what my lady friends call me. Now, you didn't answer me before. Where are you staying?"

I wheeled my suitcase behind me as I followed her down the street. The sidewalks weren't totally shoveled yet, so I walked a bit closer to her than normal in case she slipped. "I'm renting an Airbnb by the lake since I don't know how long I'm staying for, and I need access to a full kitchen."

"How did you swing an open-ended rental at the lake, of all places? That's like a golden ticket!"

I shrugged. "I emailed through the site outlining what I was looking for. I guess this place isn't too busy during the winter months, so the owners jumped on it."

The place had looked perfect online. I hoped that it wasn't some sort of scam because the rental price was dirt cheap. Of course, it was off-season, but still. Lake house, chef's kitchen, five bedrooms and I don't know how many bathrooms? It was absurd in size for one person, but how could I pass up a chance at that kitchen?

"So, you could stay for a week, or you could stay for five months," she said, handing me the bag of groceries and pushing the unlock button on her key fob.

I laughed at the idea of staying five months here. "Hold your horses, Mancini. Let's see if I can get through the week." I put her bag into the backseat along with my suitcase and duffel.

Mancini readied herself, bending slightly a few times as if

stretching out her already stretchy track pants. She was on the lowest end of five feet and I had no idea if I had to give her a boost into the truck or if she crawled in like a kid into a tree house. Just as I was about to push her, she tapped a button on the inside of the doorframe and the running board lowered. She saw my impressed expression. "If you think that's cool, hold on a second."

She stood on the running board and pushed the button again. It raised her up until she was at the perfect height to slide inside. Once off, she tapped it again and it disappeared underneath the doorframe of the car.

Before I closed the door, I smiled. "Like I said, idol."

* * *

Mancini drove at a leisurely pace through town, which was unexpected considering Henry's warning of a NASCAR experience. I got the feeling that if I wasn't in the car with her, or new to town, she wouldn't be explaining every little thing we passed by. "That's the ice-cream shop, and Henry's bookstore is that way. You know the flower shop, of course, and that's the drugstore over there. I know you know where that is," she said with a haphazard wave. The smile on her face let me know that she remembered seeing me, in that very store, just a few months back. "Now, they don't have the good weed here, just the medicinal kind. Though we're hoping Clare signs the bill for Pennsylvania to go the weed route. It'd be helpful for a lot of reasons," she said, adding a saucy wink.

"I hope Clare comes through for you," I said awkwardly, because really, how do you respond to an eightysomething who's hoping to get stoned? "By the way, who is Clare?"

She turned down another random street. "Clare? Oh, wait. I forgot you're not from here. Clare Campbell. Cooper's mother is the governor."

"Oh, I think I did know that," I said, remembering that Charlotte's other childhood friend Cooper was the town's mayor. Politics must run in that family. I yawned, glancing at my phone.

"The lake is that way?" I pointed to a sign that said HLBC for Hope Lake Brewing Company, a bar that I knew was on the lake and conveniently right down the road from my new lake house.

"Yes, I know you know where the lake is," she said, another wry grin on her cheery face.

"Okay, let's get this out of the way," I said, turning toward her. "I know that you know that I was here a lot more than I let on to my best friend."

"Parker, you can put the worry out of your pretty little head. I'll never tell your secrets to Charlotte. Now, you *should* confess, but I'm not going to be the one that lets her or that crew of besties know that you were in flagrante with the only single banana in the bunch."

I barked a laugh. "Thank you for the honesty, and for the secret-keeping. I will tell her about me and, well, everything that happened, soon. I'm just waiting to see him first."

She sighed. "In a town this size, Parker, it'll be sooner than you think."

4

Perhaps it was the years of little sleep catching up to me, or the fact that Mancini's Hummer coursed over the snow-covered streets with ease, but I soon dozed off during the short drive through the small town.

When I woke, I was outside her house—a sprawling multicolored Victorian that sat on the edge of a dead-end road. Surrounding me was an expanse of snow as far as the eye could see. To my right was a mountainside that looked like it would provide killer skiing, and Gigi's house stood sentry right next door.

Where Gigi's was a classic white Victorian, Mancini's was its nutty twin bursting with color. Speak of the devil, Mancini was on the porch and ready to descend the still-snowy stairs. I jumped out of the SUV and got to her just before she went down on an icy patch. "Whoa there, I got you."

She smiled but quickly turned serious. "Always save the lasagna first," she instructed, pushing the deep glass dish toward me. "Then me. I've got padding; the Pyrex doesn't."

"Sure," I insisted, helping her to the car. "Where are we going now?"

"Pit stop. It'll be quick."

Once inside the Hummer, Mancini made sure the lasagna was in a safe spot in the backseat. And by safe spot, I mean that she pulled a built-in car seat down from the backseat and secured the lasagna with a seat belt meant for a toddler.

She really was a character.

Mancini backed out of the driveway and pulled into Gigi's, which was *literally* next door. It was curious, though, because I knew Gigi couldn't drive, yet her place was packed with cars. Large, expensive cars.

"We could have walked." I laughed, but Mancini pointed to the deep snow between the yards.

"Parker," she said in a simpering tone that I imagined was how she sounded when any person crossed over to her bad side. "You're wearing Converses and I'm pretty sure you're not wearing socks. You'll be sick the entire time you're here if you don't make good decisions."

Make good decisions. If that wasn't a mantra for me to remember the entire time I was here, I didn't know what was.

My lips curled together in an effort to stop myself from laughing. My grandparents died before I was born, but I wagered this was what they would have sounded like. "Okay, I'll add boots to my list of stuff I have to get."

Mancini nodded and raised her hand. One by one she ticked off on her fingers, "Boots, a warmer coat—preferably one with a waterproof outer shell—a hat with earflaps, gloves, and jeans that aren't strewn with holes, please and thank you. Also, remind me to give you a warm quilt. I doubt those fancy Air Bob's have anything suitable."

"They're not called Airb— I mean they're called Airbn— You know, never mind. Thanks, Mancini. I'll be sure to remind you."

In my head, I was wondering why I was doing this to myself. It was my first day in town, and I was spending it with an eightysomething. But when she looked at me with her big brown eyes, my smile got a bit wider. I was close with my parents, but they'd traveled a lot since retirement, and with my former crazy schedule at the bakery, I didn't see them often. Being cared about by someone who barely knew me was comforting and in an odd way, I was genuinely grateful.

"Promise?"

I smiled. "Yes, I promise."

We climbed up the wide, well-shoveled steps, and I wondered who did them for Gigi. Unless she had some sort of plow rigged up to her motorized wheelchair, which wouldn't surprise me.

When we arrived at the front door, I heard voices carrying outside. It sounded like dozens of people yammering.

"What's going on here? Are we interrupting something?" I asked, hoping that we weren't crashing a party.

"Not at all. Something much better," she said, pushing the door open without a knock. "You've got front seats to the hottest ticket in town!"

"You guys got a run of *Hamilton* here?"

She bumped her hip into mine as she crossed the threshold. Lin-Manuel Miranda wasn't inside, but Gigi was speeding toward me, a wide, beaming smile on her face.

Behind her, a dozen or so card-carrying members of AARP were looking at me expectantly. I lightly elbowed Mancini, who, like Gigi, was smiling.

"Hi, everyone," I said nervously.

"Welcome to the Hope Lake Senior Citizens' Club."

Just exactly how old do I look? That's what I wanted to ask. I didn't of course because, *rude*. They were seniors, but they were also perfectly lovely.

Gigi's house was apparently the meeting spot for the group.

"This seems like the social event of the week. What am I so rudely interrupting?"

"Never an interruption. We're happy to have you here!" Gigi said, taking my hand gently. "Twice a month, or more, if we're feeling saucy, we get together to hobnob, kvetch, and organize whatever activities we want to."

I smiled. "Wow. It seems like you guys run Hope Lake."

"We do. Just don't tell Cooper," Mancini said, referring to the town's mayor.

I laughed as we walked into the next room. In Gigi's traditionally styled dining room, the club members gathered at a table that was generous enough to fit more than a dozen busybodies with room to spare. The table wasn't set for dinner per se, but there were plates stacked at one end, a pile of colorful napkins with snowflakes on them, and a runner down the center, where a profound amount of food sat atop it looking and smelling delicious. My stomach growled in delight.

Mancini was walking to the kitchen with the lasagna in her hands, talking to a woman, when she tossed over her shoulder, "I'm going to throw this into the oven to warm up, but make yourself at home, Parker."

"Mancini," I called, but she was already out of earshot. I thought this was just going to be a quick pit stop. Looks like *pit stop* was code for dinner party courtesy of the seniors of Hope Lake.

"Can I get you something to drink, dear?" a thin, diminutive woman asked. She had a severe black bob and winged eyeliner that made Adele's look amateur.

"Uh, sure. Water is fine." I smiled and waited for her to walk away. But she stayed next to me, looking on expectantly as if I'd never answered.

"Hello?" I asked, touching her arm gently.

"Oh, you're serious. Silly me. I didn't expect anyone to ask for water. I'll ask Gigi if she has any," she said, turning to walk away, but I stopped her.

"No, it's okay. I'll take whatever is handy," I insisted, looking around for a station set up with drinks.

Sure enough, a wheeled bar cart with brass fixtures and a glass top filled with liquor bottles sat in the far corner of the expansive dining room. "Holy shit, you guys are getting lit?"

The woman laughed. "We're having a drink, if that's what that means. We have the usuals: manhattans, highballs, amaretto sours, gin and tonics. The normal fare."

Normal? What year was it? But it made sense. These ladies weren't thirty-year-olds drinking IPAs and craft beers. They probably had whiskey and bourbon when they were my age. If I drank that, I'd burn up from the inside out.

"Tonic water with a lime is fine with me. In case I have to drive Mancini home," I teased, figuring anyone could back the SUV out and over a hundred feet.

She gave me the slightest eye roll and ventured off to the cart.

Under the window was another table full of food, and this spread was nothing to sneeze at either. Though this was my first senior citizens' club meeting, I had to wager that they didn't do anything small.

On the main table was a bowl that was piled high with meatballs, pasta in a separate chafing dish, the massive salad that

Mancini had brought, a partially sliced ham, scalloped potatoes, green beans, and what looked like a full assortment of desserts.

When Mancini returned from the kitchen, she carried the piping-hot lasagna with her pot-holder-covered hands, and she had a bright smile.

"Ladies, let's dig in!" she exclaimed, setting her contribution on the only empty space on the sideboard.

I took a seat at the main table, sitting next to Mancini and the woman who'd brought over my tonic water. She didn't sneer at it, but she was definitely judging me for not adding any gin. "Thanks," I said as I took a sip. "I'm Parker."

"Lillian," she said, holding out her delicate hand for me to shake. She wore a massive ring on each of her ten fingers. Emeralds, rubies, sapphires, and a diamond so large that it could probably be seen from space glittered as she signaled around the room.

"Packed house tonight," I said, trying to engage her in conversation.

She snorted. "We're missing a handful. Usually we've got thirty at this meeting, but some of the girls don't like to come out in this damn weather, even with the rides to and from."

"I could understand that, I guess. I feel bad they're missing all the food!" I quipped, earning a laugh.

"Again, this is nothing. When we have the full group, it's an embarrassing amount of riches."

I had a feeling I would be accidentally-on-purpose stopping in when they had another meeting just to see the spread.

"Allow me to introduce you to who *did* brave the snow to be here tonight. This is Pauline," Lillian said, pointing to a woman who was astonishingly pale. Her head was wrapped in a brilliantly colored scarf.

Pauline extended a thin, bony hand. "Cancer. It sucks, don't get it," she said by way of greeting. When she smiled, her eyes glittered. While her body might have been sick, her spirit clearly wasn't.

"Nice to meet you," I said, tucking into the plate of food that was handed to me. While I was hungry, I wasn't a big stuff-my-face kind of girl. They didn't seem to know that, though, because as soon as my plate was emptied, I was having another scoop of something added. If I looked away, it just appeared.

"Parker, do you want another piece of bread?"

"Parker, we know you're a famous baker, but we have cake, ice cream, cookies, pound cake, torte, cupcakes, a stollen, and I think Sadie made a Baked Alaska."

"That's it?" I teased. "I can feel the diabetes forming." I laughed when my glass was filled without me seeing the culprit. Thank God I wasn't drinking, or I would be taking the Uber or staggering home.

Another plate appeared in front of me, dropped off by a stealthy dessert fairy. On it was a sampling of what everyone had brought. "You guys really do have meetings, right?"

"Oh, hush. We always put out a spread for our meetings. You're a pastry chef, right?" Pauline asked.

"You must love to sample your own creations. I do the same. It's a perk of the job," the owner of the ice-cream shop said. She told me her name was Viola. Her hair was violet colored and spun up into a design that resembled cotton candy.

Between their names, ages, occupations, and if they were single and looking to mingle or still happily married, I was having a hard time keeping them all straight. Whether self-proclaimed or appointed, Mancini and Gigi were clearly the ringleaders, as they took charge leading the conversations. Even though the ladies had a meeting to get to, it seemed the focus of said meeting was me.

"Parker, Charlotte tells us that you are famous. It's not for one of those sex tapes, right?" a woman in the corner said, waving a finger at me. "I hear they're the new thing for you young people."

I choked on my drink, spitting a little of it onto my shirt. "Oh my God, no. Nothing like that. I was on a couple shows on the Food Network, and I was pretty popular on YouTube too."

"I saw your show," Clara said, slipping another cookie onto my plate as if I wouldn't realize it had appeared. "I was glad you beat that irritating guy you were running against. He was so pompous and didn't come close to having the skill or talent to justify the ego. I wanted to stick him in the oven."

"You and me both," I said, earning a laugh. "It was a great experience. One I'm grateful I had."

When the doorbell rang suddenly, the group grew giddy and eager. As the light *ding-dong* echoed throughout the house, I felt a sudden wave of nerves. "I'll get it," I offered, jumping up before anyone else could even set their napkins down. The reprieve from heading down memory lane was needed. I wasn't averse to sharing my life story, but it also felt like a lot to dump on people the first time I was meeting most of them.

At the door stood a smiling Henry and a harried-looking Charlotte holding a box of lopsided cupcakes. "I shouldn't have even tried, but I promised we would bring dessert."

Henry laughed. "They're perfect. They'll love it." He grinned before dropping a quick kiss on the top of Charlotte's head. As they stepped inside the foyer and the ladies started welcoming them, I noticed another couple climbing the stairs. It was Emma Peroni, Charlotte's childhood best friend, and her fiancé, Cooper Endicott, the mayor of the town. Emma was partially responsible for Charlotte leaving New York and staying in Hope Lake.

Emma was trying—in vain—to rub off the lipstick that was

smeared across her cheek. As she held the mirror up to her face, she sighed at the sight of the vibrant red stripe.

"See," she said, elbowing the guy beside her, "I told you she'd still be here." Then, "Parker!" she shouted. "Forgive my appearance, this one was handsy." Emma pointed to Cooper, who was clearly proud of the fact that he was responsible for the makeup predicament.

"I lost a bet. I said you would have been long gone by now, but it seems Emma was right. It's so good to see you again, Parker," Cooper said, reaching out to shake my hand.

"Ugh, so formal." Emma laughed, pulling me in for an awkward hug.

"I was so happy when Charlotte told us you were coming to visit! I hope it's longer than your visit last summer," Emma continued, pulling Cooper inside the foyer. "And I knew you'd be here because the ladies never let anyone leave before dinner!"

I laughed. "You're right. I couldn't turn down the food. I will say you guys sure know how to welcome a girl to town," I said, and waited on the porch for a beat until I realized that no one else would be making an appearance.

The group was still just inside the door. No one had gone back to sit at the table. I couldn't stay out here waiting much longer without it looking suspicious.

Mancini stepped outside, hands outstretched for the cake. "Just so you know, he had something else going on tonight."

I managed a small smile. One that I hoped would convey that it was no big deal even though it was—at least to me. "Oh, I'm not waiting for anyone. I wasn't . . . I mean," I began, but Mancini's face told me that no matter what lie I tried to float, she wasn't buying it. "I'll be right in."

She turned and closed the door just a bit. Enough to give me privacy to get composed, and to decide if I was disappointed or relieved that I wouldn't be running into my former flame tonight. I wrapped my arms around myself, bracing from the biting wind that whipped through the porch.

When I finally joined the rest of the meeting, I was decidedly grateful that I didn't have to see Nick Arthur. At least not yet. Not after how we ended things. Or more accurately, how we *didn't* end things.

At the table, I was pulled into another dozen conversations at once. Maybe it was a good thing so many people were here. I would only have to explain my sudden visit to Hope Lake once, especially because all the people here would disseminate my story through town.

As if hearing my thoughts, Pauline cleared her throat loudly. "Tell us about the reason for this vacation to Hope Lake, Parker," she said, subtly adjusting her scarf.

I shifted on the padded dining room chair. In what looked like a practiced move, the seniors and my friends each turned one by one until they were all facing me. Even Charlotte, who for all intents and purposes already knew the story. Everyone looked at me expectantly, and I never felt more like I was under a microscope than I did then. Which was saying something, considering I'd been on reality television.

"Well, I guess it's easier to start from the beginning," I said, watching the seniors' eyes widen excitedly. I was beginning to think their group was more about gossip than it was about, well, whatever older ladies did for fun.

"You know Charlotte's story, obviously. Well, her coming here, to Hope Lake, was sort of my fault. You know, in a roundabout sort of way." I was trying to avoid telling them that I baked a cake that ended her career when—without knowing who she was—I sent

Charlotte's boss a cake that explained, in crude detail, that her husband was having sex with her sister.

That was a major downfall of D&V. When things went awry with the deliveries and the messages, they *really* went wrong.

Gigi snorted, and Charlotte playfully admonished her grandmother with a light touch on her hand. "You mean, your cake got her fired. We all know the story." She smiled in a way that let me know that everything worked out as it should have. She got her granddaughter back home to Hope Lake because of it, and Charlotte got both her dream job *and* a great boyfriend, to boot.

"Okay good, so I can leave out the raunchy details." I laughed when some of them looked genuinely disappointed at the lack of gossip. "I'm pretty sure you can still find the video of Charlotte's old boss opening the cake box on YouTube. I'll warn you, it's vulgar and really not pretty."

Two of the ladies at the far end of the table pulled out their phones, but Pauline and Lillian were quick to sweep in and ask them to put them away. YouTube would have to wait until later.

"Anyway, prior to that incident, I was feeling a bit uninspired by the whole bakery model. The novelty had worn off. The messages and the reactions, the sometimes cruel requests from people—it was taxing my creativity and, well, my spark sort of fizzled out. I guess in hindsight it had a long time ago, but I didn't really question it until everything happened with Charlotte." I smiled, thinking about my perfectly happy best friend.

"While *I* was bored, my customers weren't. They were coming in by the droves. *I* just lost the passion for the *vicious* part of Delicious and Vicious. I wanted to focus on sweet desserts again, not what kind of crazy and nasty messages people could think up to ruin someone's day. Or worse.

"I had built a business around doing anything the customer

asked. There were no limits to the wording, only the ingredients. What started out as a funny way to get back at my own ex by sending him a carrot cake saying *It's definitely you, not me*, had morphed into something that felt out of my control. Granted, it afforded me an amazing life and opportunities that I wouldn't have had otherwise, but at what cost?"

Gigi gave me a weak smile. "At the end of the day, you can lose yourself."

"And the vicious doesn't seem like you. At least not now," Mancini said kindly, taking my hand in hers.

I shrugged. "It was. I don't want to come off like there wasn't a part of me, at one point, that liked calling people out on their crap. I just grew out of it, I guess. That, compounded with how tiring running the business was becoming, made me realize I needed a new path."

"Do you think that was before or after the Food Network appearances?" Cooper asked, mouthing *What?* when Emma nudged him in the ribs.

"Wow, you guys go right for the jugular!" I took another sip and kept the glass in my hand for comfort. It was like the adult equivalent of a stuffed teddy bear to snuggle up with at night.

"It's okay if you don't want to share, Parker," Gigi said kindly. "Though it sometimes helps to talk it out."

Ever the wise one, that Gigi.

"It's okay. *I'm* okay. The *Next Best Baker* show that I appeared on was the one that put me on the map. The other ones after that helped as well. Obviously, it was a huge boost for the business. But with it came a side to things that was less than pleasant."

"Sex tapes," the same woman at the end of the table grumbled. Someone across from her took her wineglass away.

"No, nothing so salacious," I explained with a smile. "There was some backlash, sure. People taking issue with the tone of the baked messages for one. Thinking I was being cruel by doing it, etc."

"Like what?" Clara piped up nervously. "I'm not on the sociable things like some of the other girls are. I'm not sure what you're talking about."

I smiled when she called her compatriots "girls."

"Social media was a bit of a dumpster fire. It was professionally and emotionally draining, and not something I really ever wanted to do, but it was a part of the spiel."

Mancini *tsk-tsk*ed. "I'm glad you're here and not back on the channel. It was fun to watch you, but you're too nice for the nasty business people take part in."

I smiled. "It's just a combination of all of it. All of the work led me to feeling the worst I had in ages. My trip here, well, I'm hoping it's a recharge of the old batteries. Something to kick the cobwebs off the creativity pool in my brain and help me find what's next."

"Well, the company that bought D and V gained the headache of all the nasty messages and requests, right?"

"Yep, they got all of it. So, not my problem anymore, which feels like a huge weight has been lifted. I just need to focus on my next chapter. Especially since the boredom is killing me slowly. Plus . . ." I paused, wondering if I should dump all my woes on these ladies.

"What is it, dear?" Clara asked consolingly.

"It's just, I haven't been baking. I've had a bit of what I'm calling 'baker's block.' My mojo has vanished. My creativity seems to have dried up."

They all shared looks of sympathy, and I realized no one in town understood my plight of having zero mojo or direction.

"I really know how to bring the house down, huh?"

Mancini made her little tsk-tsk noise that I realized was her way of shushing me from saying not nice things about myself. Self-deprecation was always my go-to. It was what worked on the Food Network and at D&V so magnificently. This crowd wasn't my usual audience, though.

"Well, you're more than welcome to hang around with us. Maybe we can be helpful to your, what did you say, 'mojo'? The winter months aren't nearly as exciting as the spring and summer, but regardless, the doors are always open," Mancini said, and the rest of her merry band of ladies chimed in with enthusiastic nods.

* * *

An hour or so later, I was full and sleepy. So when Cooper and Emma and Henry and Charlotte said their goodbyes, both couples offering me a ride to my Airbnb, I was ready to jump on it, but Mancini was insistent that I stay for a little while longer.

"We'll get you there, don't worry," she explained in a tone that left no question that I was to just wait it out with my new friends.

As we said our goodbyes, Charlotte reminded me about the birthday party for Henry that would happen tomorrow. "You have to come. It'll be fun, and a great time for you to see everyone again!" I hugged each of them one more time, holding on to Charlotte a beat longer than the rest. I didn't realize how much I had missed her until she was walking away again. Though this time as I waved goodbye from the porch, I knew I would see her in the morning.

After helping the ladies clean up, I noticed that they were fighting back yawns. Some were taking power naps, snoring away on various chairs throughout the house. They were as tired as I was. I knew if I didn't get to the lake house and unpacked soon that I would be wrecked tomorrow, when I hoped to stop into Charlotte's shop in town for a visit. My body was still on the four o'clock automatic wake-up call no matter how late I crashed.

"What do you guys do, just have a sleepover when the weather is lousy?" I asked, watching Gigi zip around throwing blankets haphazardly on some of the sleeping seniors.

Mancini laughed. "Not quite. Some will stay because the senior home in town has a curfew. We tend to break it often. Gigi will wake them soon so they go upstairs to sleep off the booze. Others, well, we'll get them home eventually."

"Mancini, you're the only person I know who answers a question without giving a lot of answers."

She shrugged. "It's a gift."

Once the last of the food was packed away and stored, I turned to an exhausted-looking Mancini.

"Well, it's late. I don't want you to have to drive me, Mancini, so I'll call that Uber to take me to the rental," I said with a yawn.

She looked affronted, her normally friendly face pinched and irked. "You'll do no such thing. I have a ride coming for you. A big safe one to take you to the lake. He too has nothing to do in the winter besides take care of whatever we need," Mancini explained, pulling a Tupperware container out of a bag that was at her feet. She began stuffing it full of cookies, slices of cake, and whatever else she could fit. "Such a good boy," she mumbled to herself when my cell phone dinged, distracting me from asking her what she was talking about.

Still there? Need a ride?

I hadn't realized that Charlotte texted over twenty minutes ago.

> Nope. Mancini has it "handled"

> Oh boy. What does that mean?

I was going to respond but the door swung open, letting in a gust of cold air and some flurries. The man in the doorframe was big, covered in snow, and wrapped in enough gear to hike Mount Everest.

I walked into Gigi's foyer, which was now slick with snow, as Mancini hurried along, hot on my heels.

Just as I reached him, he looked up and I got a look at two familiar brown eyes. My steps faltered when my feet hit the snowy hardwood near the door. It happened in slow motion. My foot slipped on the snow he'd trudged in, and I pitched back. I heard Gigi and Mancini shout something, but it was too late. I was already falling and headed for the floor.

A large arm slid behind my back quickly, bracing me against a solid, albeit snow-covered, body. I shivered, and we'll just go with the fact that it was the cold, and not because of the owner of said arm that was now holding me to him.

"Whoa, there." He smiled.

I huffed. "Thanks," I said brusquely, extricating myself from his arms.

He took a step away, evidently understanding my irritation. I cleared my throat, ignoring the whispers and the snickering from behind me. While I was ignoring things, the rush of warmth that had run through me when he smiled dissipated. He looked the same, though his hair was a bit longer than I remembered. He was still disarmingly handsome with his sharp jaw and warm, inviting eyes.

"Nick."

5

I stirred awake and curled up against his warm chest. "What are you thinking?"

My fingers danced across his tanned skin. I enjoyed watching the goose bumps appear where they traced. "Nick?" I asked again, but I realized he was still asleep.

Sitting up, I braced myself on my bent arms and watched his face. Nick was a force of nature when he was awake, but asleep he was surprisingly serene. Watching him for a few moments, I smiled, wondering how we had gotten here. Not just to my apartment in New York, but here together. As a unit, a couple with a potential future.

"What has you up at this ungodly hour?" he asked, groggy, his voice still sounding sleepy. His eyes were closed and he smiled as his hand dipped down, touching my rear beneath the thin bedsheet. "It's so early."

"Five in the morning is late for me," I said, glancing over at the old-fashioned clock on the bedside table. "I'm usually at the bakery by now and kneading dough."

"If I was awake, I'm sure I'd find a smartass comment for that, but I just can't come up with anything until the rest of me is up," he said, shifting his hips.

"Oh," I teased, brushing against him. "Good morning to you."

He grinned wickedly and, in a flash, he rolled us over, pinning me beneath his large body. I laughed, biting at his chin as he tucked his arms beneath the pillow I was lying on and laid a searing kiss on my lips.

"What are you thinking about?" he asked, mirroring the question that had woken him up.

With our faces so close, I could barely see the smattering of freckles across his nose and cheeks. "Your freckles are gone." With the weather finally turning to fall, his free time was opening up since landscaping was slowing down. Less time in the sun meant fading freckles.

"I kiss you good morning and you mention my freckles?"

I laughed. "It's just something I noticed since you're, you know, right on top of me."

"I'll have to try harder next time."

"I think we both know you're hard enough."

I lifted my hips to his. The sheet was awkwardly wrapped between us, preventing any real fun. I stopped teasing when he looked at me with questioning eyes.

"Parker?" he said, looking serious. "What are you thinking about?"

"You mean, about us?" I clarified.

He nodded, giving me a quick kiss on the tip of my nose.

I thought about a hundred things in a second. There were only a few that I was willing to share. "I'm thrilled that you came to visit again. If I didn't know better, I'd be starting to think you loved the city. What is this, the fourth or fifth time?"

"Sixth," he said, and my heart leapt at the idea of him counting *something. It felt very high school or puppy love but it didn't matter. It was a sweet gesture.*

"This was a surprise, though, so I guess it's different."

"It was one of the best surprises ever."

He kissed me again slowly. Considering how urgent we were last night when he showed up, this was a welcome change of pace.

"To answer your question, I'm thinking that I don't want you to leave tonight, and I'm trying to come up with a way to get you to stay another couple days."

"I can totally do that. To be honest, I wasn't sure if just dropping in was a great idea or not. Every other visit has been so well coordinated. Especially back home so no one sees you."

"I've been thinking about that too. I think I've changed—"

"Parker?"

I snapped out of the memory to find Nick waving his hand in front of me. I didn't know how long I'd been standing there, zoned out remembering the last time I saw him. A wave of sadness, anger, and more hurt than I cared to admit filled up inside me like a dam readying to burst.

"Parker?"

That was it. Just my name. Not *Hey, sorry I didn't call you back after your bazillion calls all those months ago.* Just *Parker.*

Two could play that game. "I would say that it was nice to see you . . ." I mumbled, making sure that none of the ladies heard me.

Nick did, though. "But it's not," he finished in a whisper.

"No, it's not."

He carried on as if I hadn't said a word. "I didn't know you'd be in town. In fact, no one let me know you were coming. Which is curious, because my friends tell me everything."

"Not my circus, not my monkeys," I said, mindful that Mancini and Gigi were still within earshot.

"What?" Nick asked, looking confused.

"Nothing. It's just pretty sad that we can't have a normal conversation after not seeing each other for a couple months."

He leaned in. "Yes, but things aren't normal between us."

He had me there.

"So, you're here," he said.

"I didn't think it was world news that I was showing up."

"And no one told me you were coming."

"We've established that you were in the dark, Nick."

There was no mistaking that he was irked. But why? "I didn't realize I needed to run my travel plans by you." I took a step back toward the coatrack in the foyer.

He smiled, raising a well-groomed eyebrow, but it wasn't flirty. I'd become familiar with that expression. This was irritation, pure and simple. "You're right, you don't."

"Not that I owe you an explanation," I said, eager to see his reaction to my clipped tone. But I had no idea what I was hoping for in a response. Excitement? Anger? A little bit of lust? More irritation? Any of the above would be a start. "The trip was pretty last-minute."

Nick shrugged. Aloof wasn't one of the reactions I had anticipated. I didn't let the deflated feeling take over. "Just thought someone would have mentioned it," he said lightly. "Did you take the bus?"

I nodded. I could be just as aloof.

"Henry and Charlotte picked me up in Mount Hazel and brought me to town. I've been hanging with Mancini, the ladies, Emma, Cooper, Henry, and Charlotte for the past couple hours."

That got a reaction. He crossed his arms over his broad chest and flattened his lips.

"And no one told me."

"Seems that way."

I didn't feel badly that he was in the dark. What did I care if he was irked or hurt? He hadn't returned my calls, so clearly he didn't care if *I* was irked or hurt. He pretty much ghosted me. So why would I tell him I was venturing into his neck of the woods? I didn't even think I would see him.

Lies.

Not lies. I'd *hoped* I'd see him to give him a piece of my mind, but at the moment, nothing was presenting itself to me to aid in our usual snarky banter. Plus, I didn't want to announce to the town, via the town gossips, what we had been hiding for months.

Nick glanced out the front door and I grabbed my things. "I hate to rush you, but I need to get you home." He took my coat from my hands and held it open expectantly. Well, I couldn't be rude at a chivalrous gesture. I smiled thinly in place of a thank-you.

"How long are you here for?"

I couldn't see his face, but how I wished I could.

"Cat got your tongue, Baker?" he asked, in what was perhaps an effort at being playful. Too little, too late.

"You realize that Baker isn't my name, right? Just my profession?" I murmured, stepping closer to the door. *Ex-profession,* as it were at the moment. I pulled the thin curtains back from the windows on either side of the large front door, which gave me a bird's-eye view at how blustery the weather was getting.

"Hey, Mancini?" I turned to see the ladies lined up at the door. Some just roused from their naps, others getting their serving platters, or whatever they brought their treats in, ready to leave. I began wondering again how the ladies who weren't staying would be getting home.

But when I turned the other way to see Mancini and Gigi, Nick had them all occupied, and, by the looks of it, also moony over him. "Figures." I got it, though. As much as I didn't want to, I'd also fallen hook, line, and sinker for that very same charm that he exuded in waves.

Nick had a swagger about him. Something that a lot of men tried to pull off but usually failed miserably at. He wasn't cocky, but confident. He was similar to Henry—he was handsome, kind, and he cared about people. But while Henry was the lovable, hot professor, Nick was the man you wanted to climb like a tree. So, when I met him last summer, I couldn't imagine how he was still single. It was a mystery to me.

I fished around my coat pocket for my phone to grab the rental address and give it to Nick, but he was already back in the dining room, giving the ladies a kiss on each cheek and a quick hug goodbye.

Mancini was watching it unfold. The rest of the ladies were lined up waiting their turn for some Nick lovin'. Even as bitter as I was, I could admit that it was adorable how he took the same amount of time and attention to say goodbye to each one.

"He's a sweetheart," Pauline said, coming up beside me. She teetered a little, grabbing onto my arm for support. "Sorry."

I rested my hand on hers, keeping it there. "You lean all you need, Pauline. And yes, he can be a sweetheart," I agreed, because he really could be when he wanted to.

Pauline and I watched him interact with the ladies.

Viola whispered something that made him laugh. "Viola, you know I only have eyes for you."

Until he turned to the next one. A surprisingly tall woman with ginger hair. "I know, I will. I promise," he responded to a question I couldn't hear.

He promised a few that he would see them tomorrow or another day during the week.

"It depends on how much more snow we get," he offered by

way of an answer to a question from Clara about when he would be by her place to shovel.

"Let me know when you're coming, and I'll make you dinner," she replied, giving him a sweet grin.

* * *

When he joined me again, he didn't realize that his lady friends trailed behind him like obedient ducks behind a parent. All shapes and sizes: Gigi in her wheelchair; Clara with her cane; and Viola, the ice-cream lady, who insisted that she was going to make him his favorite pistachio if he promised to shovel her driveway first. Elderly bribery at its finest.

"Wait, you open the ice-cream shop in this weather?" I asked.

She grinned, patting him on the head like a little boy. He smiled like one too, all deep dimples and a mischievous sparkle in his eyes. "For my Nick, I'll open in a blizzard."

"You *have* opened in a blizzard. Remember when I was thirteen and had to have my tonsils out?" he offered, dropping down to give her another kiss on the cheek. She beamed up at him.

Once, not that long ago, I would have beamed at a kiss from Nick too.

He gave me a moment to say my goodbyes, though the ones I got in return were not nearly as enthusiastic as Nick's.

Mancini came up to me last, holding her arms out for a hug. I melted as she pulled me tight to her. It was pure comfort and maybe, just maybe, this was what I needed. The slowed pace, the kind reassurances, and the easy-made friends who genuinely seemed like they cared.

"Now listen. The store will deliver groceries. Whatever you need, just call them up with a list. With the snow it may take a couple hours, but you'll get all the baking supplies you need to create some new treats," she said with so much confidence I wondered if she knew something I didn't.

"So, you think a snowstorm will help my eagerness to bake come back?" I asked, already thinking of what I wanted to try.

"Snow makes everything sparkle. I would wager Bertha out there"—she waved to her Hummer—"that a good storm will bring back your sparkle. It may not be this one, but you'll get there. It's not like we have a shortage of snow in this valley."

Admittedly the thought of being buried under a mountain of snow and living alone next to a lake was a bit jarring, but I was going to hope for the best.

The prospect of a little winter magic was exciting. I just prayed I could deliver.

"Ready?" Nick asked, holding open the door.

"As I'll ever be."

Nick held on to me as I descended the stairs. The gesture felt automatic: his chivalrous nature, I supposed. It wasn't something I could read into. He would have offered up a strong, muscly arm to anyone to navigate the terrain.

Muscly? Jesus, Parker.

We disconnected at the bottom of the stairs where I was firmly planted in a couple of inches of deep snow.

Shit. My feet were soaked in seconds.

Silently, we traversed the snow-covered lawn, my hands now clenched into fists in my cold pockets. The coat definitely had to be supplemented with a thick sweater if I wore it outside again, or I would just have to grab something better like Mancini suggested. Spending time in the hospital with frostbite instead of finding my mojo wasn't something I wanted to experience.

Nick's massive silver pickup truck was parked at the bottom of the driveway behind the other cars that were now well covered in sparkling powder. On the front was a plow, and an extra pair of lights mounted on top gave it a spaceship feeling.

"I've never seen that before. I didn't realize it was a real thing," I said, pointing to the chains that were wrapped around all four of the oversized tires. "Necessary?"

He pointed his finger in the air, and when I followed it to the streetlamp above us, I understood what he meant. Snow swirled around the light. More snow was coming per the alert on my phone. The flakes caught on his long eyelashes, making him look boyish. "These chains are what's going to get all of those little pearls tucked inside their warm houses tonight."

I looked at him, confused, and then what he meant dawned on me. "What do you mean? You're coming back?" I was incredulous when he nodded. "Are you nuts?"

"Well, that's a common assumption, yes, but in this case, it's necessary. Henry is meeting me here. He'll take half and I'll take the other half."

"He just left. Why would he come back?"

"Because this is what we do?" he said flatly, like I should have already known.

"Oh, makes perfect sense. Divide and conquer," I deadpanned.

"Are you worried about me?" he asked, leaning against the side of the truck, arms and legs crossed casually.

I waved him off. "No, of course not. Why would *I* be worried about you?"

It's not like you were worried about me when you stopped calling months ago.

"You'll be safe because of your *Game of Thrones* tires."

"That's a good one," he said, pushing off of the truck. "Fact is, these seniors can't drive in this weather, Parker." I didn't know if he meant to sound condescending but that's how I took it.

"I know that! I'm not suggesting that they do."

"I'm confused."

I whirled around to face him. "You don't think *I'm* confused too?" I realized that I was all over the place. Nick looked stunned, and a bit scared by my outburst.

"Nothing, just nothing," I said, trying to calm the hysterical sound to my voice. "I'm just tired and antsy to get home."

"Then why are we arguing?" He shrugged.

"I'm not arguing!"

Nick's lips curled together as if he was trying not to laugh. "Does your brain want to let your mouth know that?"

I gave him the finger. I thought I had my feelings about Nick compartmentalized. That when I rolled back into town for a visit and I saw him, I could be the bigger person. The well-adjusted adult who was ghosted by a guy she really liked and could handle it magnanimously. This brief interaction made it clear that I was completely out of my depth.

Waving toward the house, I pointed. "Why don't you take a couple of the ladies with us now? They can fit, right?"

"Don't want to be alone with me?" As soon as he said it, he looked like he wished that he could pull the words back.

My eyes narrowed, and the clapback was right on my tongue, but I wanted all of this to be over with, not drawn out.

"I'm just thinking they'll fit here in the backseat, right? Or better yet, I can sit in the back," I added quickly, thinking that sitting in the front seat next to him was probably a bad idea. "Why make so many trips?" I gave myself a mental high five for finally sounding casual.

He shook his head, taking a step back toward the truck. "Your luggage is already in the truck. I can't fit them, plus a walker, you, plus your crap—I'll just come back. No worries."

I remembered the last phone conversation we had months earlier. At the time, he ended the call with *no worries* as a farewell. I thought it was an odd phrase given the tone of our conversation. Turns out, his *no worries* actually meant *be worried*.

I had a feeling that all of the other stuff between us—the unspoken words—would be filling the car as well.

"Nick, I should have said this earlier, but maybe it's not a good idea for you to take me. I can call the Uber guy."

He sighed. "Parker, if you don't feel comfortable, I'll have Henry take you and I'll get the others. I just—"

"It's not that I'm uncomfortable, just . . . Fine. Okay, let's go," I blurted, unable to take the cold and wet snow surrounding me anymore.

"Okay." He smiled, and I knew instantly I would regret this.

"Okay, but for the record, I still think you're nuts. Noble, and maybe a little bit kind, but nuts," I said, awkwardly trudging the rest of the way through the snow to climb into the truck.

"I think that was a compliment," he snickered, following close behind me. "Need a boost?"

I cleared my throat, pulling up the collar of my coat in an effort to shield me from the elements. "Thanks, I'm good."

But I was far from good. My completely ridiculous-for-the-weather sneakers were soaked through, my hair was wet and icing up against my forehead and neck, and I was shivering from a combination of it all. A trip to the pharmacy was going to be necessary to get some vitamins and a flu shot. I hoped they delivered like the grocery store in town did. Climbing in, I waited not so patiently for him to turn the truck on and blast the heat.

I was shaking so badly that I was rattling the seat. Add in nearly blue hands and lips, and I was a Parker Pop.

"Parker, you must be freezing." He chuckled, and began aiming all the blasting vents toward my shaking hands. Turning, he took my hands in his and rubbed, the friction giving some life to my numb digits. "Take off your shoes and put them under the vents below the dash."

"C-Can't when my hands aren't free," I stammered, glancing at his hands surrounding mine.

"Oh, shit." He dropped my hands, allowing me to attempt to untie my shoes. When that didn't work because my fingers were too numb, I just pushed them off with each foot.

With all the vents pointed at me, Nick amped up the seat warmer and adjusted the direction of the heat so the blast hit my blue-painted toes.

"Thanks," I said, hating the sound of my teeth chattering. "I have to go shopping. Warmer stuff. Poor planning."

"Wasn't poor planning how Charlotte got here?" He laughed, and reached over to the glove compartment. He pulled out too-large gloves and helped me slide them on.

I nodded. "Look how good that turned out."

We were facing each other as best we could with the console between us, and my legs outstretched so my feet were under the dash.

It wasn't the first time I'd been in this car, but the circumstances were vastly different. Last time, we were headed toward his house, not my rental.

It was as if Nick had the same thought at the same moment. His hands stilled, and I missed the warmth they were generating. "Hey, listen . . ."

I shook my brain out of the fog. "I should probably tell you where I'm staying. An Airbnb down on Lakefront Drive. Can't wait. It's got a chef's kitchen," I said, pulling my hands away.

"Parker, I've got some things I want to say."

"We have to talk, I know that. I just . . ." And I did know, but was I ready to hear what he was going to say?

"Things ended poorly and I have to acknowledge that," Nick said, and for a moment, I wasn't sure if I heard him correctly. "In hindsight, I wish things ended differently."

But still . . . *ended*?

I nodded, keeping my expression guarded—at least, I hoped. I wasn't the best at a poker face, and certainly not with Nick. An apology was all I was hoping for at this point. If I was lucky, an explanation of why he decided to drop me like a hot potato.

"We have to talk. You're right. I'm just a bit of a Parkersicle at the moment and I don't know how solid my responses will be. So maybe we can put a pin in this until I defrost."

He gave me a weak grin, the sparkle missing from his eyes. "The ball can be in your court. Or maybe I'll use a different metaphor. The mixer can be in your bowl. The sheet in your oven. The sprinkles on your cupcake. The—"

"I get it," I said, smiling at his attempt at witty quips—something that I did miss about him, in spite of every wish not to.

My hands were still numb, but the warmth was finally kicking in. Shoving them under my legs, I turned and stared out the windshield and into the great outdoors. I saw snow as far as the eye could see as we drove slowly through the dark streets of town.

"Do you know where you're going? I have the address right here."

Nick gripped the steering wheel. "I know where you're staying. It's normally not far, but in this . . ."

I shrugged. "It's fine. I trust your driving."

The ride was awkwardly silent. The last time we were together, we chatted about the New York Giants' upcoming chances once we realized we cheered for the same team. Or how much he loved the banana maple cupcakes I had made and sent to Charlotte for the grand opening of her shop, which was just after our last conversation. This lack of chatting was painful.

He white-knuckled the wheel and I felt like the seat was going to swallow me up. There were the furtive glances where I would look over, get caught, and avert my eyes like an idiot. Then five minutes later, he'd do the same. I missed the conversations we had. The easiness we shared. We *should* talk about what happened. Why he stopped returning calls and why I still cared months later.

I'd had short relationships before that ended in a not-so-copacetic way, but this one seemed to have its hooks in me. Maybe Nick just managed to get under my skin in a way that no one else had. But I wasn't ready for that talk quite yet. I couldn't bear to hear why he didn't want to see me anymore. I was already in the middle of a crisis with baking. I didn't have the bandwidth to reopen my crisis of the heart as well. I'd have to actively avoid him if there was any hope of getting my baking mojo back.

About a half hour of awkward silence later, he finally pulled into the circular drive of the house on the lake. I gasped. "The photos did not do this justice," I breathed, looking at the warmly lit large triangular window at the front of the house. Inside I could see an antler chandelier hanging from a foyer ceiling. *Oh, country living . . .*

"Is someone here?" he asked.

"No, the lights are on a timer. The owners are out of town at the moment and couldn't meet me here, so they set them up."

Nick nodded. "I'll get your things and shovel you a path," he said, sliding out of the car.

Normally, I would have insisted that I could handle it myself, but I still wasn't totally defrosted, and the thought of trudging through mounds of snow to the front door was low on my list of things to do in Hope Lake.

Nick, in his massive boots and snow gear, made quick work of the snowdrifts that lined the walkway, giving me a mostly clear path right to the front door. He carried the suitcase and duffel on one side while I slipped on my still-wet socks and shoes.

When I slid out of the truck, he gave me his arm to help me out, but since it was clear, I didn't need to hang on to him like at Gigi's. I knew he was right behind me, ready to catch me as he had in the foyer.

"Be safe driving the ladies," I said with my back to him. I flipped open the mailbox and took out the key to open the front door.

"I will. No worries."

I cringed, and I was glad that he couldn't see me. I hated that phrase.

"Believe it or not, it was good to see you, Parker," he said, putting my things inside the opened front door. "If you need me to pick you up for Henry's birthday, let me know. Or let Charlotte know. We'll come get you.

"And I'm always a phone call away for when you're ready to talk."

I nodded, waiting for him to descend the steps before I closed the door behind him.

"It was good to see you too," I said, resting my forehead on the cool wood of the door.

6

The next morning, my breakfast of eggs, bacon, and toast was a success. I was grateful that the Airbnb hosts had managed to have a few essentials delivered last minute in an effort to hold me over until I could get to the store.

Thankfully, I didn't seem to have any issues with cooking, a relief since I preferred not to starve while I was here. While the baking was still a categorical bust, at least I was spending some time *successfully* in the kitchen. It wasn't ideal, but maybe it was a start in the right direction.

Plus spending the time acquainting myself in the kitchen helped kill time before my friends arrived to pick me up for Henry's party, which was thankfully nearby at HLBC.

Unfortunately for them, Charlotte and Henry had dropped by my rental to pick me up earlier than I expected in hopes of touring the house but I still hadn't cleaned up the kitchen. Their excuse was that they hadn't seen the property since it was recently refurbished. Apparently, it was a hot spot in town to scope out because of the extensive amount of work that had been done to the home.

Much to their chagrin, they still wouldn't see it because I met them at the door, dressed and ready to run out of the building.

No one, not even my best friend, needed to see the mess that was in my kitchen. Even though out of everyone, she would have appreciated what I was struggling with and would have understood the mess from my late-afternoon failed attempt at baking scones. I had a boost of confidence thanks to my breakfast success—the rest of the day was a bust.

The normally pristine and obnoxiously orderly Parker had been nowhere to be found. Disaster-riddled cupcakes were strewn across the marble island. Frosting was splattered on the doors of the top cabinets. I was pretty sure a cherry glaze was dripping from the ceiling fan.

I was a train wreck, and my kitchen—the beautiful chef's kitchen that I couldn't wait to christen—was proof.

It wasn't just the cupcake autopsy that I wanted no one to see but also the unpacked groceries the store had sent over. They were kind enough to put the refrigerated and frozen stuff away but the rest . . . well, let's say it was still in the bags on what little space was left on the counter.

My hope that Hope Lake was going to give me my baking magic back was evaporating before my eyes.

HLBC was nestled near the lake in a spot that was a prime location for a brewery. It had loads of parking, beautiful scenery no matter the season, outdoor seating, fire pits, and enough land to expand and build a larger wedding-sized venue, which Emma had mentioned in passing was something they were going to do.

When we arrived to spy a parking lot full of 4x4 vehicles, a couple of massive pickup trucks, and even a snowmobile wedged between two large oak trees, I laughed because of course these fine folks would find a way to venture out in this weather.

"We have the party room," Charlotte offered, answering my unasked question as I looked around to see where we could squeeze our group between the sea of people at the bar. "I'm glad Henry booked it. We figured people would be staying home in this weather, but I'm glad they're not. The livelier the place, the more fun we'll have."

I nodded, casually trying to scope out who else would be joining us in the party room. "I hope they serve food," I groaned, squeezing in my stomach. It growled again in protest.

She nodded enthusiastically. "It's really good. They just started working with someone new on the menu, so it's limited, but delish nonetheless. Ask Nick when he gets here for a recommendation. I think he's had everything so far."

Charlotte caught my frown before I could school my features. "What's that about?"

"What? Oh, is that Henry?" I pointed to a man who was nearly half Henry's size and height. "Let's go see what he's up to."

I walked away, leaving a mouth-agape Charlotte looking perplexed. "I hate it when you change the subject!"

Henry, who *was* coincidentally at the bar, was getting the three of us drinks while we waited for the others to get there.

Charlotte and Emma came strolling up with beer and . . . *water*? "What did you bring me?" I asked, taking the frosted beer glass from Emma.

"I took these from Henry," Emma said. "He got stopped by another teacher and they're talking shop. He said this is their Toboggan lager winter beer. I've never had it before, but Cooper swears it's the best."

I raised an eyebrow, glancing down at her water, then her other slightly shaky hand that was resting on her hip, fingers inching toward her stomach. "You haven't tried it?" I asked, offering it back up to her. "Take a sip, I don't mind."

Emma looked longingly at the glass, then side-eyed Charlotte, who seemed determined to not look at either of us in an overly conspicuous way.

I pulled the glass back, raising it and taking a sip while watching Emma's reaction. "It's really good," I said, wiping the side off with a napkin. "Sure you don't want to try it? Unless of course you can't *have* beer right now . . ."

Her eyes widened. "You know?" Emma asked, not sounding annoyed but slightly relieved. "Did this one tell you?"

"I did no such thing!" Charlotte shouted, actually stomping her foot. "I told you I wouldn't, and I didn't. Don't blame me, sister."

I held up my empty hand and took another sip. "No one told me anything. I've only ever seen a person look that longingly at something when someone who was gluten-free came into the bakery and I had just made a fresh batch of regular blueberry muffins. It was easy to squirrel out that you're preg—" I began, but she jumped forward to place her hand over my mouth. In the process she sloshed the beer out of my glass and onto the floor near my shoes.

"Don't say it out loud," she whispered, her eyes excited. "I haven't told Cooper yet, and the walls have ears." She looked around the room anxiously. No one was paying us any mind. They were just drinking and enjoying the reprieve of not having new snow falling today.

I nodded, trying not to laugh. She slid her hand away. "Sorry, my nerves. Everything is just going haywire. I can't think, I can't eat. All I want to do is sleep, which is impossible because I have a thousand things to do."

I felt a rush of sympathy for her. While I didn't know what it felt like to be preggers, I knew quite well what it was like to be perpetually exhausted. "I'd offer you a cupcake or pie to make you feel better, but I'm not even sure the wildlife outside my lake house would eat the stuff I've been baking lately."

Emma laughed. "Charlotte mentioned the baking block. Anything I can do to help? I'm an excellent tester," she offered.

"Again, you wouldn't want it even if you were starving. I tried tossing a couple scones that I had made this morning out to the squirrels. I think I might have concussed one of them. It was a miserable failure, to say the least."

Emma frowned. "That sucks. Not just because I was really hoping for those cookie dough cupcakes you sent for my birthday. I swear I was dreaming of those for a week afterward. I'm ashamed to say I ate all twelve that you sent. Poor Cooper didn't even get a crumb!"

"Well, let's hope that my mojo comes back soon. I'll bake them for your wedding. Out of curiosity, how do you plan on handling the wedding? Are you moving it back until after the . . . you know?" I said, not wanting to say *the baby* out loud for fear of eavesdroppers.

Emma shrugged as Charlotte looked at her curiously. "I have no idea. I mean, we're talking months away when I'll be enormous. I've seen pictures of my mother. If I carry the same way she did, I'll waddle down the aisle."

I smiled. Now that I knew Emma was pregnant, I could absolutely see the change in her features. She looked serene, with her long brown hair pulled back in a low ponytail and her bangs swept dramatically to the side. She was glowing, but it was more than that. It was her eyes that drew you in, wide and dark brown. Emma always had a force about her, but now she looked fierce.

"Does your mother know yet?"

Emma barked a laugh. "The whole town is still in the dark, so that would be a no. Once Sophia finds out, the entire state of Pennsylvania will know." She smiled when Charlotte nodded vigorously beside her. "I've been avoiding her. I swear the second she sees me, I think she'll figure it out. Nothing gets past that woman."

Pregnancy agreed with Emma, but at the same time, I wondered how her fiancé didn't notice the changes. "How does Cooper not know? I'm just curious because I could tell you looked different after about two minutes in your presence."

"He's been traveling a lot. Trying to get some new businesses in town. Normally, that's not a mayor's job, but he's got contacts that he thinks may be more easily persuaded if it's him doing the pitching."

"That's great."

"My folks just got home from a weekend trip themselves. I'll tell them after I spring it on Cooper."

"Tell Cooper what?" Cooper said, sidling up behind her.

Emma paled faster than I had ever seen someone lose color.

Charlotte choked on her beer, quickly excusing herself to run toward Henry at the bar. That left me, a curious Cooper, and a stunned and silent Emma, who looked like she was going to hurl. Whether that was a pregnancy thing or just the nerves of nearly getting caught, I didn't know. I sincerely hoped it was the latter.

"Hey, just the man we were talking about," I said, tossing my arm casually around Emma's shoulders. Using my thumb, I gave her a small push, hoping she'd know to play along. Not that there was a universal symbol for *Don't screw this up, I'm about to lie to your fiancé*, but what other options did we have?

"Is this going to be something positive or negative?"

Interesting choice of words, Mayor Endicott.

"I'm not a constituent, so I guess . . . positive?"

"I hope. I've had my fair share of crappy news today," he said, and Emma looked on worriedly. "We'll talk later. I don't want to bore Parker here with town talk."

"I really like what you guys are doing here. Sort of reminds me of my area of Brooklyn: family-owned stores, rent-a-bikes, and a lot of good stuff to keep the kids outside and not in front of a screen."

"Are you staying put in Brooklyn now that your shop is sold?" Emma asked, but Cooper chimed in before I could answer.

"Ever thought about opening up a bakery here in town? I have the perfect spot."

"Emma, is he always being the mayor?"

They both nodded. "Yes, yes he is," she said, laughing when Cooper looked affronted with a disbelieving frown. "Honestly, you know I love you, but you're *always* the mayor."

"Oh, it's a good thing," I said. "I think it's great that you're always looking for ways to bring Hope Lake a little further along."

Cooper smiled. "Parker gets it! Seriously, though, thank you. I appreciate that. Sometimes I get a reputation for being a bit too dog with a bone, I guess you could say."

"You mean like asking the unemployed baker if she wants to open a new bakery?"

He gave me a wry smile. "Guilty. Like I said, I've got the best spot."

"I'm in a bit of a dry spell and the baking fairy hasn't deigned me worthy yet of a visit. I hope that Hope Lake and this delightful change of scenery will be just what the doctor ordered."

Cooper looked disappointed. "So, no desserts?"

Charlotte returned carrying a pitcher of beer. "That's what you're bummed about? No sweets? My God, just ask Sophia. She'll make you whatever you want," she huffed, filling my glass, then Cooper's.

"Sophia's desserts are delicious, make sure she knows that, but

Parker, those salted caramel cupcakes were incredible. I still dream about them," Cooper said, referencing the dessert I brought to the Fourth of July festival.

Emma rolled her eyes. "He's not lying. I know you gave me the recipe, but they didn't come out the same way. Cooper was so disappointed, I think he might have cried."

Cooper scoffed. "I didn't cry, I bit my tongue and my eyes watered."

"Guys, guys, relax. Once the mojo comes back, I'll bake all the cupcakes, okay?"

"Promise?" Cooper said hopefully, and I couldn't help but laugh at the boyish expression. I was going to hold up my pinkie, when the front door opened and let in a blustery, cold breeze that we felt even at the back of the room.

"Nick's here," Charlotte said, since she was the only one facing the door to see who was coming in.

I turned to see Nick in the doorway, a snowy swirl dancing around him as if he were in a snowglobe. His large frame taking up most of the small space. He shook out his hair, sprinkles of snow falling from it as he smiled at a couple at one of the high-top tables in the corner. Nick drew attention to himself, whether intentional or not, by working the room as if he knew every person inside. It was part of his charm.

The ridiculous snowsuit that he had on last night was long gone, replaced by jeans that looked to be flannel lined, judging by the reddish patch at the bottom that stuck out over his bulky brown leather boots. He pulled off his puffy navy coat and revealed an ivory cable-knit sweater that pulled tightly over his broad chest.

Did I lick my lips?

Maybe.

Yes.

No matter how mad I was at him, I knew what was underneath all of those wintry layers. There were memories there that presented themselves at the worst possible time. That was the hardest part about seeing Nick again.

He was making his way over, stopping at random tables, high-fiving and hugging various people, but as he worked the room, his eyes kept finding mine.

"Huh, he's by himself," Charlotte said, not to anyone in particular but to the ground in general.

"Maybe because of the snow?" Emma offered. I looked between them. They seemed to be having a mental conversation that I wasn't privy to.

"What am I missing?" I asked.

Charlotte turned to me with a serious expression. Nick was almost to us, so she pulled me in close. "Nick's by himself. Jillian must have stayed home."

I racked my brain for a Jillian at the Fourth of July festivities, or at any of the times I visited in secret since then. Nothing. "Okay, you got me. Who's Jillian?"

But I knew deep down what the answer was and just as I asked, I heard heavy boots stop directly behind me.

"Jillian's my girlfriend."

7

Everything okay there, Parks? You look like you've seen a ghost,"
Cooper said, resting his hand on my shoulder and jarring me
out of my haze. I was still reeling from what I'd heard.

It felt like I'd just been stung by a bee. The initial poke is terrible, but even as it fades, it still hurts.

I shook my head and plastered on an overconfident smile. "Yep.
I'm great. Sorry, I zoned out staring at the beer menu.

"Hey," I said to Charlotte, who had just given Nick a hug,
"where's our table at? I want to grab a seat and jot some stuff
down."

Charlotte looked at me suspiciously. Her eyes slid to Nick for
the briefest of seconds. If she was working through what had just
happened, she wasn't mentioning it in mixed company. The joys of
having a best friend who knew when you wanted to keep your private stuff private.

"I'll show you," she said, taking my arm in hers. We clinked glasses as we passed a couple tables. "You sure you're okay? Is it Nick? I know you guys didn't hit it off last time, but I promise he's a good guy—"

"Yep. All good," I said, wanting to ask about Jillian and why Charlotte never mentioned her to me before. Still, as curious as I was, I didn't want the answer.

"Adjusting okay to the leisurely pace of your new life?"

I laughed. "A life of leisure isn't all it's cracked up to be. My sleep schedule is still in the pits. I'm out cold by eight-thirty and up at four like clockwork. I even took some herbal sleeping pill the other night. I made it to nine."

"Whoa, party girl. Take it easy."

I bumped her hip. "Smartass. I'm still getting used to not going to a job. Walking down the steps and stumbling into the kitchen, where I sit on a stool and stare at a snowy lake, isn't all it's cracked up to be. Believe me, it's been months of the same thing."

"Trade you," she deadpanned, stopping to say hi to a couple having dinner at a table just outside the party room. Everyone knew everyone in Hope Lake, it seemed.

"This place is literally the opposite end of the spectrum from New York, and you . . ." I paused, clinking our glasses again. "You're one of them. It's like you've always been stitched into the fabric of Hope Lake."

Emma made an excited noise behind us. "My God, you're stealthy!" I said, holding my hand to my chest. "I didn't even hear you sneak up."

"Oh, I have to write down exactly what you just said about the fabric. What was it? I'll quote you of course."

I looked at her, confused. As the rest of the partygoers started filling up the back room, Charlotte explained, "She's on a mission to get visitor quotes to use for a campaign this spring. Don't be surprised if Parker Adams, television celebrity, is used on a billboard on I-81."

My eyes grew wide. "You're kidding."

Charlotte and Emma shook their heads. "Are *you* kidding? You're a celeb! People will eat it up!"

I threw my head back and laughed. "Emma, I was on the Food Network on a baking competition show. That's hardly a celeb!"

Emma looked offended, tapping her pencil on the notepad in her hand. "You are! You're wildly popular on YouTube as well. Hell, if I had twenty followers, I'd wear a badge. You have thousands of subscribers and a fan club, for pity's sake."

"Okay," I said, laughing when she stomped her foot. "I'm Parker Adams, Food Network competitor and YouTube sensation."

"It needs work but it's a start," Emma said, and I got the feeling we would be having lessons on how to present myself as a "celebrity."

"Hey, if you think it'll help, go nuts."

"This isn't going to be a conversation that you win," Charlotte said, hooking her arm into mine. "It's easier to agree."

Henry, Cooper, and Nick strode in, followed by a couple other people that I assumed were coworkers of Henry's at the school.

"We're all here, so pick a seat and grab a beer!" Charlotte instructed, ushering people to get comfortable.

The tables filled up quickly, everyone partaking in their own conversations, which was interesting considering the party was for Henry's birthday. Our table had eight chairs, which helped me avoid being next to Nick. It was as if the Fates wanted all of us paired off. The couples took up one side of the table: Charlotte and Henry, and Emma and Cooper. Nick and I arranged ourselves on the other side of the table accordingly: Nick, two empty seats, me.

Nothing obvious about that at all.

"Now, let's get to the nitty-gritty," Emma said, flagging down our server. "We'll take three pitchers of the Toboggan. Only five glasses, though, because my stomach is still bugging me from that wonky salad I had at lunch." A concerned Cooper frowned at his "ill" fiancée. "I'll just have a ginger ale."

Charlotte smiled knowingly at Emma.

"Parker, I was thinking about everything you said last night about selling your business. You didn't say how you ended up selling D and V to The Confectionary. I looked them up. They're pretty badass," Cooper said, impressed.

I grinned. "They are, and D and V is the first dessert-centered business they bought and are franchising," I explained. The other four people leaned forward on the slightly wobbly table, all nodding.

Nick's face was full of confusion but also shock, with his mouth gaping wide. "Wait, you sold D and V?"

"Yep, sold. Signed, sealed, delivered, and the check cashed." I wanted to add *If you answered any of my calls, I would have told you, but ya didn't . . .*

Instead, I made the very adult choice to keep my mouth shut.

He shook his head in disbelief. "I've never heard of the people that bought it."

"I'd be surprised if you did. People *in* the business don't know just how much they control: they're like an octopus with twice as many tentacles. The only reason I was introduced to them in the first place was because of my connection with the Food Network. They've got an in with some of the producers to help identify potential ventures."

"So the Food Network was a really good decision, wouldn't you say?" Charlotte chided.

I laughed. "Yes, Charlotte, it was. Thank you again for forcing me to enter that first competition all those years ago."

"Christmas just passed, but I do like presents any time of the year," she said, and everyone laughed. I shook my head and continued my story.

"The Confectionary gave me two options. The first was that I could sell a majority portion of the business to them where they would maintain operating control of the business, and I would stay on as the face of D and V."

"That sounds pretty sweet, right?" Henry offered. "Face of it but none of the minutiae and nonsense that goes with running a business?"

"You're one hundred percent right. It *was* a great offer. Both monetarily and personally. Honestly, it would have given me a bit of a break from the hamster wheel I had been on for years. I could have explored different avenues, traveled to show up for openings of new franchises, whatever."

"But . . ." Cooper said.

"The *but* was the route that I chose. Their second offer."

"Sell everything and get out of Dodge," Charlotte finished for me, before reaching out her hand to take mine. "I'm proud of you for putting *you* first."

"It was the right decision. Not just because of the money, though let me tell you it is nice to not have to worry about damn near close to anything right now. But also, I didn't have a life outside of D and V, and I was sick of it. I figured if I sold the business, I'd have more time for me." I avoided looking at Nick because the idea was that if I had more *me* time I would also have more *we* time—but we know how that turned out.

"When did this all go down?" Nick asked.

I didn't know how I felt about answering his question. I decided to go with honesty. "Around Thanksgiving. Give or take a couple weeks."

Nick's eyes grew wide and we had a silent conversation while he put two and two together. Nick stopped answering my calls right around the same time I was working out the D&V deal. At the time, he was who I wanted to celebrate with. I'd be damned if I told him that now.

"So, what's the next step?" Cooper asked, breaking our silent conversation and slinging his arm over Emma's chair.

I shrugged. "I'm not sure. I came here for— Well, however long I'm here. There's no end date. I'm trying to get good at baking again. Find the zing again. I miss it. The one thing I'm good at seems to be actively avoiding me."

Nick sat up straight in the chair. "So, you're missing your mojo. What are you going to do?"

I shrugged. "I'll have to figure it out, I guess. I have no idea how to make my creativity return. I've tried making my classics, but that's the problem. They're not mine anymore."

The one and perhaps biggest thing I regretted about the sale was this fact. "When I said they bought everything, I meant they bought *everything*, my recipes included. The things I've worked on and perfected for years don't belong to me anymore. And I'm not allowed to use them. At least not commercially."

Emma's hand was at her mouth, covering her shock. "I get wanting a change, but that's so much to give up."

"I've always been a 'close one door, open another' kind of person. I figured if I was going to sell, I should sell it all. Start fresh. But somewhere along the way, I got stuck." The nail, as it were, in my buttercream coffin. "If I have no recipes, what can I bake?"

"I, uh, have a Betty Crocker book if you want it?" Nick offered kindly, and I couldn't help but laugh.

"Is it still in the plastic?" I asked, laughing when his face fell. He'd tried making us breakfast one morning on one of the few occasions he ventured into the city to visit me. Needless to say, he wasn't much better of a cook than Charlotte.

"It is. We know I'm not a great chef. My mom bought it for me when I moved into the house. I'm more of a throw-shit-together cook. Forget baking. It's all measuring and precision, and that's out of my wheelhouse. You're more than welcome to the book if you want it."

"Thanks, but I'm not sure even Betty, Martha, or Ina can kick my butt into gear."

"Is there anything we can do to help?" Cooper offered, placing his hand on top of Emma's. He toyed absently with her engagement ring and she smiled up at him.

"Nope. I'm just hoping Hope Lake has a plan in store for me."

8

During dinner, Nick's phone buzzed incessantly. Each time it started up, his fork would hover midair, his eyes would close, his chest would rise with a deep breath, and he would exhale when it finally stopped. The calls *had* to be from Jillian.

"Dude, just answer," Henry snapped, his fork clattering to his plate in frustration when the phone rang for a fourth or fifth time.

"Fine, fine," Nick groaned, pushing away from the table. Snatching the phone up, he walked off toward the bathrooms.

"Everything okay?" I whispered to Charlotte, but my whisper wasn't exactly quiet, and the rest of the table shook their heads. I immediately wanted to pull the words back. Did I even want to know?

"No," the table mumbled in unison.

I waited patiently for someone to explain what was going on. After a few moments of awkward silence, I blurted, "Is someone going to fill me in, or is this a secret? It's totally cool if it is," I said, holding up my hands.

Cooper shook his head. "No, it's not a secret."

I shoved a piece of cold chicken into my mouth. Of course there was someone else. Someone in town. Someone who wasn't me, because I clearly wasn't what he wanted. Why was I so shocked?

"So what, no one likes her?" I asked, chewing aggressively.

Charlotte bit her lip, shaking her head vigorously. "No, that's not it at all. She's nice and friendly, but she's also a lot."

"What do you mean?"

"She's sort of clingy, but I guess that's just her personality. It's not like he's complaining."

Clingy?

Here I was expecting to hear some juicy dirt. But *she's nice?* How could anyone be too nice?

"And being nice is bad, why?" I asked, with genuine confusion.

Henry scooted his chair closer to the table, leaning in. "She's very . . . *invested.*"

"'Invested'?" I clarified.

The group nodded. "She was all in with Nick on day one," Charlotte said.

"Like *all in,*" Emma contributed, earning a snort from Cooper. "Everything is about them. Him. She rearranges her schedule for him. She sends him little notes. No one is *that* nice. But she is. Ugh, she's the worst. No, worse than the worst. Is that even a thing? The worstest?" she asked, looking to Henry.

He shook his head. "Someone being *the worst* is pretty self-explanatory, Ems."

Cooper added, "And she's not the worst. He needed someone that put him first."

Ouch. I knew he didn't know my and Nick's history, but man, did that sting.

Henry jumped in. "Jillian doesn't drive, so he always has to pick her up. Before I left the house, I heard Nick arguing with her on the phone. He was busy with Mancini this afternoon and couldn't get to Barreton—that's the next town over—to pick her up and still get back here in time because of the weather. So, she was hurt she couldn't come, which I get, but the guilt trip she lays on is frustrating. Then of course he feels badly and tries to find a way to do everything. This isn't the first time something like this has happened."

"That sucks," I said, wondering if the clingy and needy type was really what Nick wanted, and if not, why was he putting up with it.

"It's just a lot of *me, me, me* from her and he isn't saying no."

"Nick obviously likes her, or he wouldn't be with her."

"Maybe. I think he's lonely. Nick has never dated someone like her. He's completely changed. He cancels our standing dinners. Forget man dates with the guys. It's like the invasion of the body snatchers," Emma said. "She calls him Nicky."

"Or Schmoopy," Charlotte added.

"It's unlike anything I've ever seen. They're a bit sickening together," Cooper said.

I looked around at everyone's faces. They were serious.

"So, let me get this straight. You're hating on her because she's . . . nice and is super into Nick?"

Emma's lips flattened. "We know we sound petty. We don't actually hate her. She's just a lot to take in . . ."

"They haven't even been together that long," Charlotte said. "But I guess when you know, you know."

"A couple months, right? Has it been that long already?" Henry added.

"I guess the clinginess makes sense. New love and all that," Cooper said sourly, waving the waitress over for the check.

"You're such a romantic, darling," Emma quipped, kissing Cooper soundly. "To be fair, it's probably the mushy-gushy honeymoon stage, blah blah."

"When did they get together?" I asked, my masochistic side winning out over self-preservation. My stomach flipped over. I turned to see Nick striding determinedly toward us.

Hearing Nick getting closer, Emma leaned in. "Right after Thanksgiving. He showed up with her one night after dinner at my folks' house."

The pieces started falling into place as I began to put two and two together. He must've met her and then immediately stopped calling me. Meaning, he ditched me for her. Glad I didn't rearrange my Thanksgiving plans when he asked me to come the last time we spoke.

When there was the possibility that the girlfriend was a nightmare, I thought it would make things with Nick easier to choke down, but if she was sweet? Nice? Overly affectionate and a lover of PDA? *No, thanks.* Actively avoiding the two of them would be paramount on this trip. I didn't need the headache or the heartache, knowing that all the lines he fed me over the few months we were together were basically bullshit. I wouldn't be rude, but I wasn't interested in the sideshow with the sidepiece.

Tonight, I resolved, would be the start of the avoidance. Even though she wasn't here, Nick and I were still walking on thin ice, and his friends, and my bestie, didn't need to witness the animosity.

I faked a yawn just as he wove his way to the table and sat back down.

"Listen, this has been fun, but I've got to bail," I said. "I have a bit of a mess to clean up in the house. Especially if I plan on trying to be productive tomorrow during all this snow that's supposedly coming."

"Oh, you're leaving?" Nick asked. "For good or just tonight?"

I laughed. "Just tonight, Romeo. Can't get rid of me that easy. Charlotte, walk me out?"

I said a quick goodbye to everyone, with a halfhearted one to Nick, as I readied to leave.

We made our way to the door, but Charlotte pulled me off to the side before I could break for it. "What's really going on?" she asked as I put on my coat. "Is it Nick? You seem odd around each other. I know you didn't exactly get along the last time you were here, but—"

"It's not him," I interrupted, not wanting to continue bringing up *when* I was here last. Guilt surged. I'd hated lying to Charlotte, but if I'd told her what was going on between me and Nick she would have had her hopes up that we would end up together. After everything that had happened since, I was glad, in a way, that I kept it from her. Still, keeping a secret that huge from my best friend left me feeling sour.

"Are you sure? There seems to be tension."

Damn observant woman.

"No, why would there be tension?" I said a little too loudly.

"Just wondering. You seemed funny when he went off to answer Jillian's call."

"Nah, just tired and trying to get my head on straight. I've got a long couple of days ahead, so I need to get some stuff done. Oh, and I promised the senior ladies I'd get to their next meeting. They said they had a couple things they wanted to discuss with me. Not sure what about."

"Wow, you don't let moss grow, do you?"

I winked. "Not if I can help it. Besides, the Golden Girls seem to think they have a way to kick the baker's block out of me. I'm going to take them up on it."

Charlotte laughed. "Well, if anyone can do it, it's them. You okay to walk home? It's a bit far to your rental. It's supposed to start snowing again soon."

"Yeah, it won't be that bad. I need to start walking again. Besides, I'm trying out my new boots," I assured her, glancing down at the new bright red winter boots I wore. "Mancini hooked me up with the 411 on the shops in town."

"You've got a friend in that one. Okay, you head out and text me when you get home!"

"Okay, Mom!" I laughed as I opened the front door. It had started flurrying as expected. This would make the stroll back to the lake house a bit longer.

As I walked, my irritation from dinner began to die down.

There was something calming about walking in the blissful silence, with snow blowing off of the bare trees and swirling around me.

I felt the tired ache in my bones just as I reached my circular gravel drive. Maybe if I stayed outside a bit longer, I'd sleep better, I rationalized. Perhaps I would shake off the discomfort.

The edge of the property had a stretch of wooden planks that led to the water. It wasn't a boat dock, but perhaps it was something to jump off of into the lake in the summer. There was a glider on it, but no cushions since it was the dead of winter. I stood at the edge, watching the water. It was eerily still, a perfect reflection of the night sky, including the crescent moon that lit up one small patch of the lake.

All this time, I was trying to figure out what went wrong with Nick and me. Why he stopped calling out of nowhere. It wasn't just that I wasn't able to spend Thanksgiving here.

He had met someone else.

9

About a week after Henry's birthday party I was on what had become my daily excursion with Mancini as we futzed about town. She called me out of the blue the morning after the party and asked if I wanted to join her for errands and Mancini'ing. It'd been our thing ever since.

No one, and I mean no one, could kill a day like Mancini. She would pick me up for breakfast, and then we'd play bingo or a couple games of cards with the girls at the senior center. Then we'd watch a little of *The Price Is Right* with Gigi before the three of us took a nap in the obnoxiously comfortable recliners Gigi had in the living room of her sprawling house.

So, when she called me again to hang out, I jumped at the chance. I had nothing else to do since Charlotte worked all day, so why not hang out with amazing people?

"Come now, we're going to my house for some cookies and a proposition. If we're lucky, we'll get there in time to see Nick shoveling the snow," Mancini insisted, pulling me toward the register to check out. We'd stopped at the grocery store for "the essentials," as she liked to call them. None of it healthy, but if I made it to eighty-something, I would eat like she did too. Little Debbie cupcakes, pretzels of every variety, and don't forget the homemade Hope Lake fudge that came in every imaginable flavor.

"Mancini, hearing you say cookies, Nick, and a proposition in the same sentence makes me want to walk the few miles back to the lake house," I said, laughing when she looked offended.

"Nick has nothing to do with the proposition, unless you want him to, of course," she said with a wink.

"Mancini," I warned playfully.

While Nick and I had yet to have a conversation about what had happened back in November, I also needed to have a discussion with Mancini about what exactly she suspected.

"Pity that he's not single anymore," Mancini said simply, as I handed over my credit card to the woman at the counter.

"Oh my God," I whispered, biting the inside of my cheek as I thanked the woman at the counter and grabbed the bagged groceries. "You're relentless."

"Are you seeing anyone, dear?"

When I turned, I prayed that my cool and collected face masked any emotion that I might have felt. "Mancini, you're about as subtle as a heart attack, anyone ever tell you that?"

"You say that like it's a bad thing, dear." She preened and headed for the door with an extra pep in her step all the way to her Hummer.

By the time we got to the house, Nick was loading Mancini's snowblower back into her garage, which held a few other cars besides his massive truck.

"Oh, damn. I suppose I can invite him in for cookies to get him to stay longer," she suggested, tapping the steering wheel.

"He's probably busy. There are a lot of needy ladies in town who rely on him to shovel their pathways."

"I feel like that should be a euphemism, but it's not, and you're right."

"You take the most innocent statements and drag them right through the gutter, Mancini."

Her hand flew to her chest. At first, I thought I had offended her. "That's the nicest thing anyone has ever said to me. Besides, all the needy ladies are here, waiting for you."

I just shook my head, and slid out of the SUV.

As Mancini opened her door, Nick rushed over to help her slide down off of the raised running boards. "You were quick today," she said sourly. "I'll fix you up some cocoa. I made your favorite chocolate cookies fresh this morning. Come in for a nosh."

He leaned down to kiss her cheek. When he pulled away, he frowned. "No can do, my favorite lady. I've got some things to do."

Things equal girlfriend, I thought.

"Now, now, you never say no to an old lady, Nicholas."

"Oh, she full-named you, Nick. You're toast." I laughed when his cheeks pinked up.

"You know I hate saying no to you, but I have to pick someone up," he explained, turning away from me and lowering his voice.

"Nick, you don't have to say *someone,*" I blurted, annoyed that he was being juvenile and awkward about this. I was a grown-up. He was mostly a grown-up. We could have a conversation without all the secrets.

Nick looked momentarily uncomfortable. "Jillian," he said quietly. "I have to pick up Jillian."

I thought back to how his friends said he dropped everything at her beck and call. "Message received. I'll see you around, Nick. Mancini, I'll wait for you inside."

I didn't wait for a response from him, choosing to bolt up the slick stairs instead, but just as I hit the first step, I slid backward.

Nick, much like he had the other evening, reached me just in time. Grabbing me by my waist, he steadied me on the icy step.

"I got you." He was close, and I was momentarily taken aback by the feeling of his hands, strong and firm, on my hips.

"Thanks," I choked out, refusing to turn around and look him in the eye. I wasn't afraid of what I would see in his but what he would see in mine. The longing that I still felt needed to be smothered, locked in a box and buried. My emotions were driving me nuts. Like him or hate him, I needed to pick one and stick with it. But when was anything crystal clear or black and white? I was allowed to be wishy-washy while I worked through what I was still feeling about him. Things would have been so much simpler if he was just a clear-cut asshead.

But he didn't make it easy, and I oh-so-wished he did.

I straightened, brushing his hands away casually. I didn't miss the look Mancini gave us. One of curiosity mixed with hope. I would need to nip that in the bud. She might have been the only other person in town who knew about the short-lived dalliance— not like we intentionally told her—but it seemed that she would need a reminder that, yes, Nick had a girlfriend and no, I wasn't looking for round two.

Nick eyed me warily. "Are you sure you're good?"

"I think we both know the answer to that." The words were out before I thought about them.

Mancini's eyes were wide as saucers.

What was I just saying about being a grown-up?

* * *

"Well, I can't say I expected this," I said, walking into Mancini's living room, where I was greeted by many familiar faces from the other night. Clara, Viola, and Pauline were sitting and chatting. When they saw me walk in, they turned and smiled.

"What's going on? An ambush? An intervention? Is this where you all tell me about your eligible grandsons and hope that we get hitched?"

There were snickers.

"My son and his husband are happily married," Viola said, taking a photo of two wildly handsome men in tuxes out of her wallet. Seriously, old people were adorable. They still had printed photos!

"So, no setup." I laughed. "What's up? This can't be another meeting of the Golden Girls Society of Hope Lake, right?"

"What did you call it?" Mancini asked, walking in from the other room. I heard Nick's truck rumbling off down the road. He really did manage to turn down her offer for cookies and cocoa. In my eyes, and perhaps Mancini's, that made his relationship with Jillian even that much more serious.

"The Golden Girls Society of Hope Lake. Sorry, I don't know what the actual name is."

"I love it," Clara said. "Viola?"

"Me too," she responded. "Suzanne?"

"Love!"

"Girls, we have a new official name. Let me text Emma and let her know to update the town website. Maybe people will join now, if it's not called the Senior Citizens' Club. Those fifty-five-year-olds scoff at joining anything that sounds stuffy."

"Happy to help," I said, laughing when Mancini pulled out her iPhone and Siri dictated the message to Emma. She ended with "Clearly, I'm the Blanche in this bunch," to which the other ladies heartily agreed.

Gigi joined us, rolling in on her motorized chair, a bottle of beer in one hand as she steered with the other. "Oh, good. You're here. We can get the meeting started," she said, pointing toward the wall.

Along it, there were two long card tables set up end to end and both were piled high with cookbooks, stacks of old, faded papers, and recipe boxes with dog-eared index cards sticking out.

"What's all this?" I asked, gently touching one of the cookbooks. It was held together by a satin ribbon because both the front and back covers were hanging on by a thread. The front read:

The Hope Lake Housewife
First Edition
1920

"You can tell this is old. A title like this would never, ever fly today," I mumbled, wishing I had a moment to look through the book. I was certain there would be "helpful hints" on how a house-wife could make life special for her husband. I quickly realized I was right.

Have dinner ready when he arrives home from a tough day at work.

Take fifteen minutes to make yourself presentable.

Let him talk first—remember, his topics of conversation are more important than yours.

Hashtag eye roll.

"This, my dear, is what we need help with," Clara said, picking up one of the boxes and holding it out for me. I set the antiquated (in more ways than one) cookbook down and carefully took the box from her. Clara peered over her reading glasses at me and smiled.

"I'm not sure I follow?" I said, examining it. It was surprisingly heavy for its size. Smaller than a tissue box, it had a small lid that sat crookedly on top. The lettering on the top of the box was faded, but you could still see that it said *Schultz Family Recipes*. The area around the name was ornately carved, and there were a set of initials carved into the bottom: *J.S.*

"These were my grandmother Josephine's recipes. My mother knew them by heart because she learned from her, but my grandmother died before I was born. Needless to say, they're *so* old that even Mancini can't decipher the measurements on the cards."

Mancini, not missing a beat, flipped her the middle finger. "I'll get you back for that one, Schultz."

"Calm down, ladies, don't make me separate you two," I teased. I set the box down and opened it, gently pulling out the first recipe. The paper it was on was incredibly thin, almost see-through, and it had an odd waxy coating on it. The recipe was for something called Oma's Apfelkuchen, and the instructions were handwritten in a classic cursive. "What does this mean?"

"The literal translation is Grandma's apple cake. I remember loving it as a kid, but I never paid attention to my mother making it," Clara said sadly. "In hindsight, I wish that twelve-year-old me learned it when I had the chance. Now we're playing catch-up."

"This is written in German?"

She nodded. "But that's not the problem," she explained, pointing to the numbers beside the words. "I can translate the ingredients—it's the measurements that don't make any sense. At least not to us. A jelly jar, fistful of flour? What kind of scale is that? Not to mention that the measurements would be in the metric system, which only makes things that much harder."

A memory popped up from my time in culinary school. "The instructors used to tell us that back in the day, people used what they had to create a recipe. So, a fistful may be a cup, or more if your gram had big hands," I said with a laugh. "I'm not too sure about the jelly jar, because if she was in Germany when she made this recipe up, the sizing would be different from here. We can play with it and see?" I suggested, but then I thought back to the table filled with books, recipe boxes, and the handwritten treasures from long ago. One recipe I could probably do, but hundreds?

I turned to the rest of the ladies, who were now chatting among themselves. "Does everyone have similar problems?"

Many nodded, while a few raised their hands as if this was a class I was holding. "Ladies, I love you, but you don't have to raise your hand. I'm not your teacher."

Mancini frowned. "But you sort of are. If you can figure these recipes out, you'll help us in a way that no one else has been able to. Believe me, we've tried."

"How? Just so I'm clear what's already been done."

Pauline stood shakily, holding an index card–sized recipe in her hand. "My granddaughter tried helping with this. She's far better at the Google than me. We watched a few YouTube videos to touch on some of what we need help with—conversions, older recipes, etc.—but we haven't had success with re-creating the old traditional favorites from the turn of the last century."

My stomach flipped. This was looking more and more difficult by the second. "So, you've already tried Google and YouTube. Short of flying to the homelands of all of these recipes, I'm not sure what else I can do."

Mancini smiled. "You're perfect for this. You're classically trained. You know the fundamentals. We're home cooks, not formally educated in the culinary arts like you."

"Hey, don't discount home cooks. I've learned a hell of a lot from people who never stepped foot in a culinary school," I insisted.

"Oh, we're not putting home cooks down," Viola said, coming forward. "We're proud of what we can do in the kitchen. But there's definitely a lack of finesse where things like this are concerned. We don't even know where to start."

She and the rest of the Golden Girls looked at me the way I imagined a deer in headlights would: terrified. Realizing the median age of the group was seventy-five, I wagered that none, save for Gigi, was Internet savvy enough to do a deep dive into YouTube or Wikipedia for an answer without the guiding hands of their grandchildren.

"I'm just saying—I mean, Google is probably going to be a lot more accurate than me, and you guys have a lot of these to go through."

But what else do I have going on that I can't help?

"We know how busy you are, Parker. We just thought maybe it would help you get some inspiration," said Mancini. "Since you don't have recipes of your own anymore, these are family heirlooms for all of us. It's win-win, you know? You help us get them in order, and you'll get your mojo back by testing all of these dishes out." Man, she was good.

"How did you know that I don't have my own recipes anymore?"

They each looked guilty in their own way. Clara looked up at the ceiling. Gigi slowly turned her wheelchair around so she was facing the corner like a scolded toddler. Pauline started filing her nails, and Viola coughed and excused herself to get water.

"Ladies," I admonished playfully. I wasn't mad, of course. More curious how they gathered their information so quickly. This place was truly in love with gossip.

Mancini cleared her throat. "Well, Emma and Charlotte were talking, and Enrico—that's Emma's dad—overheard them. He told Sophia—that's Emma's mom—who told Clara at the store, who saw Viola at canasta at the senior center, who then told Gigi, who told everyone else."

I shook my head. "I barely followed that, but thank you for the explanation. You're right. Since I don't have any recipes of my own, maybe this will help give my creativity a much-needed kick in the pants."

"Plus, if I do say so myself," Mancini continued, "we can use a little sugar around Hope Lake. Besides the restaurants, the grocery store is the only place to get any goodies unless you drive all the way to Barreton to the bakery there. And in this snow, it's so dangerous." She placed her hand delicately over her forehead. "It would be nice to have some homemade, authentic, and classic desserts to bring to meetings or social events."

"You're just laying it on thick, aren't you? Full of compliments."

She shrugged. "Is it working? If not, I have a lot more to say," she said, not an iota of shame in her statement.

The longer she talked and the thicker she laid it on, the more I just wanted to laugh. The woman was adorably relentless and admittedly, I found it endearing.

"You're one of a kind, Mancini," I said finally. "I may not know the difference between an old German jelly jar and an American measurement, but I'll figure it out."

She preened like a peacock, and the ladies cheered. "Where do we start?" one asked from the back of the room.

That was a great question.

I scratched my temple. "Give me a couple of recipes and I'll take pictures. I'd like to look online to see if I can find any sort of help for translating old measurements into current ones, and I need to find the conversions because math and I are *no bueno*. Otherwise, we'll have to just play with them until we find something that works. While that will lead to a lot of desserts for people to try, I'm not sure it's the best use of our time."

"Are you going to put us on the line?" Clara asked, taking one of her curls and twisting it in her fingers. "I've never been on the computer before."

"What do you mean? Looking things up or actually being *on* the Internet?"

"Lingo, I don't get it," she said, laughing. "I just mean if we find out that we're good at this, maybe we can have a YouTube channel. My grandkids watch these videos all the time to learn about things."

"I don't know about that," I said honestly. "Let's get through the recipes first. YouTube is a lot. I mean, maybe? Never say never, how about that?"

"We'll follow your lead, dear," Viola said, handing me one of her note cards. On it was a recipe for some sort of cake called a ciambellone that had about eight ingredients but no measurements at all except for pinch, fist, and scoop. Squinting my eyes at the recipe, I couldn't make out much other than bourbon. Lots of bourbon, apparently, as it was mentioned three times.

"This is going to be difficult."

10

When I got back to the lake house via the Uber driver that afternoon, to my surprise someone had shoveled a path from my driveway up to the front door. It wasn't necessarily newly fallen snow, but the gusts of wind blowing snow off of the piles I'd made the other day had blown it back onto the path. I hadn't yet had a chance to clear it, and now it looked like I wouldn't have to.

"Looks like you got lucky and have a shoveling angel," the driver said, pointing up to the house. Leaning against the side of the bright red door was a shovel with a bow attached to the handle.

"I guess you're right. I'll have to thank them with some cookies," I said, but then realized the likelihood was slim. Unless there was a note on the shovel, I had no idea who had done the good deed. I had a feeling it could have been Nick, but just because he shoveled a lot of other places didn't mean that he was here.

When I got into the house, I set the folder of photocopied recipes I brought with me on the table in the foyer to keep it safe.

Thank God Mancini had a copy machine. The Golden Girls wanted me to take the originals, but something so old and precious wasn't safe in this house. Not in its current state of disarray.

Since I spent most of my time with the Golden Girls, in the kitchen, or with my laptop in bed trying to come up with inspiration, I still hadn't unpacked my suitcase. Instead, I just chose to rummage around in it for what I needed.

Maybe it was self-preservation. I could make a quick escape by just closing it up instead of taking the time to repack. Granted, I didn't have much with me anyway. Most of what I was wearing now were the new items I bought with Mancini so I didn't "catch pneumonia."

The other rooms were as spotless as the day I'd arrived. I hadn't ventured into the living room, and I hadn't had guests over yet to give me a reason to tidy the other rooms. A housecleaner would be stopping by on Friday, so there wasn't much for me to do there either.

Still, afraid of giving the person a heart attack when they saw the kitchen, I decided to have a good, long look at the state of it and to do a pre-tidy before they got there. At this rate, I wouldn't be getting my deposit back because everything was a mess. Dishes were piled in the sink, my refrigerator had the most pathetic stack of bowls filled with mediocre frosting, and I didn't yet have the gumption to look in the oven, where I knew my once famous chocolate chip cookies lay sad and flat and stuck to the Silpat.

They were a test. Since I hadn't been successful at making anything new, I figured I'd try something I was old hat at: a recipe that I created back at the Culinary Institute of America a decade ago and had made at least a thousand times from memory.

It should have been a guaranteed success. Instead, the cookies didn't rise and were dry.

Walking into the kitchen, I felt a sudden urge of panic seeing the mess I had left behind that morning.

"What to do, where to start?" I asked the quiet, empty kitchen. My phone buzzed in what felt like strangely perfect timing.

I had texted Mancini earlier asking for some advice. Nothing specific, just some of her wise words to carry me through the day.

Two words from her decided the course of action for the next bit of my afternoon.

Keep trying

Easier said than done. I was distracted, and it showed in my lazy baking. Knowing that I needed to focus, I racked my brain for another approach. I was never any good at meditation, but I tried anyway. Sitting on the counter in the kitchen, I took a couple deep breaths and thought about the joy that I used to get from baking. How fun it was for me. Engaging with clients, creating the recipes, and just overall getting my hands dirty. I missed that.

Instead of focusing on where I erred during my last attempt, I took Mancini's advice to carry on and realigned all the ingredients on the counter as I tucked in. I started with room temperature butter, sliding it into the mixing bowl, then oil and a thick block of brown sugar followed by a delightful sprinkle of white. Once the rest of the ingredients made it into the bowl, and a couple of chocolate chips made their way into my mouth, I let the mixer do its work with the gentle whirring sound that I always found calming.

While it was mixing, I set up the cookie sheets, lining them with the new Silpat pan liners that I had bought at the store, and turned the oven on to preheat. The dough in the bowl looked perfect, and a sense of pride washed over me. Granted it was mixed with a heaping spoonful of trepidation, but I ignored that.

Traditionally, I would have used a dough scooper for the cookies, but I didn't have one handy. Using my hands actually felt like I was back in culinary school. The dough was nice and sticky as I shaped it into quarter-sized balls. I placed each one on the Silpat in even rows until the sheet was filled.

Once both cookie sheets were covered, I slid them into the oven with a silent prayer on my lips. The timer was set, so I made coffee and sat at the island watching the light snow fall as I waited.

There was a constant peace out here—one that I hoped would reinvigorate me—unlike anything I'd experienced while living in the city. Sure, I missed the constant stream of sounds that floated up to my Brooklyn apartment, but I loved that here everything was still.

Looking out the window over the sink, I marveled at the mountains of sparkling snow that covered the entirety of my backyard. To the right was a wide-slab stone path, which was currently blanketed in snow, that led to the boat tie area. I knew that there was a small boat in the garage, not that I had a clue how to take it out. Even if the weather was good, with my luck I'd get stuck in the center of the lake with no way of getting back.

The property extended back into a wooded area on both sides of the house. Having had years of crazy work hours with little sleep, being here, surrounded by blissfully quiet woods, I was sleeping better than I had with every sleeping pill on the market I'd tried. With the nearest neighbor down the block, this home really was a bit of an oasis to escape to.

The timer dinged while I was lost in thought. I slid off the stool, eager to see how the cookies turned out, but when I got to the oven door, I immediately knew that something was wrong.

Pulling them out of the oven, I transferred one pan quickly to a cooling rack and waited. I was relieved to see that they weren't burned, but the coloring wasn't right either. They were supposed to have a sugary coating on the outside from the brown sugar baking up and out of the cookie, but that was missing. After a few minutes, when I took a bite out of one, the natural moisture it usually had was absent.

Not typical Parker quality, but still edible. Progress, I guess.

Today's attempt was both a success and a failure. A success because this was new and I tried. But a failure because it wasn't up to par with what I was used to making. Feeling dejected, I spent a few hours scouring the kitchen, putting everything back the way I found it when I arrived. Making another list for the grocery store, I put it on the fridge using an adorable Hope Lake magnet. The groceries would be delivered as soon as I called: a surprisingly modern touch for the town. Apparently the boom of Airbnb visitors created a need, and the store rose to the occasion.

Still, I thought, *I should go to the store soon*. The reason was motivation. I was sorely lacking exercise, and after living in the city, where I walked constantly, I was feeling the laziness creep in. Plus, as an added bonus of getting out of the house, I'd be able to see more of the town that I had previously only wandered around at night.

When I visited Nick, each time was the epitome of *sneaking around*. I always took the last bus into Mount Hazel, where he would pick me up and bring me back to his place. If Henry was home, or God forbid Charlotte was around, we'd drive to the edge of town, lie in the bed of his truck, and talk about anything and everything. It was part of what I missed the most about this Nick-less trip here.

Focusing on him and what had happened between us months

ago wasn't helping my mood. If anything, thinking about him and his relationship with Jillian deteriorated it. My phone and laptop were staring at me from the breakfast nook. The bright green folder that contained all of the ladies' recipes was taunting me from the foyer. It was only four in the afternoon and I had the whole night ahead of me with nothing to do but talk to myself or try to make a dent in the work I'd signed up for with the recipes and research.

"Stronger coffee first," I decided, pulling the French press from the cabinet to get that started. I set my laptop up at the corner of the countertop and sat on a stool.

Opening up the laptop, I went straight to YouTube because it was my natural default. The process reminded me of how I used to have a routine every morning. Back in the day before the business got wildly busy, I would relish spending a half hour just watching random videos. In fact, the more mind-numbing, the better. Laughing at cat videos or adorable babies giggling was a great way to decompress.

I dusted off the proverbial cobwebs that were on my YouTube home page and fought the urge to check out what The Confectionary had done with D&V's channel. Running two pages had never been fun, but it was necessary in order for me to keep my personal space.

Now without having to deal with the D&V social accounts, I knew I needed a fresh start. Instead of focusing on what D&V was doing, I changed the name of my personal page to Parker Phase Two. Parker Wakes and Bakes was no more. I was older, wiser, and this felt like the right move.

Once that was done, I set out to search for solutions to the measurement problem that all of the ladies' recipes seemed to have.

With cooking, you could almost always wing it. A pinch and a dash didn't make a whole hell of a lot of difference. But baking was a science. A teaspoon versus a tablespoon of baking soda could prove a disaster if interchanged. Even something as seemingly innocuous as not leveling your flour or using large versus medium eggs could throw things off. Everything had to be followed to the letter.

So how do you make a recipe with no measurements?

I looked down at my own hands, nicked from cutting fondant and chapped from constantly scrubbing off caked-on flour. There were burn marks and a perpetual pinkish tint on my hands that wasn't quite natural thanks to all the food coloring I used. Making a fist, I realized that's what they were doing. If they didn't have a measuring cup they used what they had.

Their hands.

The cartoon lightbulb went on over my head and I had the urge to get started again. Motivation to use my hands filled my veins. I glanced at the clock on the oven, and then at the weather outside with the light snow falling. Luckily, it wasn't accumulating.

The list from the store would take a novice a while to put together, but a seasoned vet like me could fly through the baking aisle and get everything with ease.

Without a second thought, I grabbed my phone and the keys to the lake house and headed for the door.

* * *

I should have had them deliver the groceries.

When I walked in, I heard his voice first and the hair on my arms stood at attention. I stopped short.

Can I run for the Uber driver and have the groceries delivered after all?

Nick was at the checkout counter with a woman draped over his arm, making it almost impossible for him to bag the groceries he was buying. He was smiling, and she looked positively moony over him, whispering something in his ear that made him blush. Admittedly, it was hard to watch as she peppered his cheek with light kisses every time he leaned close enough. Jillian.

I wasn't sure what I was expecting, but it wasn't her. I didn't want to admit it, but Jillian was the opposite of what I looked like. Short, dark bobbed haircut, fine, narrow features with wide brown eyes. She was pretty, and she was built a little more on the average side whereas I was tall and athletic.

Thankfully, Nick didn't see me hidden behind a stand filled with bags of chips. It was the perfect spot to watch their exchange. I couldn't make out what she was saying other than a semi-nasal "Nicky," to which he gave a beaming smile in return. His friends were right—he did look happy with her.

The people surrounding them looked on as if they were the perfect couple. Even though it sucked to admit it, they did look good together.

As it turned out, Nick wasn't bagging the groceries for him and Jillian but for the elderly couple who was in line with them.

"No, we don't mind at all," Jillian gushed to the elderly woman. "He'll carry everything out for you. He loves helping. Isn't he the sweetest?"

"He's always been such a good boy," the older man said, patting Jillian on the hand. "You're a lucky young lady." They said their goodbyes and Nick proceeded to leave his girlfriend in line while he carried the bags out to their waiting van.

Jillian turned back to the cashier and grinned, tapping the conveyor belt with her long nail as her and Nick's items were scanned.

When he was walking back to the doors he stopped short, and for a second I thought he saw me through the window, but he was looking at Jillian with another heart-stopping smile. She welcomed him back in with a hug.

"You're the sweetest, Nicky," she said, and I rolled my eyes. Her voice wasn't just obnoxiously nasal, but it also had that baby-like sound that grated on my last nerve. It reminded me of that character Janice from *Friends* who dated Chandler, but without the New York accent. *Or maybe I'm just being petty.*

He rubbed her arms and smiled. "Sorry for leaving you, Jilly, he was my second-grade teacher. I love that guy. I had to do it."

"Yes, you did, because you're a gem of a boyfriend and everyone loves you."

Is this chick for real? Now I know what everyone meant by *too* nice.

"So, what do you want to do tonight? Let's get snacks and watch *Real Housewives*," she said in that singsong voice.

Nick cringed a bit. "Uh, sure, if that's what you want." It was clear that was the last thing he wanted to do.

"Nicky, if you don't want to do it, just tell me. I just thought we could spend some quality time together. You've been awfully busy lately. Don't you want to spend time with me?" she asked, moving farther away with her back toward him.

"No, no, it's not that. Of course I want to spend time together. It's just that I promised Henry that we'd get Cooper together for a guys' night. We haven't had one in months." He rubbed the sides of her arms gently. "Come on, Jilly . . . you'll be at the house when I get back. We won't be gone long."

Her lower lip started quivering, her eyes fluttered, and a racking sob that was so loud the entire front of the store turned to see what was the matter erupted from her small frame.

She turned to face him, sniffling. "Nicky," she said, her shoulders quaking.

Nick seemed panicked, his eyes darting between her and the dozen people watching them. His body went stiff and he paled.

"Jillian, it's fine. I don't have to go."

"It's just," she sniffed, laying her head on his shoulder. "It's just . . . You remember what happened the last time you guys had a night out."

Nick's head fell back against the sliding door of the store. With a deep breath, he wrapped his arms around her completely. "Okay. I won't go."

She smiled up at him and squealed. "Oh, yay! We'll snuggle on the couch all night and you won't miss those guys at all."

But he would. It was clear as day on his face. He was just going along with it to make her happy. I raised my hands toward the sky in frustration but, as my arms went up, I proceeded to knock into the chip rack, sending it clattering to the floor.

The entire store turned to look. Including Nick, who looked at me, then at Jillian, and then back to me and then to the scattered display of chips all over the floor.

Parker? he mouthed, taking the tiniest step away from Jillian. She one hundred percent noticed his movement, and whatever tears she had left dried up faster than pie dough left on a counter uncovered. I was the Grinch in that moment, because the nugget of pettiness in me grew about three sizes.

I gave him a small wave and mouthed *Hey* before bending to assist the employee who had come over to help clean up the mess I made. "I'm so sorry," I said, stacking the bags in his arms.

"Believe it or not, it happens all the time," he said, setting the bags on an unused conveyor belt beside us.

There was an empty cart behind me, so I tossed in the reusable bags that I had brought from the house and took off down the aisle before Nick decided to come and chat.

I made it to the baking aisle before he caught up to me, with Jillian, a smile plastered on her face, trailing behind him.

"Parker, what's up?" he said, sounding a bit out of breath. "How've you been? You look good. How'd you get here? Do you need a ride home?" he rambled, and for a second I was tempted to put my hand over his mouth and tell him to shut up, because we had an audience.

"Nicky? Who is this?" Jillian asked sweetly.

"What?" Nick said, clearly not paying attention. She gave him big eyes and a head nod to me, and then he realized that he hadn't introduced us. "Sorry. Parker, this is Jillian. Jillian, Parker."

I never cared for the phrase *if looks could kill*. It always seemed like such a goofy sentiment. Who would actually be able to kill someone with their eyes, besides Superman? In that moment, though, I knew exactly what it meant. Because for the briefest moment, Jillian's eyes narrowed, her face forming a deep frown. Then it melted away as quickly as it had begun. In a matter of two seconds, she looked like she had earlier: pleasant, sweet, and happily in love with Nick.

That realization stung more than I cared to admit and I attempted to school my features to make sure everything appeared perfectly fine. Even though I felt anything *but* fine.

"Oh, *Parker*! You're the famous baker whom I've heard *so* much about from Nicky and our friends."

Well, this is going to be awkward.

I could have handled a catfight in the middle of aisle eight, but not some kind of sorority-level bonding. Nick seemed relieved, his body relaxing. Slowly, and if I had to guess methodically, judging by Jillian's wry smile, she grabbed his hand in hers and twined their fingers together.

She was a dog marking her territory. I didn't know what Nick had told her about me, but I wasn't eager to continue this conversation longer than I had to.

My eyes flickered down to where their hands were connected, and my stomach lurched.

I grinned tightly. "Yep, that's me."

I turned to Nick to answer his questions. "No, I'm good, thanks," I said, turning my back to Jillian. "I took an Uber to get some supplies, so I'll just take one back. I'm doing some research for the Golden Girls."

"Oh, that's so nice," Jillian said. "I just love those ladies. And they sure do love my Nicky, don't they, baby?" she cooed, kissing his cheek noisily.

Nick shrugged her off so delicately, I don't think she even noticed. "Did you get the shovel?"

"So that *was* from you," I said, tamping down the flicker of glee that I felt.

"I thought you said the shovel was to help an old lady?" Jillian asked, trying to hide her annoyance. This wasn't good. While I still hadn't made up my mind about her, I did not want to be in the middle of a lovers' quarrel.

"I said it was for a friend," he corrected, rubbing the back of his neck.

"I distinctly remember you saying *old* friend."

Oh boy. I needed to get out of the crossfire.

"Anyway," I interrupted, not wanting to get between them. "Thanks for the shovel. It was helpful."

Nick glanced down at his shoes, and I saw the faintest of smiles on his lips. "I'm not busy in the winter months. It's mostly shoveling and plowing, so if you need a ride—you know, a free one—I'm always around. You don't even have to rate me on an app."

My heart skipped a little at the invitation. Nick smiled, a slow, shy grin that shot a feeling of warmth through me that I felt down to my toes. I couldn't help but return it. When my eyes met his, I wanted to say something. Anything. But it all fell apart when the sound of a throat clearing brought me out of my fog. Jillian gave me a pointed look.

I suddenly remembered that I was supposed to be angry with Nick. He stopped talking to me when he met this woman. Why was I allowing a simple act of kindness—one that he would have done for anyone in my position—to almost make me forget?

Nick looked to Jillian, almost as if he had forgotten she was there. "Hey, I know you want to get back for the show. I forgot about grabbing the snacks, so I'll meet you at the register to check out again, okay?"

She didn't huff or pitch a fit. Instead, she smiled. "Sure, Nicky." Then, turning her attention to me, she smiled even broader.

"Parker, it was positively delightful to meet you. I can't wait to see you again." And then, as if this wasn't *Twilight Zone*-y enough for me, she pulled me into a crippling hug.

It wasn't firm and friendly like Mancini's, but stiff and uncomfortable. When she released me, I stumbled backward.

"Nick," she purred, "I'll see you up there." She planted a kiss on him that was anything short of PG, and when she moaned I might have thrown up in my mouth a little.

As soon as she walked away, I deadpanned, "Well, she's . . . nice."

Nick's face fell, and he rubbed the back of his neck again. "I know she seems like a lot, but she's great. Really. I think if you spent time with her you'd really like her, Parker."

"Nick, we've always been honest with each other, so I'm just going to shoot straight. In this situation, I can't imagine that she and I will ever be friends."

He looked like I just kicked his puppy. "Ouch."

I tried to smile consolingly. "I figured honesty was better than being fake." Jillian seemed to sense that there was something more between us, and she felt threatened. I wasn't about to reassure her that she had nothing to worry about. That was not my problem.

Nick winced. "I guess I understand. If you had someone else, I don't know that I'd be gung ho to be his friend."

"Exactly. And to be honest, I wouldn't blame you. I know your natural default is to be friends with everyone—"

"That's not a bad thing—I just want everyone to get along."

I bit down on my lip. "I didn't say it was a bad thing, but just because that works for you doesn't mean I have to follow suit. You've got your friends to welcome her into the fold."

He shook his head. "I can tell that Em and Charlotte think she's a bit over the top. I don't see it but . . ." he said sourly. Clearly, it bothered him that his friends didn't see his girlfriend the way he did.

"Listen, it doesn't matter what they think. You're the one dating her," I said, giving myself an imaginary pat on the back for being mature.

"Listen, Parker, I wanted to apolo—" he began, but I held my hand up when I saw Jillian rounding the corner, heading back our way.

"I'll see you around," I said dismissively, just as she sidled up next to him carrying enough snacks to stock a movie theater.

"See you, Parker," he said, and I wandered down the aisle in search of something to make me feel a little better.

"Yes, see you soon, Parker!" Jillian added brightly.

It wasn't the conversation I wanted to have with Nick. If we were going to move on in any sort of positive way, I knew that we'd have to hash it out eventually: get to the bottom of why what happened happened. Just for my own peace of mind and closure.

I made easy work of the shopping list and then discovered that there was a light at the end of the tunnel.

Some grocery stores in Pennsylvania sold wine.

11

I was going stir-crazy in my Airbnb. Mancini was busy with senior planning, so I hadn't seen her for our daily outings. I'd walked the property so much that I was convinced the neighbors thought Bigfoot was in Hope Lake.

My baking was on overdrive, thanks to the momentum and improvements and all the snow that had fallen. With not much to do outside the house, I made due with what was *in* the house. Though I was quickly running out of friends and neighbors within walking distance whom I could gift the cakes and treats to. The best and worst part about the Golden Girls recipe and testing experience was how much dessert it all yielded. My cup runneth way, way over.

Each gifted dessert was sent with a card and a caveat explaining that while this wasn't Parker's best, it wasn't Parker's worst. The ones that went to Charlotte, Emma, Henry, and Cooper had a bonus caveat that read:

At least these aren't as bad as what Charlotte makes . . .
You won't become physically ill from this . . .
No dental reconstruction necessary . . .

These were the types of messages that were easy and fun to come up with—I didn't have to tell anyone that they were getting dumped or fired, like I did with D&V. I was still struggling in the creativity department for my original recipes, but what I was managing to make weren't the worst things I'd done.

Exactly what every trained, professional baker wants to hear: "You're not the worst."

Whatever I was—worst, not awful, or classic Parker—anything was better than me not baking at all.

Baby steps.

There was more that I needed to work out, though. It wasn't just the recipes but the ladies themselves. They were some of the most interesting people I had ever met. Last night, while I perused websites to help figure out their odd recipes and measurements, I stumbled upon a YouTube series called *Pasta Grannies,* a professionally produced venture that followed the dying art of making homemade pasta.

It was genius. Simple and short videos that gave you a smidge of background information on the granny, as well as the region she was from, and it all went along with a delectable pasta recipe.

Looking down at the stack of recipes, I realized that was it. The ladies and their recipes were the best part of this entire venture. Clara was right—maybe they *could* be on YouTube, much like *Pasta Grannies.* It was clearly a popular channel. Could we make something old new again?

I shook my head out of my daydreams. Before I put the cart before the horse, I needed to perfect their recipes first.

One of Mancini's recipes for traditional Italian cookies that were almost like mini fruitcakes was proving to be the most difficult to figure out. They featured honey, chocolate, *actual* shortening—which I hadn't used in ages—and an obscene amount of candied fruit.

I was sure I had the measurements right, but they were still coming out too dry. The cookies were loaded with flavor, but they were also brittle. Taking a sampling of the last batch that came out decent, I decided that a change of venue was in order and summoned an Uber. I needed a friend to kvetch with, so I was off to Late Bloomers. Charlotte would understand my excitement and either encourage me to run with it or calm me down and get me to refocus my energy.

I was secretly hoping for the encouragement.

"You need to answer three questions for me," I said to Charlotte the moment I stepped into her floral shop. "Wait, no, I take that back. Four questions."

"Hello, Charlotte! You're looking smashing today. Love the color of the shirt. Are those new jeans you're wearing? Your ass looks great in them, order two pairs," Charlotte said, mocking my lack of conversational skills. She continued when I didn't offer any clapbacks. "Thanks, Parker! You're looking marvelous yourself. How's the baking?"

"Okay, okay, I get it. I'm terrible at idle conversation lately, but I have something to discuss," I explained, taking a seat on the metal stool at her counter. The top of her workstation was about as messy as my island. Whereas mine was splattered with flour, hers was decorated haphazardly with flower stems and petals from whatever centerpiece she was creating. It was full of vivid pink and purple flowers and the simplest green vines that billowed over the planter she was shoving them into.

"I'm very busy. And stressed," she said, looking tired.

"Why don't you take a couple days and go to my apartment in the city? You need a break, girl," I said, pulling her nicked fingers away from the floral foam she was pulling apart. "Hit the old haunts, enjoy a day or three at a spa. My treat. Just do something to relax."

She sighed. "Oh, wouldn't that be amazing. I'd love to, but I really want to be able to go with Henry. Maybe we can sneak away during a weekend after I'm mostly caught up on orders and work. Even an overnight trip would make a difference."

I winked at her. "Is Nellie still out of commission with the finger injury?" I asked, not seeing her college assistant around anywhere.

Charlotte shook her head. "Her finger is better, but now she's got the flu. Just when I think she's going to come back, something knocks her on her ass again and we have to postpone orders."

"Can I help?" I offered, though after eyeing what she was doing, I didn't think I'd be capable.

"I wish, but it sounds like you've got your hands full with the ladies." She laughed when I nodded aggressively.

"It's been a challenging but fun experience. This is about the most math I've done since college, and it's taxing my brain. But I'm making progress! Out of the original twelve recipes I took the other day, I've managed to figure out ten of them."

"That's amazing! Henry said you dropped off some treats at the school. That was really kind. I know the teachers appreciated the goodies. They also thought your note was hilarious."

I laughed, remembering what the note to the high school teachers said:

These won't land you in detention . . .

"Speaking of goodies, put this in your mouth," I said, handing her a cookie from the tin I had brought with me. It looked perfect, but I knew it would be slightly dry.

"Seriously? 'Put this in your mouth'? How about some wine? Cheese? Dinner first?"

I guffawed. "You're hanging out with Mancini too much. All of you are taking the piglet route lately. Nothing is safe!"

"Parker, think about what you just said."

"Okay, okay, I guess we're all hanging out with Mancini too much."

"There's nothing wrong with that. She adds color to the dreary winter. All of them do. I can't help but crack up when they're around."

"I know what you mean. They've been a huge help with giving me something to focus on while I'm here. Case in point," I said, pushing the cookie toward her again.

"This is so pretty, I don't want to eat it," she said, still proceeding to take a giant bite. She chewed slowly, her eyes closing as she swallowed.

The anticipation was killing me. "Well?"

"It's really good! I'm not usually a fan of the fruit-filled-cookie thing, but this is delish. What is it?"

I blew out a sigh of relief. "It was one of Mancini's recipes. Something her grandmother made in the old country. I don't remember the name, but it's basically a fruit cake cookie and it was a pain in the ass to figure out."

She gave me a high five. "Well, I say you succeeded."

"Not too dry?"

She took another bite, again chewing slowly to savor it. When she shook her head, I felt some of the tension leave me.

"Not at all. Why? Do you think it is?"

I shrugged. "A little, I guess. I just want these to be perfect for them."

"I love that you're doing this. They're so excited. They'll tell anyone who will listen that a famous baker is in town and helping them re-create their old recipes. People have even requested some lessons from you after trying some of the treats that you've been sending around town."

"Really?" That was interesting. I puffed out my chest a bit at the praise. "That could be fun. I don't have space in the house, and Airbnb has stipulations about using the rentals for anything commercial. But I would certainly consider baking at Mancini's or somewhere close by."

"That would be awesome. Don't worry, I won't sign up if you start lessons or classes."

"Even though you should."

"Ass."

I pretended to wipe my brow. "We'd have to have Hope Lake Fire Department on standby."

She flipped me off and popped the rest of the cookie into her mouth. "There's a bunch of places where you could host classes. Is that really something you might be interested in?"

Was it? Didn't I have enough going on without teaching too? "Maybe?"

"Henry could come, and Cooper. Although they're already good cooks. Nick should sign up. He's a hot mess like I am," she said, rooting in the container for another cookie.

I laughed.

"What?" she said around a mouthful. "They're good, and I haven't eaten breakfast or lunch. Anyway, what's next? You figure out these recipes and then what?"

There again was the million-dollar question. "Well, I dusted off the old YouTube channel. Changed the name, updated my contact information, and got rid of the D and V connection. I haven't posted anything new lately, but I have some ideas."

"Wow, really? Parker, that's amazing. You loved doing the weekly videos you used to do before you got too busy. Bringing that back is a great idea. When do you think you'll start?"

"Whoa, hang on. I haven't decided one hundred percent that I'm doing it yet. It's just nice to have it there just in case, you know?"

"Good point. Well, when you're ready, you know I'll hold the camera. Even if I do a shitty job, you can count on me!" she said.

"I'm really glad I came to Hope Lake, Charlotte. This place has been good for the mojo. I can't explain why, but maybe this place is magic like Emma insists."

"It's the pace, I think," said Charlotte. "It's slower than we're used to in New York and, at least for me, that's energizing. I feel calmer, even though I'm swamped. It doesn't feel as frenetic as it did in the city."

I thought about it. Maybe that was it. "Perhaps. I'm sleeping better. Or, I should say, actually sleeping. While there are a ton of distractions, none are stressful. I guess it's the perfect storm."

"Soak it up while you can. It'll only help for when you eventually head back."

"Eventually. For now, maybe I'll look into teaching some baking lessons."

She clapped. "Look at you, professor! Cooking classes, dusting off the old YouTube channel. The new Parker Phase Two is just what you needed."

I smiled. "Mancini and Gigi and I were talking about it briefly. I'm guessing Gigi told you about the idea?" I smiled when she nodded.

"I thought about doing their recipes on-camera, but then I thought that maybe I should use these guys as part of my channel. I have to chat with them about it."

Charlotte's eyes widened. "You thought about highlighting them!"

I laughed. We might not have lived together anymore, but we still were able to finish each other's sentences every now and then. It was comforting that we still had that.

"I did," I said. I proceeded to explain how I'd found *Pasta Grannies,* and how that had sparked my idea to use the Golden Girls' recipes for a series.

She came around the workstation, waving some sort of purple flower in her hand. "The Golden Girls would kill it online. I mean, obviously you can't call them that, but what if they're on the show . . . or they *are* the show on your channel? Then to bulk it up, you can feature videos of just you baking, if that's the direction you want to go in. Parker and the ladies. You're the face that people recognize. But because everyone already knows you and your skills . . ." She paused when I tipped my head. "It makes sense why the ladies and their recipes would be the focus. I don't think anything like them exists on the Internet."

"You're scary sometimes, you know that? I rolled in here with a wink and a prayer that I might be onto something and here you are figuring it all out yourself!" I said, the wheels now turning on how I could make this work.

"Give it a shot. You seemed excited about the prospect of doing videos again." Charlotte tucked the stem of the flower behind my ear and grinned. "I think you have your answer about how to get your mojo back. Use the process of trying to redo the Golden Girls' recipes as a way to relaunch your own platform. You can finally tell your fans that you sold D and V and that you aren't affiliated with them anymore, but that you also have a new project now. I think you'll be surprised. People will be supportive. Anyway, now that we've sorted out your life, why did you come in? Or was this amazing idea the whole reason?"

I laughed. "You think I remember now? I'm having a senior moment. Blame it on all the seniors that I'm BFFs with."

She gave me a look.

"I'm kidding, but they are rubbing off on me—in the very best way."

She walked back around to her workstation and began snipping stems and fitting them delicately into the foam. "Can I guess?" she asked knowingly.

"I'm guessing that by you offering to guess, you know what I was going to ask in the first place," I said, and while it made sense in my head, hearing it out loud was confusing.

"What? Never mind. I think you came in to gossip about Nick and Jillian."

I was as transparent as Saran Wrap. "Wow, you're blunt," I said, shocked that she figured it out. "I ran into them at the store. It was an unexpected experience, to say the least."

"I heard. Nick called me on his way home after driving her back to Barreton. Which is a ridiculously selfless thing to do, by the way, and—"

"He does it because he's genuine," I finished. "And she's . . ." I paused, looking for the right word. "Something."

"She is. She does dote on him, which is what Emma says he needs. It's a little much in my opinion, but I'll admit that only to you."

"You mean the 'Nicky' whining? Or maybe the constant kisses on the cheek like he's a Labrador instead of a man?"

"That's very specific, but yes. I mean, if he likes it? He's had short relationships, but nothing has been serious like Jillian."

I did everything I could to keep my face unaffected by what she was saying.

"It doesn't matter what I think. If Nick is happy, great. She seems to genuinely like him and vice versa."

"That's just it, though. I don't know if he *is* happy."

"What do you mean?" I asked.

She shrugged. "Maybe it's in my head, but he's been different since he's been with her. Distant and passing on things that he normally wouldn't, like dinners or nights out with the guys. We used to see him all the time but since Jillian, he begs off by saying he's busy."

I nodded. "I get it. Maybe he's just trying to make it work, and spending all his time with her is how he thinks he wants to do it. She mentioned something at the store about not wanting him to go to guys' night. He agreed not to."

"Yeah. Cooper and Henry were disappointed. He hasn't been hanging out with them lately. I know he felt left out after we all coupled off, but—"

"Left out? Of what? You guys are always all together. You're like the real-life equivalent of *Friends*."

Charlotte stood, walking over to the front windows of her shop. She stared out at the bookstore directly across from her place, where Henry worked part-time.

"I mean," she said slowly, "we *were* always together, but I think that was the problem. He was the fifth wheel for months. I figured he wanted someone to spend time with, so he wasn't always the odd man out."

I frowned. "That would make sense, I guess. Seeing you guys all happy and moving forward maybe made him feel left behind."

The more I learned about Nick and Jillian, the more I realized what we'd been missing. We never hung out with his friends, because we were a secret. But then again, he never did give us a chance, did he?

"Well, you certainly don't have to spend time with her if you don't want to," said Charlotte, breaking me out of my thoughts. "We just do so we all get along."

"You're right. If you guys think she's okay-ish and Nick is happy, go nuts. I was clear to Nick that she and I wouldn't be friends, though."

"Why?"

I shrugged. "She's just not my cup of tea. Nick and I—" I stopped myself, almost admitting to her what I had said to him.

"Nick and you, what?" Charlotte asked, and I could practically see the wheels turning in her head, trying to figure out what I stopped myself from saying.

We don't lie to each other. But that wouldn't have made sense to Charlotte. To the best of her knowledge, Nick and I had only met once before I got to town.

"Truth is, I think deep down Nick is probably a good guy. We're very similar, which usually leads to havoc." *Or passion.* "You saw us at the Fourth of July shindig."

She nodded. "You guys were combustible. Emma and I had bets on whether you hooked up."

"Say what now?"

"Cooper and Henry were adamantly opposed, saying there was no way you would have fallen for Nick's flirting, but Emma was convinced that you guys wandered off to the woods to bone."

"Are you twelve?"

"Why? Because I said 'bone'? Are you blushing? Oh, my hell, *did* you bone?"

I scoffed. "Bone. I can't believe you just said that," I mumbled, shaking my head and trying to keep my voice even. It would have been the perfect time to just come out and say *Yes, we did hook up*, but then it would have led to more questions when it didn't even matter. No, thanks.

"Huh, interesting," she said, eyeing me skeptically. Crap, she was fishing, and I was being too honest. I just had to keep everything vanilla and even tempered or she'd smell blood and pounce. "Anyway, you guys were like oil and water, but it was fun to watch you bicker. Jillian's just . . . I don't know, *there*. I mean, I'm glad she's all about Nick, but there's zero spark between them. You two, on the other hand, could have set the park on fire."

"You're exaggerating, Charlotte."

"Am not. You didn't see what we saw," she said, and again I was reminded of why I didn't tell her we were together. In Charlotte's, and likely Emma's, eyes, Nick and I would have been perfect for each other, and they would have put pressure on us. Instead of a relationship of two, it would've been one of four. And that wasn't something we wanted, especially in the early stages.

"You really think she's good for him?" I asked.

She shrugged. "Last fall, after Henry and I got together, Nick was . . . happy. We knew something was up with him, but he didn't say anything and didn't *seem* to be dating anyone. And then as the holidays approached, he became moodier. Actually, he was not that fun to be around. Then right after Thanksgiving, Jillian appeared." She shrugged.

"What did you ask? If he's happy? I guess? I mean, she's nice all the time, so I can't imagine them having problems." She picked up a pair of shears and I wondered if she realized she was holding them like a character in a Stephen King novel: aggressively.

"Oh, one of the witnesses who saw you talking to them told me Jillian was talking about you all the way around the store after you left. She couldn't believe she met you. Nick, of course, left all of that out of our conversation."

"What, is there some sort of sophisticated spy network around town that reports through a switchboard? My God, you guys are quick on the gossip," I said, standing up and taking a turn around the shop. "I can't imagine why she'd say anything about me."

"Maybe she's jealous and she can feel the tension between you and Nick."

"There is no tension." *At least, not on his end.* I glanced away, not wanting her to see my face. "That seems farfetched. Maybe there's some jealousy, though. He did buy me a shovel."

"A shovel? For grave robbing or snow removal?"

"What goes on in that head of yours is mind-boggling."

"I'm aware. It's a mess up there," she said, tapping her temple with her fingertip. "And yes, there is a spy network and your lady friends are at the helm of it. They rival MI6 and the CIA when it comes to extracting information."

"Noted," I added, turning to look in the coolers where the ready-made bouquets and arrangements were. I wanted to distract myself from Nick and Jillian. Thinking about them too much was going to give me a migraine.

"Maybe a couple vases of flowers would help lighten the mood in the house and help me further the process along. I need a punch of color in that kitchen in case I do a video. I'll be sure to plug your business."

I pulled two squatty glass vases from the cooler and set them on the counter near the register. Charlotte looked surprised at first but quickly rallied. "Ooh! Thanks, I like free marketing. I can make you something custom if you want. You don't need to buy from the cooler, Parks."

I leveled her with a glare. "You're busy enough as it is. I don't need to be adding to your stress with flowers for my kitchen. And be sure to charge me what you would any person off the street. I don't want any best-friend discounts."

"No deal," she said, jumping when a loud crash sounded from the exit that led into the rest of the building.

Charlotte's shop was located in one of the spaces in a recently renovated bank building. The once-dilapidated building was something the town took over thanks to Emma and Cooper, and their team at the Community Development Office. I still wasn't quite sure about all the ins and outs of what Emma did, but basically, if something happened in Hope Lake—a new business, a parade, a town hall—the safe bet was that she had something to do with it.

"What's going on next door?" I asked, craning my neck to see through the windows on the side entrance. Charlotte's customers predominantly came in from the street since she was currently the only space that was open for business in the building, but eventually, when someone else joined her, they would use the side entrance that led out to the main hallway.

"I'm not sure yet. Emma mentioned that something was supposed to go in there, so they readied it according to that plan but then it fell through. It's move-in ready with a great kitchen in the back, and it has everything else a *bakery* could need," she explained, looking at me expectantly. "Now it's just waiting for the right owner . . ."

"Really? Is it bigger than this space?" I asked, ignoring her intimation for me to go in there as Parker the Baker. "It looks about twice the size, right?"

She nodded. "It's an odd design, if I'm being honest. I didn't quite understand what they were doing when they were renovating it, but I guess the thought was that if it was some kind of coffee shop or café, you could have tables in front with a counter for sales, and the kitchen in the farthest part of the shop to keep it out of the customers' way. It's big enough to have a meeting space, depending on how they set it up, I guess. We'll have to wait and see what they get in there."

I walked over to the shop windows that led into the hallway. "What do you think about Cooper's idea about putting a bakery over there?"

Charlotte tried to feign innocence. "Surely I don't have any idea what you're talking about," she lied, unconvincingly.

She slid off her stool and joined me at the window. I could feel her vibrating with excitement, though she tried to play it off like she was nonchalant. "Sounds cool. Good idea. Sure, why not."

"Tell me how you really feel."

I laughed when she lunged, pulling me into a hug. "I think it's amazing, whether it's you or someone else. It's a great spot for something like that. But obviously I hope it's you."

"I don't know what I'm thinking. I have to be crazy."

"Cryptic, Batman. Explain, please," she said.

"I've been kicking around some ideas—they're vague—but I can't stop thinking about them."

"Still cryptic. Just spit it out."

I sighed. "While making and testing all the recipes for the ladies, I gave a lot of it away, and ate more than my fair share too, but I've been running out of people to give the treats to. Then I re-membered Cooper's idea."

"Oh boy," she said, rubbing her hands together.

"I have no idea if this is feasible. I'm not being coy; I really can't imagine starting another bakery this soon. I would have to be crazy . . ." I paused when I saw her face. "Okay, crazier than I al-ready am to jump in with both feet again, but—"

"But what?"

"But I love the Golden Girls, and the excitement is there for something else."

She nodded. "But it would be totally different than before, right? Just normal goodies."

"Yeah, definitely not anything close to D and V. You know I'd get sued if it resembled that at all. The Confectionary doesn't mess around, and I'm not in the mood for them to take away everything they just gave me."

"So, an actual take-orders-and-bake-cakes bakery?"

I shook my head. "No, that was always go, go, go. I think people need to slow down a bit. Myself included. A slower pace has been good for me. We all just need a place to sit, to take a breather. Relax and, I don't know, feel calm. Everything is such a rat race. It sounds like even Hope Lake can be in the summer, from what Emma's told me. What this place needs is a spot where people can just hang out and chat. Kick their feet up, have a cup of coffee and a scone and . . ." I paused, wanting to follow the thread that my mind had started unraveling.

The stark-white, peaceful shop next door called to me. In my head, I saw it filled with delicious homemade food and cute tables with people talking. No phones clogging up their conversation, no outside distractions. Just simple conversation.

"I think I may be onto something, but it's not quite there yet."

Charlotte touched my arm. "I think it's a great idea."

"It's not even fully formed yet," I said, placing my hand over hers.

"I know. That's how I know it'll be great."

* * *

Talking to Charlotte got me thinking. I was in the mood to go old-school baking, and nothing beat a classic. Charlotte suggested visiting Henry and the bookstore for inspiration. Buying a cook-book might have seemed old-fashioned, but it was how *I* learned to bake. Sometimes returning to the basics was necessary to move forward.

Henry greeted me as I walked in the front door of the book-store, the tinkling sound of the bell fading into the sounds of classi-cal music that played throughout the store.

"What brings you in today?" he asked, coming over to give me a one-armed hug. He was well over six feet, and to someone like Charlotte, he must have seemed massive. I was grateful for my five-nine frame so that I wasn't constantly looking up at everyone.

"No school today?" I asked, forgetting entirely that it was Satur-day morning. "Never mind. Without a booked schedule, I seem to lose track of the days of the week, unfortunately."

"Understandable. If I'm off my routine thanks to a snow day or something, I'm messed up as well. Any progress on the baking front? That's me asking as a friend, not as a hungry would-be patron," he insisted, smiling so that his dimples showed promi-nently.

I shook my head. "Yes, lots. I'm not back to myself, but it's get-ting there. I'm actually here because I'm helping some of the ladies decipher their recipes. I'm thinking an old-school cookbook may help if I can find similar recipes for comparison."

"What about Nick and his Betty Crocker?"

"I'll get that one too. If you wouldn't mind, could you get it from him and give it to Charlotte? She can get it to me and then I'll have it."

Henry's eyes grew wide. "That's a lot of steps."

I thought back through what I had said. "Yes, well, I'd love to borrow it, but I'm sure he's busy and you see him often, and Char-lotte too, and I see her, so yeah . . ."

If he wanted to ask something else, he opted not to, instead scratching his head while working out how convoluted a process I had just made of getting a simple book.

"I'll take it any way I get it," I said finally.

"That's great, because he's had it sitting in his living room since he offered it to you. I was starting to think he was going to read it himself for tips, but I saw that it was still wrapped in plastic."

"That's kind of him. Maybe I'll poke around and see what your selection is like. I may want a couple others." I didn't want to call Nick or have to see him to get the book. It was awkward enough the way it was between us. Plus, I really didn't want to be the one to drive a wedge between him and Jillian, because it was clear she was not my number-one fan.

"Well, his is a classic. In fact, I don't know if that edition is in print anymore. If you're looking for the basics, that may be your best bet. Either way, the cookbooks are back there." He began to walk toward the spot to show me, but the front door opened and a stream of six or seven marching snowsuits entered screaming for Mr. Henry.

"Oh, my group is here for story time. Feel free to look around. If you have any questions, I'll be done in about a half hour. I can help once they start the craft project since their parents participate in that."

"I'll be quick. Heading to Mancini's after this. Thanks," I said, gently pushing him toward the kids. The moment he made his way over to them, they enveloped him in a rush of hugs and giggles.

The cookbook area was bigger than I'd anticipated for such a small shop. They took up an entire bookcase along the back wall. Every current celebrity cookbook was in stock, as well as the classics like *The Bread Bible, The Flavor Bible,* and *The Cake Bible*—clearly, the culinary world had a theme going. What was surprisingly missing was the classic *Betty Crocker Cookbook*. The one that was a staple for newlyweds or single folks who were living on their own and whose parents didn't want them to live on ramen and frozen dinners. The book that I knew was filled with obscure measurements and tips for newbies.

The one that Nick had.

Henry was still occupied with his small-fry friends. He was reading something about a box of crayons, and they were eating it up because he was doing different voices for each color.

As quietly as I could so as not to interrupt his story time, I looked around for another employee but came up empty. It was so slow that Henry could probably handle whoever came in, I figured. I walked over to the checkout area that bordered a large wall of mugs and complicated-looking coffee machines and left him a note asking him to order me a copy of the *Better Homes and Gardens New Cook Book* because I didn't want the Betty Crocker one. Yes, it would have been better to just ask Nick for his copy, but . . . *What are you afraid of?*

"Oh, screw it," I mumbled, and shot off a text.

> Hey, will take you up on the Betty Crocker book offer.

> I think it may help me out after all.

> If you're around, you can leave it on the porch.

> Or leave it with Charlotte.

Thanks.

I dropped the phone into my purse and left, taking the Uber back to the lake house. Several hours later, around dinnertime, I remembered to check it. Stupidly, I expected to see a message from Nick. Much like the last text I sent him, this one too went unanswered.

12

The good thing about a small town like Hope Lake was that you learned your way around pretty quickly.

The downside was that you always ran into people whom you might not necessarily have wanted to see.

"Parker," Nick said, jogging up the sidewalk so he could hold open the door to the library for me as I walked in to find something to help with the research and baking. "Fancy meeting you here."

"Thanks," I said, sliding past him and into the warm building. It was thankfully not snowing, but the temperature had dipped to somewhere around twenty degrees, and it was absurdly cold with the wind chill.

"What brings you to the library?" he asked, catching up with me easily as I tried to walk past him. I wasn't trying to outrun him, but I wasn't waiting around either.

"Research," I said, quickly scanning the signs above the rows of books for direction.

"I like research. Want some help?"

I stopped short, causing him to run into my back. When I turned, he held up his hands and apologized. "Sorry, I wasn't paying attention."

"Nick, what is this? The shovel, the offer of rides, asking to help? It's okay to ignore me. You're usually really good at pretending I don't exist."

It was a poor shot, but I was tired, a bit hangry, and I just wanted to get the work done I had set out to do.

"Parker," he began loudly, and the librarian behind the counter shushed him with "Nicholas, you know better."

"Sorry," he said, pulling me toward the corner of the stacks that held DVDs for rent. "I wanted to talk to you. To explain, but there hasn't been time so I'm trying to make it a point."

"So, you're what? Following me?"

"What? No, I was around the corner, and I saw the Uber drop you off." I pursed my lips and rolled my eyes.

"Okay, yes, I guess I did follow you in here, but it's not creepy or anything."

I closed my eyes. "Nick, what is it?" Even to my own ears, I sounded exasperated. How was he not getting the hint?

"I miss you," he blurted, and again the librarian sent out a warning shush. "Sorry, that wasn't appropriate. I just can't think straight."

I laughed, but it held no mirth.

"That makes two of us, but now is not the time for this. I'm tired, and I have work to do."

He reached out, ushering me closer to the wall and away from the eavesdropping librarian. "I didn't want to interrupt your day," he said quietly. "I've just been trying to find a second to talk, and it's been impossible—"

"Because all your time is spent with Jillian," I shot back.

"That's unfair. Jillian has nothing to do with this."

"She has everything to do with it!" I whisper-yelled, storming off down a narrow passageway that was under the stairs.

Nick followed, his heavy footsteps echoing down the dark hall. "Parker, stop."

I turned on him, jabbing my finger into his chest. "How dare you follow me? How dare you try to make amends for leaving me high and dry and clueless?" Another jab, and my finger was beginning to hurt. Nick's chest was solid, and with him stressed and angry, he was even more rigid. "How dare you?"

"I'm sorry, Parker," he said, taking a step back.

"It's not good enough," I said, storming past him to get back into the main part of the library.

There weren't any heavy footfalls following me out. I didn't bother searching for what I needed. I wasn't about to run the risk of bumping into Nick Arthur again.

* * *

After the library, I needed a friendly face. Charlotte was busy, Emma was in a meeting, and I knew my favorite lady in town would squeeze in a minute to see me. "Mrs. Mancini, are you here?" I shouted into the open doorway. "I brought you a surprise."

Stepping inside, I closed the door behind me and wondered why she had left it open in the first place, considering how cold it was outside. Worry started to build when I walked through the entirety of her first floor and still couldn't find her. "Mrs. Mancini?" I called again, heading up the stairs.

On the second level, a place I had yet to venture in her home, I was pleasantly surprised to hear some amazingly bad singing from down the hallway. "Oh, thank goodness."

Pushing open the door, I laughed when I found her singing and dancing along to an exercise video on a very large, very pricey television mounted on her wall. "Oh, hello, dear. I didn't hear you," she huffed, clomping over to turn off the TV. "What brings you by?"

"I just thought I'd come and visit. I had a couple things to run by you," I said as I walked around the well-decorated space. Photos of her friends, my friends, and the town were hung all along the walls or set atop the various pieces of furniture. Some old black-and-white photos were there too—ones of her family, I suspected, when they first arrived in Hope Lake.

"Let me guess. There are cookies in that tin?" she asked, pointing to the round tin in my hands.

"Yep, though I realize it's pretty bad of me to hand them over while you're in the middle of your workout. I can leave them down—"

"You'll do no such thing," she insisted, snatching the container from my hands and lifting the lid. "I've been eager to try these ever since you said you were working on them! They look just like the ones I had as a child!"

Carefully, she lifted the lid and took a deep inhale. "They smell delicious. They look delicious," she said, taking one out of the wax paper I had wrapped them in. As she sank her teeth into it, her eyes rolled back and she groaned. "They taste delicious. Perfect. They're perfect," she mumbled.

"You've got the final product. There were a couple test runs that Charlotte enjoyed, but these—well, I'm damn proud of these, Suzanne."

"As you should be. They're just like I remember from Nonna Mary," she said, wiping a tear from her eye. "Thank you for giving this back to me, Parker."

"You're welcome. I'm glad I was able to."

"I owe you one, or five. Whatever you want, it's yours."

I smiled. "I did this for you, but now that you mention it, I could use a favor."

"Name it," she said, walking over to sit on one of the brown leather Queen Anne chairs that didn't match the décor of the room. They seemed out of place. Classic for a not-so-classic lady.

I took a seat in the chair opposite her. "You know I used to have a YouTube channel and be on the Food Network, right?" She nodded and motioned for me to continue. "I was thinking of starting it up again. I did a couple of test videos using your recipe, and I wanted to know if you'd let me—"

"Yes," she interrupted. She stood, ignoring my gaping mouth and anxious eyes.

"Yes? But you didn't even know what I was going to ask." I laughed, but she wasn't kidding.

"Parker, if you want to do something, go for it. Record it, publish it in a cookbook—I don't care, as long as it helps you move your needle."

"Move my needle?"

She sat back down, taking my hand in hers. "Yes, dear. Move your needle. Get your fire lit, put some air in your tires. Whatever metaphor you need, use it. I want you to have some spark back in those gorgeous blue eyes of yours, and if the YouTubey or whatever is the way to get it, go for it. I want to see happy Parker again. Like the one I saw last fall before you stopped coming around."

I smiled, wringing my hands together in my lap. Last fall, I'd been running around town with Nick trying not to get caught. Of course, that failed because we ran into the one person who could have told everyone: Mancini. Surprisingly, though, she didn't say a word, because if she had, the entirety of Hope Lake—both permanent resident and tourist—would have known about Nick and me.

"We'll chat about *that* another day. You know that I know about you and Nicholas, but I see that talking about him dims your light and we're not about that right now. We want you to shine, Parker."

I nodded, grateful to not have to get into a Nick-related conversation right now. "Thanks, Mancini. I was thinking that if I did a video featuring your recipe, maybe you could appear with me as a costar of sorts. Or even better, I could interview you and you could explain the recipe and how you got it from your family. I had some ideas about videos and the recipes to run by you ladies, and this was one of them."

Her eyes lit up. "Me, on a video? Well, I think that would be exciting. Are you sure? Wouldn't you get more whatevers—thumbs-up, compliments—if it's just you? I mean, I'm a bit old for the You-Tubes, right? I'm almost seventy."

I leveled her with a disbelieving look. "Okay, seventy plus twelve," she sighed. "But really, Parker. What does a seasoned woman like me do on a video?"

I stood side by side with her as we faced a large oval mirror that hung on the wall before us. "Well, for starters, just be you. I think that alone would be a hoot. You may be seventy plus twelve, but you're sharp as a tack and your humor is off the charts. Add in an awesome family history and a kick-ass recipe, and I think we've got a winner."

She smiled and patted my hand. "You know how to make an old lady feel, well, not so old. Okay, we'll do it. I want to make sure my hair is done, so I'll call Giavanna to get an appointment. I need to look my best for my appearance on the line."

I pulled her into a bone-crushing hug. "I don't know that the line is ready for you, but I can't wait to see how much you guys kick ass once you're on it."

13

The following day, I was getting out of the Uber to visit Mancini when I stopped abruptly in her driveway. Nick was standing outside of Mancini's front door, smiling like I hadn't yelled at him in the library. He offered a small wave.

"This is a surprise," I mumbled, as I climbed the steps to her house. I knew full well he would be there for dinner tonight, I just didn't anticipate being met at the door. Nick's truck wasn't in the driveway or the garage. Where had he come from? I considered staying inside the Uber and heading back to the lake house. Weren't we just saying that we had no time to chat because people were always around? How did he manage to find the one minute when no one was eavesdropping?

"Parker, listen," he began, but I shook my head.

"Please don't. I came here to see my friend. Not to argue, or whatever else will happen if we continue talking."

"I just want to explain a few things. Things I should have months ago."

Nail meet head. "That's just it. You should have done it months ago. Or even the other day when I texted you and you, once again, didn't respond."

I surged up the stairs, saying a prayer that I wouldn't slip this time. Thankfully, I made it to the front door unscathed. Turning, I said, "Nick, I—"

"You asked for the cookbook so I figured I would bring it today. I stopped by my house on the way over here. I don't want to push you into talking to me any more than I think you want me to, but we have to talk and I want to make things right. We have the same friends, and while you're in town, I don't want to avoid you or have you avoiding me."

"I'm not," I lied.

"Parker, you hid behind a mailbox so you wouldn't have to talk to me and Jillian the other day."

"I wasn't hiding, I was tying my shoe."

"What about at the pharmacy when you dodged behind the reading glasses display when I came over to say hello?"

"I was, uh . . ."

"If you'd rather I pretend you don't exist, I'll try, but that's pretty hard to do. We have a history—" he began, but the door opened, and Mancini stepped outside.

"It's too cold out here for a deep conversation. What are you two standing there for? You'll catch your death," she said, ushering us into her front room as she closed the door. "Kids today. You think you're invincible." I was feeling anything but.

We crossed the threshold into the formal sitting area, which faced Gigi's house next door. Mancini said she'd be right back, but by her time standards that could mean twenty seconds or an hour.

I slid off my coat and hung it in the closet, then waited with my hands in my pockets while he did the same with his. "So," I started, prompting him to give me some reason why he was here besides the book. Which he could have just as easily left on my porch and not tracked me down with.

"So, that?" I asked, pointing to the thick tome in his hands. "I'll take it and put it with my coat so I don't forget."

It was almost as if he had forgotten he was carrying it. He looked down at it before handing it over. At first, he didn't let go, giving the impression that we were engaged in a tug-of-war.

"Thanks for this. I'll be sure to give it back when I'm done," I said, strengthening my hold on the book.

He looked confused, with furrowed brows and flattened lips and with his hands still gripping the book. "I don't need it back. I'm just hopeful it helps. I'm miserable in the kitchen, and a book like this won't help."

I took a small step back, tugging the book along with me and forcing him to let it go. I pulled the plastic off and stuffed it into my pocket before opening the book. The spine creaked the way brand-new books do.

"Told you I never used it," he said with a laugh.

Nick rolled back on his heels as I perused. Just as I thought, it had a good amount of odd and old-fashioned measurements that weren't used in today's recipes. Only certain editions had them listed these days. Closing it, I tucked it under my arm and said thank you. Again.

But with nothing left in the conversational wallet, the room felt stifling with thorny tension. We stood there staring at each other. Mancini hadn't come back in, and I didn't know if she was giving us space on purpose or if she was still getting ready for dinner.

Whatever she was doing was keeping Nick and me alone together, and God, it was awkward. I wanted to say that to him. "Why is this so weird? Why can't we act like normal, rational, thinking adults?"

He frowned, and I realized that I had said it out loud. "I don't mean for things to be awkward or uncomfortable for you. If you'd rather I not be here, Parker, all you have to do is say so."

"No, no, it's not that. They're your friends too. It's just hard for me."

I almost wondered if Nick would be easier to deal with if he was being a dick about everything. Like the first night I met him, he was a bit of a pompous shit, but it didn't stop me from having a one-night stand with him that ended up lasting months. What could I say? I had a type, and he was it.

He stepped toward me, his hand reaching out before he yanked it back. "I'm sorry, I wish—"

I shook my head. "Now isn't the time or place, but—"

We didn't get to continue the conversation because Mancini decided, with her impeccable timing, to join us.

"Table is set, I'm just waiting on the timer to ding. Oh, and Clara stopped by. She wanted to talk to you quickly before dinner," she explained, and Clara popped out from behind her.

"Parker!" Clara beamed. "How is my favorite baker?"

Clara pulled me into a huge hug. The others stood by, with Mancini hovering just behind them watching. "Thanks for everything you're doing," Clara said, letting me go but keeping my hand in hers. "I'm just so grateful that you figured out the recipe the way it was intended. I can't ever repay you for what you've done for me. My kids are thrilled to have their great-grandmother's recipes."

I pulled her into another gentle hug, and quickly wiped my tears away while no one was the wiser. Bringing joy to people like Clara was the whole reason I had agreed to help in the first place.

Dinner was stuffed shells, both meat and cheese, and dessert was Mancini's cookies that I'd made. Charlotte had two, insisting that Henry do the same. "They're so good, they'll all be gone tonight and you'll be sorry."

"There are plenty," Mancini explained. "I have Parker here to thank for that."

"Seriously, Parker. That's really great," Nick said, before taking a bite of the cookie. When he moaned around the mouthful, I looked down, not wanting to see that face again: the one of pure delight, his handsome face serene.

"It's too bad you're appalling in the kitchen, Nick. You could learn a thing or two from this one," Mancini said, laughing when Nick jutted out his bottom lip in mock sadness.

"I'm not terrible. Charlotte is worse," he said, pointing a cookie at my friend.

"You're not wrong. She's hopeless. You, on the other hand, have at least *some* skills in the kitchen. Your ideas for mixing ingredients are great," I said, and immediately felt all eyes turn toward me.

"How do you know Nick has skills?" Charlotte asked, not missing a beat.

Emma's eyes narrowed as she waited for my answer. Henry and Cooper continued eating cookies, having no idea the mental war games their girlfriend and fiancée were putting me through.

Nick didn't know where to look. It was anywhere but at me, because he knew if our eyes locked, the memory of me trying to teach him how to bake while we were semi-naked would come soaring back, and I wouldn't be able to hide the look on my face. He might not have been able to look me in the eye, but I watched as he discreetly rubbed a spot on his leg. A spot that I knew had left a small mark thanks to a splash of hot oil hitting him.

"Parker?" Charlotte asked again.

I pushed aside a memory of Nick wearing my apron with nothing underneath, but trying to ignore the past wasn't helping. "At the Fourth he made me a hot dog, and it wasn't burned to a crisp. Besides, no one is worse than you, Charlotte."

Charlotte seemed mollified but Emma didn't look convinced. Instead, she raised an eyebrow and pursed her lips. "So, Parker. Charlotte said you tried recording some new material for your YouTube channel. Have you thought about bringing on someone else as a student? Someone to teach in a video to help to make it more exciting?"

The idea had merit. "Well, I was talking to Mancini about doing some cooking shows with the Golden Girls, almost like a channel within a channel."

Emma took the bait and ran with it. "I love that idea. We could help promote it throughout town. But you can't have the ladies in your videos. They already know how to bake and cook. They're rock stars. You need a hot mess like Charlotte to make the videos interesting."

"Yeah, no, thanks," Charlotte said. "I've actively avoided her recording me for years. I'm not going to put myself through the ringer now. Besides, we want people to tune in for help, not to see how shitty I am. The focus needs to be on Parker's vast knowledge and ability to help people get through the process of baking. And then the ladies and their recipes. Focus on the classics with some classics."

"I think I love that. Classics with the classics," I said, blushing under the compliment. "I do like to help."

Charlotte laughed. "Of course you do. Did you know that in culinary school she used to tutor some of her classmates to make sure that they made it through their lessons? Everyone is jockeying for position to be the best of the best in each course, and here's Parker just trying to make sure that people aren't failing."

Emma smiled. "That sounds like a great hook for a series. Helping the woefully inept bakers create a masterpiece."

"I'll do it," Nick blurted, and everyone turned toward him. "You can teach me how to bake."

I swallowed hard, feeling the lump sit right in the middle of my throat. "Nick, that's a kind offer, but—"

"Oh my God, that's an amazing idea. You guys have great banter, and the tension will read really well on-camera. I mean, hell, it reads well in real life. How can it not show up online too?" Emma cheered.

"Emma, I didn't realize you were a pro at what works on-camera?" I said, snappier than I intended, but as a person thrown, quite effectively, under a bus, I wasn't in the mood to mince words.

She smiled. "I like to think I have a good idea of what is interesting to see, yes. Don't you think it's a good idea? I mean, you and Nick are *friends*—right?"

My smile was thin and positively fake. "I think it's a swell idea. Can't wait to get started."

* * *

"What the fuck were you thinking?" I howled the moment I sank into the passenger seat of Nick's truck. Charlotte's car had been filled with boxes of vases, Mancini had been busy cleaning up her kitchen, and Emma had been headed in the opposite direction, which meant Nick was my only option for a ride.

Which was perfect because it gave me a minute to unload on him.

"Why would you offer yourself up for this?"

Nick white-knuckled the steering wheel, staring straight ahead. "Nick?"

"You're making me crazy. You being here again is literally driving me mad. I can't think straight," he said very matter-of-factly, as if me being there wasn't weighing heavily on me too. He continued staring out the windshield as we sat in the driveway.

"Let me get this straight. Me being here is driving you insane, and your bright idea is to spend *more* time with me? I'm in the Twilight Zone."

"Not insane. Mad, crazy, wild—I can't get my head on straight with you here again, Parker. It's brought up a lot of—"

"Don't you dare say feelings!"

"They're not all good feelings! Most of them are bad. I'm angry that you're here. I'm sad that you're here. I'm confused that you're fucking here!"

I yelled right back. "Then why the hell did you volunteer?!" I couldn't take him not looking at me anymore so I shoved his shoulder as I shouted. "Why, Nick? Why would you willingly spend time with me if I'm making you crazy?"

"Because I *want* to spend time with you. Jesus Christ, Parker. I've been trying to see you since you got here and you keep running away."

I slumped back against the seat. "Where was this urge to see me in November, huh? When you cut off contact like I was some random woman you met on Tinder, not someone who spent months with you in every way imaginable?"

"Parker, I wanted to—"

"Just drive me home, Nick. I don't want to talk about it now."

He laughed. "Of course you don't, Parker. You don't want to talk about anything that's not pretty and wrapped in a goddamn bow."

"Now's not the time for this."

"Why the hell not? What are you waiting for? Jillian isn't here. Mancini, Emma, Charlotte, or any random witnesses aren't here to watch us implode all over again. Let's get this over with."

I turned, pointing an angry finger at him. "Want to know why? I'll tell you. I wanted to talk about this months ago, and where the hell were you? You dropped me like a bad habit. You don't get to dictate when we talk about all the crap that went down. We do it on my terms, and right now, I don't have it in me to go down a memory lane that's covered in spikes." I took a quick breath before continuing. "What you need to know is that you hurt me. Whether it was intentional or not, you did it and you haven't apologized for it. I need that. I need to know that you even hazarded an errant thought about what you did to me over the past two months. I want to know that it bothers you that you left me high and dry without an explanation. I want to know that you thought about me at all."

Nick looked pained, the skin beneath his eyes dark, giving him a haunted and tired look. His hands were still gripping the steering wheel tightly, and his breathing was labored. A few moments of silence passed. I groaned in frustration.

"Fine, don't say anything—it doesn't matter."

He shook his head. It was a small move, but I still caught it.

"Parker, I think about you all the time. It's not right and it's not fair. I'm more than well aware of this."

14

After days of stewing about how I ended things with Nick, I finally returned one of his calls. There had been a half dozen, plus texts and even a Snapchat. Ignoring wasn't my style, but inviting him over to record the video wasn't high on my list of things to do either.

But it was what I had to get done.

Of course, I could have said no. Insisted that someone else do it or just not have a guest at all, but I guess I wanted to prove to myself that I could do it.

When the doorbell finally rang on the day we were set to record, my stomach bottomed out.

I shouldn't do this here. I should go to Mancini's or literally anywhere else, I thought on my way to the door. My place had become something of a sanctuary. A home away from home that calmed me down and made me feel like I wasn't so adrift in the ocean. And yet here I was, about to let the guy who made me feel anything *but* calm into my safe haven.

On the other side of the door was Nick, looking too good for words. I hated myself for thinking it. "Come on in," I said, trying not to remember his phrasing from the other night.

"Working on this video is all I've thought about," Nick said.

"Same," I said honestly. Something told me that we weren't thinking about it the same way.

"Are you sure this is cool?" he asked quietly.

"I wouldn't have done all this if I was having second thoughts, Nick."

Making my way into the kitchen, I stopped to be sure he was following me. When I turned, he smacked into me. He was closer than I had thought.

"My bad." He reached up and tugged on his dark hair, sending it flying in different directions.

"We're going to have to fix that if you're going to be recorded," I said, pointing at the waywardness of his hair.

"I brought a couple things for that. I was going to have Jil— Never mind."

"Jillian fix it. I'm surprised she's not here with you for your You-Tube debut," I said, proud I didn't choke on the words.

He shook his head. "She was going to come but I couldn't get there to pick her up and then back here in time. I didn't want to take up your whole day by having you wait around for us."

"How thoughtful," I said, uninterested in hearing about the goings-on of Nick and Jillian. Who wanted a front-row seat to her ex and his current girlfriend's show? Not me. "There's a bathroom over there if you want to fix your hair. Thanks for wearing a dark color. It picks up better on-camera." I motioned to his jeans and the navy dress shirt he wore. "Just fix your hair and I'll be waiting in the kitchen." He nodded and headed for the small half bath at the end of the hallway.

While waiting for him, I futzed around rechecking the bowls of ingredients and fixing the setup, making sure that all the utensils were readily accessible and that I didn't have any part of my spinach omelet from breakfast stuck in my teeth.

My shirt was newly ironed, my hair was straight and pinned back, and I was wearing a new apron because I would be damned if I used the same one I did when Nick and I once baked brownies naked at two in the morning. I was as ready as I'd ever be for this.

When Nick returned, he looked at the space in awe. "You did a lot of work to make this look like a studio kitchen," he said, clearly impressed.

The far end of the kitchen, across from the windows, was transformed into the "studio space." I had a makeshift island in front of it and the equipment set up facing it. I had added homey touches, like flowers from Charlotte's and some wintry Martha Stewart accents against the wall so it looked more studio and less home kitchen. I'd cleaned and polished all the equipment and bought new utensils so that everything looked as professional as could be.

"Thanks. It's all borrowed equipment, thanks to Henry's friend at the high school. They're not using the trusses or lighting or the camera this weekend, but we have to be careful because there are some faulty issues with the remote and connectivity. If the series and my channel pick up speed again, I'll buy new equipment for myself and the ladies to use, but this is good enough for now."

He nodded. "So where do you want me, Chef?"

"Over there is fine," I said, waving a hand over to the corner where his apron was. I couldn't look at him just yet. I needed to center myself to get through the next hour.

He donned the apron, tying it crookedly. "Here," I offered, re-tying it so it looked like a bow, not a knot.

"Are you nervous?" he asked, touching my hand lightly. His skin was warm, rough against mine.

"Yes," I said honestly. "I'm afraid this is a terrible idea."

He looked down. "I'm sorry you feel that way. If you'd rather not do it . . ."

"It's fine."

He laughed. "I'll be good, I promise."

That's not what I'm worried about.

Ignoring my fluttery belly, I put on my own apron and got the cue cards that I had made earlier ready. I didn't want to leave anything to chance or have it run away with too much banter and no content.

"Let me give the rundown of what we'll be doing. The goal, like with any cooking show, is to have a completed display piece ready to show the viewers, so they know what the end result should look like. Even on YouTube it's helpful because the videos should be informative, but not exhaustive with information. *Should* being the operative word. I already made the cake you requested this morning, and it's ready for its debut. We'll just use that one as the final product after I edit everything. Okay?"

He nodded.

"Nervous?" I asked.

"Not at all. Is that weird?"

"No. You're wildly confident, Nick. I would be more surprised if you *weren't* excited and ready to roll."

Nick laughed, and I caught myself smiling along with him.

"Let's get this show on the road," he said.

"I'm going to walk to the camera, hit record, and come back. I'll edit that part out."

"Why don't you just use this?" Nick asked, holding up a small black remote.

"Henry said the record button doesn't work and sometimes the other ones stick."

He shrugged, and I straightened my shirt for the umpteenth time as I walked to the camera. With an unexplainably shaky finger, I pushed record and slowly walked back into view. One more deep breath, and a smile and . . . we were on.

"Hello, everyone, and welcome to Parker Phase Two. I'm with my friend Nick here. Say hello, Nick."

"Hello, Nick," he said, and I chuckled. I'd be editing that out later.

"Funny. Today, we'll be making Nick's favorite cake. It's called a hummingbird cake, and while it isn't difficult to make—"

"It's impossible," he interrupted, looking directly at the camera and smiling.

I shook my head. "I'm going to get you through this," I said, patting his hand.

Before I could pull it away, he laid his hand on mine, patting it quickly. It was so fast that I was sure the camera wouldn't have caught it, but I did, and my reaction was to be stunned momentarily.

That would also need to be edited out.

I cleared my throat and continued trying to keep my heart from bursting through my chest. "Our ingredients will be listed on the site; the link is below. Nick, you're going to point to the ingredients and drop them in order into the mixing bowl."

"Aye, aye, Captain!" He saluted, and again I fought back a smile. Damn him.

The space against the pantry wall that I'd allotted for the two of us to film didn't quite work. Maybe I forgot how broadly Nick was built, or maybe subconsciously, I wanted to be close to him, but needless to say, we were practically on top of each other throughout the entire recording.

I would have to squeeze behind him to get a utensil that I needed, or he would have to lean over me to pick up a measuring cup. My fear was that the entire exchange would look intimate—which was the opposite of what I wanted, or needed.

Thankfully or not, depending on how I looked at it, Nick added a comedic element to the process. For every slice of the banana that ended up in the bowl, Nick would eat one. "Nick, you're not supposed to eat the bananas before you smoosh them up."

"Is smoosh a baking term?" he quipped, pointing the peeled banana he was readying to slice at me.

Without a thought, I leaned over and bit it.

And wished immediately that I could have spit it back out.

His nostrils flared, and inwardly, I kicked myself in the ass for not thinking before doing.

I cleared my throat. "Now drop in the pecans, and fold them into the batter slowly with the spatula."

"Like this?" he asked, but he was mixing a bit too rough for the delicate batter.

I shook my head. "Not quite. Here, a bit gentler," I explained, putting my hands over his. One on the bowl and one on the spatula. "Like this."

We moved our hands slowly, and I hoped that I didn't look as nervous on-camera as I felt. It wasn't just being this close that was getting to me but having my hands atop his. It was almost like that scene that everyone swooned at in *Ghost*. Except instead of a pottery wheel bringing us together, it was a mixing bowl.

Awkwardly, I backed away, slightly staying in frame and smiling at the camera and *not* at Nick. "Good, keep up with that for another few seconds."

I wanted to dab the sweat off my forehead. Or strip off my apron to be able to cool down. Both of which would give me away on-camera and which couldn't be easily edited out.

We continued the video, me using whatever small distance I could to avoid touching Nick, who, once again, seemed completely and frustratingly unaffected.

Nick did everything I instructed. Well, almost everything.

"You've got to be careful when measuring the flour," I said, handing him a paper towel to wipe a smudge from his cheek.

"Also, make sure the mixer is off when you plug it—"

"Oops," he said, looking around for a towel to wipe off the batter that splashed onto his apron.

I had one draped over my shoulder, which I handed him. "Accidents happen."

Overall the mix looked great, and I was just glad that we hadn't killed each other or burned the rental down yet. We put the cake in the oven and I said a little prayer that it would be fine even with all the hiccups.

"Now we wait," I said, hitting the remote on the camera to pause filming.

"This is fun. I've never been a fan of baking, but this—thanks for letting me do this, Parker."

I nodded. "Come here," I said, holding up a tea towel toward him. "You've got a little smudge of flour."

Taking my time, I dusted the flour off of his cheek. Even after it was gone, I swept the towel gently across one more time. Lowering it, I rubbed the splotches on his apron where the batter splashed up. Nick was closer than he should have been, making it difficult to clean off the spot.

Abort. Abort. Abort.

As I looked up at him, my breath caught. He was staring down at my lips. "Nick," I warned. This was a bad idea.

"Is the red camera light supposed to be on?" he whispered, tucking a strand of hair behind my ear.

I turned and squinted. Sure enough, the red recording light was still on and blinking. Damn it. If all of these moments were on video, I wouldn't be able to edit everything out without leaving us with a two-minute show. I slid to the side and grabbed the remote, pushing pause two more times; it worked, and the red light finally turned off.

"Come on, we've got to get ready for the icing."

"That's it? Icing and we're done? This wasn't nearly as hard as I thought it would be."

"What do you mean?" I asked, curious to know what he had expected.

He looked nervous. "Well, and don't get mad at Charlotte, but she said you were a hard-ass in the kitchen. Especially when instructing."

I smiled. "I take that as a compliment, not a fault. This isn't an easy job, and if I'm going to show someone how to bake, I want them to do it the right way and learn something from it. If you were to have someone help you with your landscaping work, would you do it for them, or help them understand the tools they need to complete the task on their own?"

Nick nodded. "I see what you're saying. I'm glad you agreed to do this, albeit begrudgingly." He snickered, but stopped smiling when I didn't join him in laughter.

"Sorry, I can't seem to keep my foot out of my mouth with you."

I shrugged. "I get that. I don't know that I'm acting right with you either. I guess natural banter isn't an option."

"So . . ." he began, and I stepped back to focus on the task of cleaning up the mess. Luckily, he took the hint and joined me in silence.

"So . . . any feedback? Need more equipment or need me to re-angle the lights? I can help if you think you need it," he said, pulling out some paper towels and Clorox wipes.

"Nick, you don't have to help me clean up," I said, avoiding the question. I didn't have much by way of feedback other than *I think I've made a huge mistake thinking I could work with you side by side without feeling epically confused over all of my feelings.*

"I do. It's my mess too," he said, and I wondered which mess he was referring to. The mess between us, or the mess in the kitchen from filming.

"So, feedback?" he asked again, and I paused my towel-drying.

"This space is too small for the two of us. Think about if it's me, Mancini, and Viola or Pauline filming all together. We wouldn't all fit. As much as I'd like to say it would work, it won't. I have to figure it out. We need something bigger, but not an actual studio. I still want it to have that home feel but also show viewers that we know what we're doing."

"True. It's a tight squeeze," he agreed, and I remembered that the last time we were in the kitchen together, a tight squeeze was perfectly fine.

It seemed by the flash of fire in his eyes that Nick too was re-membering it. He cleared his throat and stepped away. "So, what's the plan for you and the Golden Girls, then?"

I shrugged. "There's the space next to Charlotte that would work. It would be perfect for both a bakery and a teaching space, which I've been considering too."

"Really?" he asked uneasily. "So, you're going to stay?"

"That's the million-dollar question, isn't it?" It was before as well, when Nick and I were still together. I knew if our relationship was going to move forward, coming here even part-time was something I was going to have to consider. It's what we'd talked about before he stopped talking altogether. Selling D&V was supposed to make that decision easier, since I didn't have any reason to stay in New York. Then things fell apart.

Nick's phone buzzed. Setting the bowl down on the towel, he stepped into the foyer to take the call.

In the time he was gone, I made the icing, decorated the cake, and put it in the camera frame to shoot since the video would be too long if we took the time to have Nick do the work. He'd only have to show it off and bid farewell to the viewing audience.

I looked over at Nick, who was just saying goodbye to the caller.

"We're good here. Just pop on, say how fun this was, and follow the script on the cards. Then wave goodbye."

He finished in one take and helped pack the cake away in the storage box for transport once we were all done. He was taking it home with him as his treat for agreeing to do the video.

"Hey, are you busy after this?" I said, feeling guilty when he quickly slid the phone into his pocket. "Never mind. I'll call Uber."

Nick was exasperated. "Don't be silly. I'll take you wherever you want to go. I know it may not seem like it now, but we can be friends, Parker. And I know we need to talk . . ."

"Do we, though?"

"What?"

I motioned between us. "Do we need to talk? I don't want to sound ungrateful for your willingness to explain yourself, but really, Nick. What good will it do us now?"

He looked confused. "I thought you wanted to hash it out?"

I shrugged. "I did, and maybe I still do, but honestly why am I going to put myself through hearing what happened? You've got Jillian now. Us discussing the past isn't going to change what happened."

"But I don't want it to be awkward when we're together. I want us to be able to be friends, Parker."

I nodded reluctantly. If I was considering staying longer in Hope Lake and we were going to be seeing more of each other with all of our mutual friends, I would have to get over things or at least put them aside enough to be civil.

"I told you," said Nick, "I have nothing to do today besides helping with the video. Let's go for a drive. Talk through it. We have to sooner rather than later."

"But what about—" I began, but he cut me off, stepping closer and putting his hands on my arms.

"She'd be fine with it. Relax. She knows I'm always eager to help."

"Are you sure?"

He nodded as we headed for the door. "I just want us to be able to be friends."

Easier said than done.

I grabbed my phone from the small table by the front door and saw the no-battery sign flash when I tried to turn it on. *Great.*

"Hey, my phone died when we were filming. Can I use yours to text Emma?"

"Of course," he said, handing it to me.

As he walked outside toward the car, I realized that I should have had him open his phone first, since it needed a pass code or face ID. I glanced at his phone background. The photo that appeared was a simple landscape of the river with the mountainside in the distance and the sun setting behind it.

The lock screen wasn't him and Jillian, as I expected it to be. It was a photo that I had sent him, taken on my first clandestine visit to Hope Lake to be with him. I didn't know how to feel about it.

Touched that he kept it? Relieved that it wasn't a picture of him and his annoying girlfriend? A mix of both?

I headed outside to find Nick, who was sitting in his truck, and I walked around the car to slide into the passenger seat. Once inside his truck, I held up the phone. "Um, smile," I said. Instead of a smile, he stuck his tongue out but the phone still unlocked.

"Smartass."

He shrugged as he backed out of the drive. "Guilty. Where should we go, anyway? I probably should have asked that before we left."

I took a deep breath. "I have a suggestion."

"Hit me," he said, smirking when I pretended to punch his arm.

"Remember the conversation from ten minutes ago? About the space by Charlotte?"

He scratched his head. "No, doesn't ring any bells."

"Funny. I don't know if it'll work, but what if we turned it into a community bakery? Something regulated, of course—it couldn't be a free-for-all. Instead, it could sort of be like a community garden."

"I'm not following."

"We had them at school when I was growing up. The PTA used to have bake sales where parents would contribute various desserts, and all the money would go back to the school. That's what I'm thinking. Something where people provide treats and the money rolls back into the business. I want some advice about it, and Charlotte, Emma, and Cooper are the ones who are going to give it to me."

He looked at me with thinly veiled shock. "I thought you said that you weren't ready for another D and V. I believe those were your exact words."

"You're right. I'm not ready for that level of a business, where I'm both owning and operating. If the community bakery works out, though, I would still own it, but it would be operated almost like a nonprofit once I got my investment back."

"Like on *Shark Tank.*"

I laughed. "Yes, like *Shark Tank,* but I'm the poorest Shark there is. They've got tons of money. I'm just looking for ways to invest."

"Parker, that's a nice idea, but it's also impulsive. You need an actual plan. I know you know that, but you're also someone who throws both feet into the fire and then wonders why they're burned." Nick knew me too well.

"Well, you're not wrong there."

"How would you make your money back? Mark Cuban always looks for that. You should too."

"Obviously. Like I told the Golden Girls, I promise I won't put the cart before the horse. None of this may even be feasible."

"Guess there's only one way to find out." He smiled.

From Nick's phone, I shot off a quick text to Cooper and Emma and included my number for Cooper to return the message—not that it mattered, though, since it was dead at the bottom of my bag. I was asking them to meet me at Charlotte's shop because I had questions about the unit next door. I'm sure Cooper would know what that meant.

"You know, I'd be happy to help you get this started if you needed. I've run my own business for years. I can help you work through your thoughts while we're driving to Charlotte's," he offered, slowing his truck a bit to account for the snow squall that was currently swirling around us.

"You know, I ran my own too. So successfully, in fact, that a *big* company bought me out for a lot of money," I shot back, laughing lightly when his ears turned pink.

"I didn't mean to imply anything. I just thought it might help to talk it out," he apologized.

"Nick, I was teasing. You *can* help," I assured him. "You run a business *here,* in a small town that's what, an eighteenth of the size of New York City? There are bound to be differences in operations, management, hiring, sales, and pricing. I can sell a dozen cupcakes in the city for almost forty bucks but I know that wouldn't fly here."

His face was aghast. "You're not serious."

"Dead serious."

"It would fly here. Right into a wall."

I laughed. This was the part of Nick I missed: his quick wit and brutal honesty.

I nodded. "I priced nine-inch pies at thirty-four bucks, a single brownie at four. That's why I think you can help. I would get lambasted if I did that here. Even during the height of tourist season."

"If you charged me thirty bucks for a banana cupcake, I might die before getting to eat it."

"I remember banana was a favorite. I assumed that's why you chose to make a hummingbird cake today?" I asked, curious.

"I'm easy so anything delicious is my ultimate fave, but Mancini loves hummingbirds and I thought she'd get a kick out of us making it," he said, and I smiled at his sweet nature.

"Now, if you pull out a salted caramel PB, C and B cake, I'll do anything you ask," he said, sliding a wry smile my way as we reached the stop sign on the outskirts of the town proper. "And honestly, I'm happy to help. There are a lot of moving pieces for this to work. Who would do the baking at this community bakery? How would you regulate it to make sure no one's not making pot brownies?"

I laughed. "That sounds exactly like something Mancini would do."

"I wouldn't doubt that she has some in her house right now."

I shook my head. "I think I need to draw up a plan. See what would actually work and what is a pipe dream."

When we pulled behind the bank building, he eyed my sneakers warily. "We'll have to walk up the sidewalks."

Seeing what he was looking at, I got defensive. "Listen, Mancini Jr., I didn't think we'd be adventuring today so I didn't wear the good boots."

"It may be a problem," he said, pulling into the back lot next to Cooper's BMW.

I looked over the dash to see mounds of ankle-deep snow. "Shit."

He opened his door and hopped out. Before shutting it, he instructed, "Sit tight a minute."

Nick made his way over to my door, rubbing his hands together. Opening it, he turned his back to me. "Hop on, Parker."

When he said it, I blushed white hot. The heat rush from my face down to my chest settled into the pit of my stomach. I was so glad that he couldn't see me because I'm sure I was beet red.

"Nick," I started, my voice shaking. The last time we did this, my shirt was half off, my shorts were all off, and we were charging into the lake to skinny-dip and scare the fish.

"It's not a big deal, come on. You can't walk through the snow with Chucks on, Parker. I'm wearing waterproof boots. This is a no-brainer."

"Fine." I let out a deep sigh and climbed on. He bounced me up once to hook his arms under my legs better and turned so he could close the door behind us. He made easy work of the trek through the snow. It was a lot deeper than I thought from my vantage point in the car.

"Don't drop me. I'll kick your ass," I said, flicking his ear.

"You mean like this," he teased, pretending to loosen his grip on my legs.

I squeezed as much as I could around his thick coat. "Nicholas, don't you dare!" I howled, and before I knew it, he was doing squats near a pile of snow near the curb.

"What's the matter? A little snowball fight may do you some good," he said, getting precariously close to the mound. There was a newspaper vending rack near the curb. His arms were still tucked under my legs, but he managed to scoop up the snow and hold it in his gloved hands.

I grabbed his chin, turning his face toward mine. "Don't you dare. I can't defend myself up here on Mount Saint Nick."

We both laughed, and for a moment, it felt like it had pre-Jillian.

The snow was falling again, but it was just a flurry that coated his hatless head. I brushed it off, mussing his hair and earning a chuckle. "Hey, I worked hard on this hair."

"It looks better now. I de-snowed you," I explained, giving his hair one more run-through with my hand just as he rounded the corner onto Main Street.

"I'll take your word for it— Hey!" he said, sounding shocked. I looked up to see Jillian at the front door of the building with Emma and Cooper, the three of them chatting amiably. When Jillian saw me, her expression darkened for a moment.

Nick squeezed my legs once before allowing me to slide down onto the one patch of shoveled sidewalk.

"What a surprise," he said, walking over to give Jillian a quick kiss on the cheek. She turned her head, giving him a mouthful of her hair. Perhaps trying to save face in front of his friends, and I supposed me too. "I thought you said you couldn't make it up this weekend?" he asked.

"Parker," she said, ignoring Nick's comments entirely. "So nice to see you again." Then, much to my horror, she hugged me.

Okay, now I was beginning to think she gave hugs as a way to handle awkward situations. I guess it could be worse. If I saw my boyfriend carrying another woman on his back, laughing and teasing, I'd be pretty annoyed, not giving her a hug. "Good to see you too, Jillian. How did you get here? I thought you didn't drive."

"I didn't drive. I used Nick's Uber account," she explained, turning to Nick, who looked a bit wan. "I thought we agreed that we were meeting up today to finish our conversation from the other night?"

Covering my discomfort with a pretend cough, I asked Cooper and Emma to join me inside for a chat. Turning to Nick, I smiled. "Thanks again for the ride here. You saved me from having to walk all that way." Sure, I exaggerated a little, but I hoped that Jillian wouldn't be too hard on him, considering the friendly and flirty position she caught us in.

"You're welcome, but I can come in too? To chat about what we discussed? I'd love to be a part of it too," he said hopefully, turning to Jillian. "Babe, do you want to wait in my truck? Or you can come in? See what's going on?"

"If I go to the truck, are you going to carry me too?" she asked, trying to sound sweet, but it was heavily laced with bitterness. She was uncrossing and recrossing her arms over her chest. There it was. I actually felt relieved that she wasn't pretending she was okay. *She has human emotions, ladies and gentlemen!*

She smiled at me, and then planted a searing kiss on Nick's lips. I looked away just as he closed his eyes. He didn't lean into it, but the whole scenario was impossible to watch.

"Parker, lovely to see you again. Nicky, I'll be in the truck keeping it warm." As she walked off, not waiting for his response, I was struck by how passive-aggressive she was being. Again, I tried to imagine myself in that position, and I felt a pang of empathy. Once she was around the corner heading back to the alley, I stopped Nick from following Cooper and Emma inside.

"Listen, I appreciate you wanting to help with everything and I'll definitely take you up on it, but not now. You can't with her here. It's awkward enough without me getting in the middle of you guys. I can fill you in on what we talked about later."

He smiled thoughtfully, and I sunk inside a little, assuming that he was going to heed my advice and leave. "I promise," he began, "it'll be okay if I stay. I want to help. Besides, Jillian knows that you and I hung out a bit in the past and that we're friends now."

"So she knows? About . . ." I pointed my finger back and forth between us.

He looked down, rubbing the back of his neck. "She doesn't know much. Just that you and I . . . well, that there was a you and me at one point," he whispered, looking around to make sure no one heard.

I took a deep breath. Nick was delusional if he thought she wasn't bothered. The fact that she knew *something* happened between us explained a lot, and I almost felt bad for her. This was the kind of thing I wanted to avoid at all cost. Jealous girlfriends were not my favorite thing to deal with. When I ran D&V, I constantly got requests from jealous exes, or even current girlfriends, trying to ferret out information. I would always pawn those off on another baker to handle. And I did not want to deal with that drama now.

"Nick, I don't want to tell you what to do, but you've got to know that coming inside and leaving her there is not the best move right now. Especially with her knowing about us. I mean, there is nothing for her to worry about, right?"

"Yeah," he said slowly, rubbing his neck again. "Nothing to worry about."

But the way he said it had me thinking that maybe he wasn't being honest—and that felt scarier than the truth.

15

Nick looked at his friends, then at me and then back at Jillian, who was already around the corner headed toward his truck. "I should go," he said.

Which meant he left me on the sidewalk, mouth agape as he jogged through the snow toward his truck.

Two steps forward seemed to always bring us three steps back.

Instead of wondering what was going on, I joined Cooper and Emma in the main part of the room next door to Charlotte's shop, leaving Nick and Jillian to hash it out in the cold. The place was exactly as Charlotte had described it. It reminded me of her space but it was much larger. The space was an empty canvas of whites and grays, which actually worked really well for what I had in mind. It wouldn't need anything bold and audacious to make it special. Particularly if the goal was keeping things *classic*.

"So, Parker. What's up? You called a meeting," Emma said, and I got the impression that she was used to being the one who called meetings, not vice versa.

"I did," I said excitedly. "I've got an idea."

As I ran down the main points of what Nick and I had discussed in the car, and what Charlotte and I had discussed previously about the classes, Emma and Cooper were riveted. "I'm assuming you'll draw up a formal plan for this venture?" Cooper asked, smirking.

"Of course! But you know about all of this already, don't you," I said, rolling my eyes. "Let me guess, Charlotte?"

"I'm the mayor; of course I know all of this. In fact, I believe my future mother-in-law wants to come for a class."

"Please, from what I hear, she can teach the classes. Which leads to another point, but I'll get to that in a minute."

"Apologies, we know how to sidetrack a conversation better than anyone else," Emma offered before holding her hand up to her mouth as if she was going to be sick.

"Do you want to sit down?" I asked, pushing her toward a metal folding chair that was in the corner at the front of the space.

"Thanks, I'm just a bit woozy today. No big deal," she said, casting a wary glance at Cooper.

When he was preoccupied with his phone, I whispered, "You haven't told him yet. Why?"

She shook her head and raised her index finger to her mouth. "Waiting for the right time. Please don't say anything."

I made an X over my heart and mouthed *Promise.*

"Sorry, carry on," Cooper said, coming over to stand with a comforting hand on his fiancée's shoulder.

I walked in a circle around the largest part of the room. In my mind's eye, I could see it coming together nicely.

"The goal is to use everything that we make for the YouTube videos and sell it here in the shop. Every week the menu changes except for the core staples. The classics! People can bang those out easily during the week, but we'll keep the changing specialties a surprise."

"By classics you mean, like, bagels? Sorry, I don't want to sound clueless, I'm just trying to get a handle on what you're thinking. You remind me a lot of Emma. Your brains operate at a speed ten times mine does, so it takes me a bit to catch up." Cooper chuckled.

"Aw, babe!" Emma sang from her perch in the corner. "That's the sweetest thing you've ever said to me."

"No bagels. Think muffins, scones, traditional cupcakes: chocolate, vanilla, maybe hummingbirds because that's old-school. Just simple things that people love."

"Okay, seems simple enough."

"Yes, it's pretty straightforward, and we'll use social media to drive traffic to the store. It'll depend on who our guest baker is."

"Oh, guest baker? That's fun!" Emma said.

Cooper nodded. "Where'd you come up with that?"

"Viola. She mentioned that she does a celebrity scooper at the ice-cream shop every now and then, so I just changed it. The businesses go hand in hand, so instead of this being competitive, it's collaborative. It works if people take ownership of the place. The social media is the easy part in all of this. It acts as a commercial for the business."

"Do you mean someone will just pop in sporadically, or is it a set thing? Like, every Monday is Sophia. Or holidays with Henry?" Emma asked, and I loved that she used Henry as the example. As much as I loved her, crappy crêpes with Charlotte probably wouldn't fly.

"Both!" I grinned. "It depends on who wants to volunteer and how much time they have to devote to the bakery, but I see no reason why we can't have both scheduled and seasonal guests helping out."

"I'm following you now," Emma said, her fingers moving lightning fast as she took copious notes on her phone. "This sort of sounds like a community garden."

I clapped my hands. "That's exactly what this is like! Except instead of renting spaces to grow your crops, you're baking goodies and showing off your skills."

"So how does this tie into the YouTube videos?" Cooper asked.

"The new version of my videos will highlight the Golden Girls, and have me giving lessons like I did today with Nick, except instead of featuring one person, they'll feature the entire class. We'll run those here too. Charging for the classes is part of how the place will make money. We can use the large space in the back by the kitchen for the class setting, and maybe we can bring in a handful of decorative chairs or small tables for displaying photos, or flowers from Charlotte's place. It'll be more of an in-and-out–style shop. Grab a muffin and you're off." I paused and looked around once more.

"This all seems so easy and yet complicated," Cooper noted, before kneeling beside Emma to check on her.

"You're not wrong. But I think with a little help, this could be really cool, not too expensive, and overall good for the people in town to have something new and vibrant for them to not only be a part of but also to fill a need that Hope Lake has."

Cooper puffed out his chest knowingly.

"Don't let your ego get too inflated. I'll admit that you were right, but this bakery is not *exactly* what you're thinking."

"I'm listening," he said with a mock smugness that made me want to both laugh and slap him.

"You both know that I sold Delicious and Vicious for a pretty penny. I put a lot in savings. I bought a couple stupid things, but that's all I've done with it."

"Parker, what are you saying?" Emma asked, standing to put an arm around Cooper's waist as they waited for me to explain.

I smiled and let out a cleansing breath. This would feel good, and I wagered it would go a long way to helping me try to find myself again. "I'll be the financier of this little ditty. An investor until I get my initial money back. I'll help get it started and make sure it's running on all cylinders, but then I'm going to turn it over to the Golden Girls to run. Think of me as a silent partner whom everyone knows about. I'll be what Lucille was to Charlotte," I explained, referring to the woman who owned Charlotte's store. "Once I earn back my investment, we can have a plan in place to roll the money back into the bakery or we can donate it after expenses. I don't particularly care as long as it's a group decision."

"Parker, that is more than generous. But what will you get out of this?" Cooper asked, genuinely concerned for me. It was sweet and, for the first time, it made me realize that Cooper, Emma, Henry, and even Nick were *my* friends, not just Charlotte's. They all cared about me. It warmed my heart.

"I'm enjoying just spending time with the Golden Girls, but I'm not being entirely altruistic. I don't need the money. Once I recoup my investment, everything will roll into the bakery."

They nodded. "That's good. As long as it makes sense for everyone in the long term," Cooper insisted.

"I think I've finally figured out what Parker Phase Two is. This space is still open, right?" I asked, placing my hand against the cool window of the empty shop. When I pulled it away, a print was left smudged against the glass.

They looked at one another warily. "Yes, but we'd have to move faster than you may want to."

I shrugged. "I'm from New York. Fast is what we do. I'll talk to the ladies and see what they think."

16

After my brainstorm session with Cooper and Emma yesterday, the idea of the bakery was fresh in my mind. But today I needed to focus on the videos with the Golden Girls. We were filming our first one.

When I got to Mancini's I was relieved to see Nick's massive truck parked in the driveway next to her cherry-red Hummer. We hadn't spoken since the ill-fated piggyback ride, except for a text to say that he was coming to help with the video that day. Still, with things as uncertain as ever between us, I hadn't been sure if he would really come by.

I climbed the stairs, absently smoothing my hair back. When I knocked, my hand barely left the wood before Mancini whipped open the door looking excited.

"Hi!" I said, feeling as nervous as I had the first time I'd been on-camera for the Food Network. I hoped Clara wasn't feeling the same pressure, since she was on deck for a video today. Just as I thought about her, she appeared.

Clara joined us looking lovely with her short, curly hair smoothed back. "All set?" I asked, and she beamed.

"I am. I'm excited, is that funny? I never thought I'd do this and yet, here I am, eager to get this show on the road."

"That's good. I'm glad! Just keep that positivity and excitement in your pocket while you're filming. People will love you. I know it."

We moved everyone into the kitchen, where I immediately pulled up short. Inside was the kitchen I remembered, but it had been transformed into a makeshift studio. Cameras were rigged up with lights shining down onto the marble island. On it were brand-new supplies: a state-of-the-art KitchenAid Artisan, Le Creuset bakeware, and a handful of Williams-Sonoma utensils, which must have been bought for the occasion, some still having price tags on them. Hanging in the corner was a new rack that included a half dozen aprons with *The Baked Nanas* stitched onto them.

"Um, Mancini?" I asked, concerned. "What happened to keeping things simple?"

She laughed. "Well . . ."

"Where did all of this come from?" I asked.

She was looking slightly put off by my question. "Not to worry; we borrowed the camera and lighting equipment from Viola's son and husband. The aprons were donated by a friend, and the kids at the high school embroidered our names on them as part of a home-ec assignment that Henry set up. We did buy all the bakeware, but that's only because mine was so old that it would have looked terrible on-camera. Besides, who knows, maybe we'll get sponsored and we can get more stuff for free."

"Talk about putting the cart before the horse," I said, and Nick, who had sidled in quietly, elbowed me.

"You said that out loud too, in case you didn't mean for it to be," he explained, his dimples deepening while he tried not to laugh as he reminded me of the last time I blurted a thought.

I elbowed him back lightly. "I meant for them to hear that one."

Turning toward him, I whispered, "I haven't heard from you since yesterday. Everything okay?"

He leaned in. "Worried about me?"

I laughed, taking a much-needed step back. "I just didn't know if you'd show. Without you here, I wouldn't have a cameraman."

When I turned to face Mancini and her league of extraordinary grannies, I found them watching us, with smirks and wide, glittering eyes.

"Oh, don't mind us," Mancini teased.

"Carry on," Clara encouraged.

"Don't let us stop you," Viola quipped.

"So!" I shouted, clapping my hands. "Let's get started." It was the only thing I could think of to get them back on track and not thinking about Nick and me as *Nick and me*.

"Clara, the first thing you're going to do is follow the apple cake recipe as we have it. I'll give you the ingredients to open up some dialogue between us so it sounds natural, not rehearsed and stiff. This is the same format as Nick's video, except you're doing more of the baking than he did."

"It helps that it's already not rehearsed," Clara quipped.

I laughed. "Hey, save those one-liners for the filming. I'll come off as a trained baker, but the thing to remember is that we want people to feel that these recipes are accessible, vintage, and from the heart. That's where your spin will come in handy. Talk about how it was making these recipes with your grams, and be sure to mention the old-world measurements. I know you don't remember all of it, but some snippets will go a long way. I think it's a hook that people will appreciate. Once the apple cake is done and you put it in the oven, we'll stop the filming and watch what we've just recorded to see what needs to be enhanced. Maybe you'll think of a better memory to include, or just something that we need to iron out. Then we'll get started all over again and hopefully film what will be a perfect cut. Remember, I'll edit the video before uploading it too, so it's in the best possible shape."

"Then what?" Mancini asked, leaning over the counter with her cell phone in hand. "How do we see how many hits the video's getting? Or subscribers?"

"Again, cart-horse," I said, laughing. "We'll get you guys there, don't worry."

* * *

Once Clara had the first cake in the oven, I said a silent prayer that the "real video" was going to go as smoothly as the first.

"You ready for round two?" I asked as she took out index cards from her pocket to read through her notes again. "Here's the thing, it's okay to be nervous. It's totally normal to fumble. I've done it, and I can tell you this: in my experience, people react more positively when you're real and approachable. Stiff and emotionless are never a good look. So, if you flub or say 'um' and 'like' a bunch, who cares!"

"I know. I'm not really nervous. I just keep thinking about Nick's video and how fun and fast and loose it was. I just hope this isn't dorky," she said worriedly.

"It won't be at all," I said, wondering when they'd seen it, since I'd just posted it last night. I sent it to him for notes. Mainly to see if he thought Jillian would take issue with it, but when he didn't respond, I let it go out. He didn't bring it up today, and I assumed no one—at least not in Hope Lake—had seen it yet. I had been actively avoiding my social media to see how it was doing.

"The Nick video was most likely a one-off. I doubt we'll do another unless it's really well received and, well, if the stars align and all that jazz." *Meaning if Jillian doesn't watch it, swallow her tongue, and somehow gives her blessing to do another.*

Admittedly, the video with Nick was . . . charming, for lack of a better word. Of course, I wouldn't admit that we did have on-screen chemistry or that the banter was funny and at times flirtatious. I tried editing that out as much as I could, but if I was being honest with myself, there were a lot of moments that had me pausing the video to overanalyze the look on his face. Or the longing in my eyes.

What ended up being uploaded was a fraction of the original baking time, but it was the best I could do, all things considered. It was probably part of the reason that I didn't want to check the comments.

I wasn't as worried about the videos with the ladies.

"I think your videos are going to be fantastic. I've got a good feeling, and I'm usually never wrong when I get those," I said, squeezing Clara's hand.

"Thanks, Parker, this means so much. I can't ever repay you for what you've done for me. My kids are thrilled to have their great-grandmother's recipes. Plus, I think these videos are going to be a lot of fun."

The YouTube side was a bonus. With the videos, we got to help the ladies while helping others at the same time. Plus, I really did believe people would find them as endearing as I did. Once the world fell in love with the Golden Girls like I had, I knew that people would want one of their aprons too.

17

Around midnight, someone knocked at the front door of the lake house. The noise startled me and sent the spatula in my hand sailing across the kitchen, along with a stream of expletives flying out of my mouth. Unfortunately, that meant the nearly perfect batch of cream cheese frosting I'd been working on went with it.

"I'm hearing things," I said to myself, grabbing a knife from the block on the counter.

Just in case.

I tiptoed toward the darkened front door and prayed that I remembered to lock it after the kid from Casey's Pub delivered my pizza.

Burglars don't usually knock, Parker.

Peeking out the small side window next to the door, I was relieved to see Nick sitting on the stoop.

Okay, not relieved, per se, but it was better than some woodland murderer who preyed on single girls in lakefront rentals. I would have to ask Henry if there was a book on that because it's definitely something I would read. During the daytime.

When I was back home safe and sound in the city.

Opening the door, I hid the knife behind my back like a serial killer in the movies and smiled. "Nick."

I wasn't mad at him for stopping by, but I wasn't not mad at him either. I knew there was still a lot of resentment and feelings that were unresolved.

"Can I come in?" he asked, keeping his eyes trained on his shoes. "We didn't have a chance earlier, and I wanted to talk about yesterday."

I sighed.

"Parker, please? Five minutes."

"Nick, it's midnight. Can't this wait until tomorrow?" *When I'm dressed and caffeinated?*

His eyes met mine, and it seemed like he'd been drinking. "Did you drive here drunk?" I asked, furious.

"What? No, I drove here, then drank. In your driveway."

"You were drinking by yourself in my driveway? For how long?" I got home at four, the pizza came at eight, and his truck wasn't there at the time.

He looked embarrassed. "A six-pack worth of time?" Nick took a deep breath and hiccuped. "It's okay, I'll sleep it off in the car and we'll talk tomorrow. How about at breakfast? I can make eggs?"

"Nick, why were you drinking by yourself in my driveway?"

"If I said it's a long story, would that be enough of an answer?"

"Nick," I said again, but I wasn't sure what else to say.

Turning to go back to his car, he slipped down the first step and had to grab the log railing to steady himself. I looked at the sky, which was clear and smattered with stars. *Give me some kind of strength for dealing with this man,* I silently begged whatever was up there, hoping she'd give me an iota of self-preservation and courage.

"Come on in, Nick," I said, setting the knife on the side table. If I was going to have to help him up, I didn't want to accidentally stab him too.

"It's okay," he said, slumping on the step. "I'm not drunk; they were light beers. I just didn't eat and I'm really tired. I'll sleep it off in the truck and see you in the morning."

My sneakers were thankfully by the door. I pushed my feet inside and went out into the blustery cold. The wind picked up again, and I knew there was no way I could let him stay outside overnight. He'd be a Nicksicle in the morning.

"Let's go, big guy," I said, pulling him up. He was heavier than I expected, and the two of us almost flopped backward down the stairs. "I got you."

"You do, Parker. That's the problem. You got me."

Ignoring his nonsensical rambling, I focused on moving him into the house. "Help me out here, Nick. I'm not going to be able to pick you up."

Once I got him safely into the kitchen, I pushed him to sit at the breakfast nook by the windows. He slumped over and, looking at him in the light, I realized that he was likely less drunk than he thought, and melancholy more than anything else. He didn't have that sloshed look that he had when we had gotten drunk together in the city around Halloween. Drunk Nick was pretty obvious.

"Coffee or tea?"

He shrugged. "Doesn't matter."

"It does, though. These are things people know about each other if they're eventually going to be friends. We never really discussed things like this." I wanted to keep him talking so I could maybe get at what was bothering him. "Maybe you like coffee with a little bit of sugar. Or tea with honey? Am I getting warmer?"

He smiled, and while it didn't quite seem sincere, it was better than him looking so morose. "Coffee would be fine. But don't go to any trouble," he insisted, putting his hand over mine on the table. "I'll be fine outside. Just let me say what I came to say first."

Slipping my hand out, I placed it on his shoulder. "In a bit. I'm in the middle of something, and I need a pick-me-up too."

Which was not the case at all, but I couldn't let him leave without hearing him out first.

I already had the coffeepot ready for the morning, so I just pushed the button to start it. There were scones that I'd made earlier sitting on the counter, so I put them and some jam on a plate and handed it to him in case he had the urge to nibble.

"Try those. They're delish and a potential for the bakery," I said proudly. "Or I can heat up some pizza. Do you want a slice?"

That perked him up. "Pizza? From Casey's?" he asked, seemingly more awake than a second ago. When I nodded, he smiled, and this time it was genuine. "I'll never, ever pass up Casey's pizza. Although the scone sounds good too."

"Eat both. I'll heat them up for us and you can start talking when you're ready." I placed the pizza and scones on a cookie sheet and slid it into the oven. The coffee was ready, so I poured two cups and made up a little tray with cups, a sugar bowl, and a small ceramic cow carafe with cream.

"How about I start?" I asked, setting the tray down. "If you want to chime in, you do it."

Nick took one of the cups and slid his hands around it. When he nodded, I figured I would ask the awkward questions first, since that's how we rolled. Maybe he needed time to figure out what he was hoping to say to me.

"Did you get to talk to Jillian after you left yesterday?" I took a sip, keeping my eyes glued to the liquid.

He nodded, taking a giant scoop of sugar and plopping it into his cup. His mood had shifted from possibly drunk and exhausted to irritated, judging by the way his lips flattened and his eyes narrowed.

"First things first, I wanted to apologize for butting in. It's none of my business what goes on in your relationship."

He swallowed, keeping his eyes trained on the cup. He wrapped his hands around it and mumbled, "S'okay. You're the only one who's honest with me."

"But I'm not," I began. "I don't know you as well as your friends do, so I should be the last person to pry. It was rude and I apologize."

"Parker," he began, reaching out for my hand before pulling his back sharply. "I'm sorry for the way I reacted. It's just she—"

"It's none of my business. You don't have to tell me," I urged.

"I have to, though," he whispered, and let out a deep yawn. Tonight was not the time for this conversation.

But when is, Parker? You've been putting it off since you arrived.

"Jillian's . . . *annoyed*."

"Expected and understandable," I began, trying to gather the strength to be the bigger person in all of this. I kept repeating *I will not get in the middle,* and yet here I was, firmly planted *in the middle.*

"What do you mean, expected?" he asked. "You expected her to be annoyed with you, but why?"

I shook my head. Men didn't understand feelings like jealousy and insecurity when they were in a relationship. "I hoped she wouldn't be, but really, I'm not surprised. When you told me she knew something happened between us, I didn't doubt she was pissed. I would likely be as well, if I saw my boyfriend carrying his . . . *whatever* on his back and having a heigh-ho time."

He frowned, nodding solemnly. "I told her nothing was going on but . . ." Nick's large hands rubbed over his face, pushing on his temples.

I had no idea where he was going with this, so I had to be more strategic with my questions to get answers out of him before he crashed for the night. "I'm sorry about that. If you'd like me to talk to her about it, I will. Tell her that you were just doing me a favor because of the sneakers."

"Well, that would've been great until she saw the video . . ."

"So you *did* see it. I waited for you to respond, but when you didn't, I just assumed you didn't care, so I posted it."

"No, I saw it and thought it was fine. Great, even. But she must've analyzed it frame by frame because she claimed to see all these feelings and emotions from the two of us. I just saw flour on my face."

Ugh. As much as I wanted to prove her wrong, I knew deep down that Jillian was right. Again. I tried editing out as much of the flirtation as I could but even I, Captain Denial, could admit there was a spark in that video.

"Tell her we won't make any more."

He scoffed. "I tried that. She actually said that she, you know . . ."

"No, I don't know," I explained, wondering if he wanted me to guess.

"She asked that I not see you anymore."

Shocked, I dropped the spoon that I was using to stir my coffee, sending it clattering to the table and dotting my shirt with droplets of brown liquid.

"Is that so?" I asked, as calmly as I possibly could. "I get it, given our history. It *would* make it difficult for us to continue to record tutorials with the Golden Girls, though. Unless . . ."

He shook his head. "I told her that not seeing each other was impossible. We've got the same friends. You're in town for, well— however long you're here, and it wouldn't work because I really liked working with you."

I swallowed a bubble in my throat. There wasn't anything in there about how *he* wanted to stay friends—not just that we shared friends. Admittedly, that hurt more than I thought it would. The hurt would ease eventually, but for now it was lingering.

"Anyway, we talked about it, and she understood that it's a small town and we have the same friends. So, we compromised and I said that I'd avoid spending time alone with you except for the videos, where we'll be surrounded by lots of people."

I almost laughed. He did realize he was sitting in my kitchen at midnight and it was just the two of us, right? "And yet, here you are . . ."

The oven timer dinged, and I was grateful for the interruption.

Sliding on oven mitts, I took the cookie sheet out and plated two slices for him and one for me. At this point, I wanted my mouth full. Otherwise, I would say something vicious, like I used to write on cupcakes.

He smiled up at me wearily after I placed a plate in front of him. His normally clear eyes were bloodshot and veiny. He looked exhausted.

"We need to talk about more than just Jillian," he said around a mouthful of pizza. He moaned, while I focused on pulling apart my crust.

"I know." I took a bite of my own slice.

"It's just . . . I find myself haunted by the way I left things with you in November," he blurted, setting his slice down.

Okay, we're doing this.

He folded his hands on the table and stared straight ahead as if

I wasn't in front of him. Maybe it was easier to tell me what happened if he wasn't looking directly at me. "Okay, maybe 'haunted' is a bit dramatic," he sighed. "But it *is* the first word that comes to mind when I think about you." I stayed silent, urging him to continue.

"Parker, I need you to understand that I really enjoyed our time together. Beyond the sex—which, don't get me wrong, was fucking great—but it was more than that. I really thought—" He paused, his Adam's apple bouncing as he worked through what he wanted to say. "I really thought that we had a connection. It wasn't just a physical thing, though it's clear we're attracted to each other."

We're, as in we are. Not *were,* as in past tense.

I blushed, and if he noticed, he ignored it.

"Even though I visited New York and you came here, it bothered me that you kept it—me—a secret. I thought maybe we could have done the long-distance thing because really, it's not that long of a distance, but it didn't seem like you were interested in continuing with the traveling. You were always too busy—"

"Nick, I knew we couldn't continue doing what we were doing if we were going to have anything more permanent. I *was* trying to give us a shot, but then you stopped returning my calls. Quitting cold turkey was rough for me to deal with."

"You kept blowing off our plans leading up to the holidays. I figured it was your way of signaling to me that you were over it."

"What?" I asked, dropping the pizza onto the plate with a *thwap.* "We had one conversation about the holidays, and I couldn't commit because I needed to figure out my baking schedule. I never said I didn't want to spend them with you."

"I still felt like you weren't feeling the same things I was. That you weren't as invested—"

I cut him off. "I sold my business for you!" I screamed, realizing that I was in a little bit of denial at just how much my relationship with Nick had affected my decision to sell D&V.

There was complete silence. Nick's eyes looked like they were going to come out of their sockets.

"I never asked you to—" Nick started.

"I didn't mean that. Well, not entirely," I sighed, suddenly exhausted. "I didn't sell it for you, exactly. But what we had—what we started—showed me I wanted more in life besides the shop and the hours, the stress and the hectic lifestyle. It made me realize that I wasn't really *living*. Not in any way that made me feel great at the end of the day. And I couldn't have the type of life I wanted with you if I was still living and breathing D and V. All the other reasons for selling are true, but if I'm being honest, you did play a role. I was excited to tell you about it, but . . ."

"I never gave you the chance," Nick finished my sentence, and his face morphed into one of anguish. "We were never really great at communication, were we?"

"That would be correct," I said. Our conversation was too little too late.

"I was definitely feeling the same things. I don't know how you thought differently."

Thinking back to late summer and early fall, I remembered the hope I felt with each text he sent. Each time he showed up on my doorstep unexpected or when he pulled me into his house with a searing kiss. Maybe things would have worked out if we'd tried harder. Maybe if I'd told him how much I enjoyed spending time with him, things would have turned out differently.

"But I am sorry for that," I said. "I know I wasn't always timely on replying to things, but our hours didn't sync very well with me being up at four and asleep at nine. But I always answered the following day."

He reached across the table and laid his hand on mine. "I guess we were just lousy at communicating. I wanted to spend time with you whenever I could, and I just felt like you didn't rank me very high on the priority list. That hurt."

His candid answer made my stomach flip. "But why didn't you tell me that instead of leaving me in the dark? You could have just explained what you were thinking. Instead, I was completely caught off guard by your behavior. That hurt so much."

"I'm so sorry for that. It's one of the things I regret the most. I honestly don't have an answer for why I ghosted you. I think maybe it was my pride. I didn't want to hear that you didn't feel the way I did." He laughed, but there was no humor in it. "When I say that out loud, it sounds incredibly stupid."

I kept my head down, not wanting to look him in the eye. "Maybe it was just the wrong time for us. It wasn't meant to be. I do believe that everything happens for a reason. Maybe in the cosmic game of chess, our pieces weren't meant to exist on the same board after all. I just wish you told me this then. Even if we weren't meant to continue, leaving me hanging like that was an awful thing to do."

His pizza long forgotten, Nick's left hand joined the right and clasped around mine. He nodded. "I feel terrible. Maybe that's why I feel haunted when I think about it. I handled it poorly, and I know it's all on me."

Scooching forward, I leaned closer to him. "I don't need you to apologize now or feel guilty about it. I'm just telling you so that maybe we *can* move on to being friends," I said, repeating his words from earlier.

"I'm going to be blunt," he said, rubbing his thumb against the top of my hand. "There are a lot of feelings that I have for you that aren't *just* friendly. It's why I told Jillian I'd avoid being alone with you. It's because I know there is some validity to her concerns."

I bit the inside of my cheek to stop myself from agreeing. From saying *I know, me too.* That would have gotten us in trouble.

We could ignore the tension. Or allow it to fade as it surely would. *Eventually.*

"I won't confirm or deny having similar thoughts," I said slowly. "But, Nick, I've dealt with a lot of terrible breakup messages to home wreckers and I'm not going to be that person. You're with Jillian now."

"I know."

"And that makes things really complicated," I continued, needing that extra reminder that we could not, we *would* not, be crossing that line again while I was here and he was with her. "Not to mention that we can't seem to get our shit together to have an honest conversation. Why couldn't we do this in November?"

"I don't know. I wish we did. Things might have been different. But I also hope you know that I would never cheat," he said seriously. "Never."

I swallowed. "Then answer me this. When did you get together with her?"

"What?" he asked, looking up. His eyes were even more bloodshot than before. He looked exhausted, and for a second, I felt guilty bringing it up. But what better time was there than the present when you were looking for deep answers?

"I'll repeat the question. When did you get together with Jillian? Before, during, or after us?"

He took a deep breath, his hand stilled over mine. "After. I would never have cheated on you."

"I believe you." It was the truth. Nick and I were similar—loyal and monogamous. Even though whatever we had last fall wasn't "serious," we'd had a talk early on that we'd be monogamous. He must've stopped calling and messaging me when he met her. Granted, he left me confused, but we were undefined and long-distance, and it wasn't like there was a conversation in which we outlined what the relationship was.

"I won't pretend that I'm not still hurt or mad, because I am, but I don't have the urge to grind your nuts in a food processor anymore."

He smiled. "I wish I could take things back, Parker. I've missed you."

I couldn't respond. Not that I wasn't feeling the same way, but the lump in my throat wouldn't let the words come out.

"Are you feeling a little less drunk?" I asked him, just as the clock in the foyer chimed one. I yawned. The coffee hadn't had its intended effect on me. And not on Nick either, judging by the fact that he too was covering up a yawn with his hand.

"Here's what I suggest," I said. "You crash here. Either stay on the couch or in one of the guest rooms, and in the morning, we can forget this over some eggs and bacon? That *I* make, because we both know you can't make eggs *or* bacon," I said, remembering his well-intentioned but sad attempt at breakfast after one of our nights together.

He smiled brightly, his dimples deep. "Deal," he said, sliding out of the breakfast nook.

Nick helped me clean up the table, tossing the trash away and filling up the dishwasher. He even helped scrape the icing off the counter from my previous baking attempt and licked his finger. "This is delicious. What is it?"

"Cream cheese frosting. I'm trying to create new recipes that are mine again. It's not perfect yet, but it's still pretty good," I explained, feeling a deep sense of relief that maybe, just maybe, my mojo tide was coming back to shore.

"What do you put it on?" he asked.

"Cakes, cupcakes. Number-one rule of baking, friends don't eat all of the icing without sharing."

Nick smirked, his eyebrow rising slightly. "Sorry about that. Maybe we can pack it up and eat it tomorrow with breakfast."

"Deal."

We made quick work of the dishes, mixing bowls, and blades.

I walked to the front door, Nick right behind me as I locked it. He spied the knife sitting on the small side table and tipped his head in question.

"Something you want to tell me?" he asked, picking up the large chef's knife.

I smiled, taking it from him and bringing it into the kitchen. "I thought you were a burglar earlier. It was midnight and a man was knocking on my door. I was going to use it for protection."

Nick laughed. "Parker, I don't know anyone else who makes me laugh as much as you do. Truly, you're one of a kind."

"Funny, I say that about Mancini all the time," I explained, and his expression softened at the mention of his number-one fan.

"I owe a lot to that woman," he said, waving his hand for me to go first up the wide wooden staircase.

He paused on the landing. "Are you sure you don't mind if I crash here? I can call an Uber if you prefer."

I turned. From my vantage point, two steps above him, I was able to get a really good look at him. His skin still held its summer glow, though maybe not quite as rich and golden as it had been in July. The slight laugh lines around his eyes deepened as he waited nervously for my answer.

"It's almost two in the morning and I have guest rooms. It's what friends do," I insisted.

"We're friends, right, Parker?" Though he asked the question with conviction, I still didn't believe it was all he wanted, and that was bad for both of us.

"Almost, Nick."

The steps didn't creak as we climbed, but I was still aware of every footstep as we reached the second floor. This felt like a turning point for us—in a good way, I hoped. It would be good to lose the undercurrent of sexual tension and work on our friendship. We needed to be able to play nice.

Besides, Nick left me confused once. Was I really willing to risk feeling that way all over again? We could be friends—I just needed to make sure that anything else that lingered was ignored.

Because that always worked.

18

Nick had cleared out of the guest room sometime after I crashed upstairs. So quietly that I didn't hear a peep. At least he was considerate. He left the room so spotless that I thought I had imagined him being there.

There was no note, no text. Just like last November. The only proof that he was here last night was the shoveled path to where his truck was parked and the fading boot prints left in the snow where he escaped.

I took five minutes. Five minutes to be annoyed and a little bit hurt that we literally had just decided to be friends. To act like normal people. And here he went, fleeing in the middle of the night.

He really knew how to bruise a girl's ego.

Instead of ruminating, I decided to move on. I made coffee, extra strong, a bagel, extra butter, and a plate of bacon, extra crispy.

All of it made me feel exponentially better until I checked the paper that was so kindly delivered to my rental. Flipping it open, my buttery finger smeared the black ink across the front page. It was an article about the available spaces in the bank building, and the companies that the town council was hoping would occupy them.

The largest available unit was almost done with its remodel. It would be an upscale restaurant called The Vault—an aptly named restaurant with modern fare that was brilliantly using the fact that the original bank vault was still inside. It was being billed as the centerpiece of an out-of-the-box dining experience.

The other spaces were also *supposedly* spoken for. Though I was under the impression after my conversation with Cooper and Emma that the unit next to Charlotte's was still up for grabs.

A town council member was quoted in the article as telling the reporter that a chain pharmacy was interested in the space next to Charlotte's shop, and that the council was sure to approve it. The opposing opinion came from Cooper, the mayor himself, stating that all options were being considered and that nothing would be finalized until they entertained all offers from interested parties.

"Okay, well, that's good news," I said around a mouthful of bacon.

With no time like the present, and with no time to dawdle, I grabbed my cell phone and called Mancini.

She picked up on the first ring. "Hello, dear!" she said, sounding out of breath.

"Mancini, did I catch you at a bad time?"

"No, no," she puffed, and I heard her tell someone to wait a moment. "I'm at my senior aerobics class, but we're almost done. How are you?"

I swallowed the rest of the bacon, along with the nerves that had built up. This wasn't what I had originally discussed with the ladies, but I wondered how they'd react.

I often blamed Mancini for putting the cart before the horse. Was I guilty of the same thing?

"Dear?" she asked again nervously.

"Sorry. I'm okay, I just wanted to chat with you and the rest of the ladies about another idea I had before we headed to your house for another video."

"Oh! An idea. We love those. Girls, we're meeting Parker after class!" she shouted, and I could hear a flurry of activity through the phone. "How's an hour from now? I could come get you or . . . ?"

"No, no. I'll call an Uber and meet you guys at Charlotte's shop. Is that okay? It's near your aerobics class, right?" I asked, hoping that I wouldn't be putting them out too much.

"Perfect. Oh, we're all so excited. See you soon, sweetie!"

*   *   *

I arrived at the shop with time to kill before the ladies got there, and texted Cooper to see if he could meet me.

Emma had given me a key, so I walked the space wondering again if this was a good idea. "Yes, but D and V started with a squirrelly idea, and look where that ended up," I said to myself.

There was a light rap on the door, and I turned to see Nick looking through the glass.

I opened it for him and stepped back, letting him decide if he wanted to stay inside or outside. I crossed my arms and continued walking around the space, my back to him.

"Do you want to be alone?" he asked.

I shrugged in response, the sting from this morning still fresh.

"How've you been?"

I snorted, not helping the blunt response. "I just saw you a couple hours ago. Not much has changed."

Turning, I watched him rub the back of his neck.

"So, fine, I guess?"

"Yes, I'm fine," I stated coolly. "Are you here for Mancini? She'll be here soon. How did you know I was here?"

I was confused as to why he was here, since he wasn't supposed to spend time alone with me. Perhaps that was why he'd bolted before dawn. Jillian's warning was to be heeded, not ignored, if he wanted to keep himself in her good graces.

"I know. Mrs. M. let me know you were going to be here. I thought maybe I could help since we didn't, uh, get to talk the other day about the business idea. Unless you don't want my input anymore, since, you know."

I stiffened, not liking that conflicting feelings were brewing. There was a large part of me that wanted to spend time with Nick, but not at the expense of my own self-preservation. Plus, I didn't want distractions when I needed to be sharp for my announcement. "Sure, Nick. Whatever you'd like to do." It came out bitchier than I'd intended, but what was the point of friendship if it was a one-way street?

"Parker, I'm sorry about this morning," he said. "I really am. I should have stayed."

"Okay."

"I *am* sorry, whether you believe it or not. I woke up and panicked when I realized where I was. Jillian had called a couple times. I—"

He paused, and I was grateful that he did, because I really didn't want to hear that Jillian, the super-sweet girlfriend who was the opposite of me, was the reason that he'd left.

"Nick, it's fine. Maybe it's better if we try to avoid each other while I'm here or whenever I visit. I really don't want to be the cause of any fights you and she may have. I don't really have the time or energy for it." I couldn't bring myself to say her name. Petty, sure, but a girl could only take so much.

"It's not that. We talked, and I explained that we're just friends and that we were going to be seeing each other. She doesn't know *everything* that happened between us. I don't want to tell her that. I don't think she'd understand."

That makes two of us.

"You do whatever you've got to do. I appreciate the offer, but you don't have to stay if you think it's going to cause an issue. We're not in a group setting, so this isn't allowed anyway."

I took off, walking toward the back of the space, where there was a heavy door that led into what I was visualizing as the classroom setting. The lights in the building weren't on, and this room had no windows to provide outside light like the front space did. When I walked in, I realized too late that I couldn't find a switch, and the door shut behind me.

"Shit." I felt around for the doorknob and came up empty. My phone was in my purse in the main area, and I prayed that Nick didn't heed my urging to leave or I'd be stuck until Mancini and the ladies showed up.

Banging on the door, I called out. I heard him shuffle over. "Parker?" he asked, his voice muffled by the thick door.

"Yeah. I'm glad you're still here. I got locked in, and it's completely black in here. I don't have my phone to use as a flashlight. I can't find a light switch anywhere."

I could hear him jimmying the door, but it wasn't opening. "Okay, well, the bad news is the door is stuck," he explained, continuing to wiggle the handle. Following the sound, I found the inside handle, but it was also stuck.

"What am I going to do?" I asked, a rush of panic making me nauseous. I didn't like the dark and feeling like I was trapped in it.

"Take a step back. I'm going to slam my weight into the door to try to get it to open," he instructed.

I took two tentative steps back, since I couldn't see where I was going and if anything was behind me. My heart was racing from being in the dark. I'd hated it since I was a kid and got locked in the basement by accident.

Sweat collected on my forehead and my palms were slick. The only thing saving me from a full-blown panic attack was hearing Nick struggling to get in by slamming his body weight against the door.

"I feel like I'm almost the—"

Nick flew in through the doorway, his large body slamming into me. With an uncomfortable *oof,* we collided and tumbled to the floor, his arms wrapped protectively around me. We rolled once, and I ended up lying half on top of him.

"Thanks," I mumbled into his chest.

Just enough light was coming in from the front room and windows for me to see him clearly. Luckily the door hadn't closed after he barreled in.

His hand was lying on my bare skin, just above where my jeans ended and below where my shirt had rolled up from the tumble. His palm felt hot and slick against my skin, which was odd considering how cold it was outside and in the room. When I looked down at him, his eyes were squeezed shut, and his mouth was open, lips pursed as he exhaled slowly.

"Nick," I choked out. "Did I break you?"

"Almost," he said with a smile. "I'm pretty sure everything is still where it belongs."

"Do you want to check?"

"Did you really just ask me if I wanted to check?"

I shook my head. "Never mind. Forget I said anything."

His hand fisted the back of my shirt for a second before he released it and opened his eyes slowly.

"I'm going to slide off of you, okay?" I asked, bracing my hands on either side of him to make it easier to shove off of his body.

"Pickle chips. Pickle pizza. Pickle juice. Pickle—"

"Are you hungry?"

He laughed. "I'm trying to make something go away."

"Ohhh!" I said, stretching out the word. "So, you're saying not to move?"

He didn't respond with words, just a curt nod.

"What if I just hop up?" I tried to get up in one smooth motion, but it didn't work as planned and I ended up pushing off of him by placing my hands on his chest. His muscles flexed beneath my palms. When I finally got to my feet, I held out my hand for him to take it so I could help him up.

He shook his head and held up a finger. "Just need a second," he explained, staring at the ceiling and breathing heavily.

Don't look down. Don't look down. Don't look down.

I looked down.

Oh. *Oh!*

A throat cleared from the doorway and we both turned to see Mancini, Viola, and Clara standing there with confused expressions.

"Are we interrupting, dears?" Mancini asked, eyeing Nick and me. "I know you said to meet at Charlotte's place but we thought we heard a ruckus. We came to investigate."

Of course you did.

Nick sprang up from the floor and backed away as if I was on fire and he needed to keep a safe distance.

"Nope," I said, taking my own step away from him. Which, of course, didn't go unnoticed by any of them.

"I got locked in and Nick had to ram the door open. Then we fell."

"Uh-huh," Mancini murmured. I took a step toward them, and Clara grinned. I would need to nip this gossip in the bud before the whole town found out, and our collision turned into a story about the ladies catching Nick and me in a passionate embrace.

"Ladies, I'm glad you're here," I said, changing the subject as I marched past them and into the main part of the shop. I turned to see the three of them looking excited and following me. Nick, for whatever reason, stayed in the back room.

"Parker, is there anything you need to tell us?" Mancini was fishing.

I shook my head, hoping to appear nonchalant. "Nope."

As if sensing that I needed a bit of salvation, Clara piped up, "You share when you've got something to share."

"I do have some things to discuss about the—"

"Parker, if this is about the videos," Mancini began, "we were thinking—"

"Yes?"

"Well, we were just thinking that we're a bit . . ." she said, sounding nervous.

"Oh no, you're rethinking it? If you're not comfortable, we can do something else. Maybe you just stand and hand me ingredients and I do the talking? We'll work it out so you're all on board and feeling great about this," I rambled, hoping that this could be salvaged.

"That's not it at all," Mancini explained, reaching out and taking my hand. "We were just thinking that we should maybe record a couple videos in advance so we can stick to the once-a-week posting schedule." She took out a notepad. "We made some notes last night about ideas for upcoming shows."

My relief was immediate. "This is great!" I said excitedly. "I'm glad you guys are taking the lead on this. After all, this is all about you."

"Oh, good. We were worried that you'd be mad," Viola said sheepishly. "Or back out because Nick's video was so cute and you want to do a solo project with him." She elbowed Mancini and smiled. "I think we were afraid that you thought we were edging you out."

"No, never! Besides, this is *your* venture. I'm just helping. This brings me to my idea and unfortunately, due to timing, it's something we need to act on quickly."

"Oh, really?" Mancini said gleefully. "What could it possibly be?"

I watched the three of them exchange knowing glances.

"You already know, don't you?" I asked, wondering who had spilled the beans before I was able to run it by them.

Mancini at least had the decency to look guilty. "Oh, talk gets around town quickly, dear. Don't be mad at Cooper. He didn't spill the beans, necessarily. Viola's daughter is the town solicitor, so she happened to overhear when Cooper mentioned it at the office, and she happened to mention it to Viola, who told me and Clara at aerobics earlier."

"What else?" I asked, seeing that they were still bouncing to say something else.

Mancini smiled. "Emma was more forthcoming when we saw her at the pharmacy. She said it'll be similarly set up to a community garden. Parker, that's genius. We used to have a garden, you know. Back in the sixties over by where you're living, funnily enough."

My God, this town left no stone unturned. "I had no idea. I've never had much of a green thumb so I can't help kick-start that again, but why not this? It's a good investment for the town and for my soul."

"Parker, are you sure? I mean, that's a big task that you'd be taking on," Viola said, brows furrowed.

"Viola, you look worried." I walked over to her to put my arm around her.

She nodded. "I'm very busy with the ice-cream shop. Maybe not now because of the off-season, but come April, it'll start to pick up again. I don't know that I'll have time to devote to this," she explained sadly. Her friends looked on with concern.

"I thought about that. I figure that if you ladies and your league of extraordinary women are the faces of it, we can work out a schedule that makes sense for everyone. If, and this is a huge if, you're willing to do it. I can help too when I'm here, and ultimately, it'll only draw more business to the ice-cream parlor too. My hope is that every small business in Hope Lake has an uptick in patrons thanks to The Baked Nanas."

Mancini clapped her hands excitedly, and when Cooper walked in a few minutes later, they rushed over to tell him they were in and spent the next ten minutes bombarding him with questions.

"I think this sounds amazing, Parker," Cooper said, looking up from the ladies. "So, are you officially going to make an offer on this place?"

Their enthusiasm was immediate, but it wasn't without a sense of worry.

"I need to look at my finances—"

"If I move some things around, I can—"

"I'll sell some stocks—"

I smiled. "Ladies, stop! We didn't get to this part yet, for good reason." I shot a glance at Cooper, who looked apologetic for the gaffe. "Like I said earlier, I'm using this as an investment property. Not just financially, but emotionally too. If I have something like this feeding my soul, I think it'll help me figure out the next phase of my life."

Mancini started to interject but I raised my hand.

"I've been thinking about this. I'll front the money for start-up costs and then we'll work out a plan to pay me back once the bakery is profitable. I'll take a small percentage, but then the rest of the profits will go back to the store. I want to do this. I can't explain it, but I feel like it's something that I have to do."

Nick finally came out of the back room, surprising Cooper, who immediately engaged him in silent conversation using only his eyes, a raised eyebrow, and a subtle head tilt.

The art of a silent broversation was something that mystified me.

"If we're done here," Cooper began, holding the door open for us all to file out, "my fiancée wants to meet us at the diner for a quick meeting and a bite to eat. Mancini, it was a joy to see you, as always."

"Parker, do you need a ride?" Cooper offered, and Mancini looked on expectantly. "Or you can go with Nick. Whatever is easier."

"I've got to grab my stuff, but I'll see you there in a bit," I said, eyeing Nick, who lingered by the door. If he wanted to talk again, I would have to gently explain that now wasn't the time. The conversational whiplash was getting to me.

Viola, Mancini, and Clara filed out behind Cooper, chatting away about how excited they were.

That left Nick and me alone again.

"Instead of calling an Uber, if you want, I can take you. We can discuss the business," he said.

"Nick, you know that nothing between us is ever *just* one thing. It's never *just* a conversation. It's not *just* a trip to your house. It's not *just* a dip in the lake. It's an impossible combination of things and a slippery slope that I can't slide down again. I'm still recovering from the first time around."

He rolled back on his heels. "I don't want us to walk on eggshells around each other. That's actually the last thing I want. That and awkwardness. I miss the friendship that went along with everything else. It's just navigating the new terrain that's confusing me."

"Me too. I want to try being friends."

I still couldn't help but think that the back-and-forth and the hot-and-cold between us was getting to him as much as it was getting to me.

19

The 81 Diner was a traditional East Coast diner filled with linoleum floors and plastic-covered booths. Needless to say, I loved it and the menu. Classic diner food was always something I gravitated toward when the opportunity arose.

The truck was barely in the parking spot before I was sliding out of it and away from a stunned-looking Nick.

The diner was packed with locals yammering about whatever made the town tick. Cooper, Emma, Charlotte, and Henry were already seated, and Henry and Cooper stood when I arrived at the table.

"Well, that's awfully old-fashioned," I said, giving both a one-armed hug. "I sort of love it." I turned to Emma and Charlotte and grinned. "Ladies."

"Parker," they said in unison. Charlotte was smiling, but poor Emma looked a bit green.

I mouthed *Okay?* to her when Cooper wasn't looking. She nodded, smiling at Charlotte.

"Sit anywhere. We're just here to chat about a couple of things as a group."

As a group. I wanted to disinvite myself as I was only a tiny part of this, but I figured they wouldn't have asked if they didn't really want me there. For the briefest of seconds, I felt the slightest bit guilty that Jillian wasn't here for Nick, but I got over it when he held the chair out for me to take a seat. Rome wasn't built in a day, and Nick and I weren't going to magically be fixed after one conversation.

Taking the seat across from me, Nick set his phone on the table and it lit up immediately with a stream of messages. I couldn't read them, but I could see that they were all text notifications from the same name.

Jillian.

He wasn't breaking his promise, I guess, since we were in a group setting. However, I couldn't help but wonder if she was going to jump out in surprise and randomly show up again. If that was the case, I wanted to be nowhere in sight. I had had about enough of the Jillian-Nick saga for a lifetime.

Once the waitress came to take our orders and left, Emma looked at Cooper and smiled. He nodded and she turned to the group.

"So, the reason we asked you all here today was because we have a lot to discuss," Emma started, and Charlotte shifted anxiously in her seat.

I had a feeling that Emma would be discussing the pregnancy and I had a feeling that Cooper finally knew since he was beaming, but Nick and Henry still seemed to be in the dark.

"First things first, Cooper and I want to let you know that

everything for the wedding is going on as planned. We'll be hitched at the end of July, and Parker, we'd like to ask if you'd help us out with the wedding desserts. I know wedding cakes aren't what you're used to doing, but we're not going traditional anyway. We're thinking individual desserts that the guests can pick and choose from."

"Oh wow, I'd love to! That is an honor, truly."

Nick smiled, the first genuine one I had seen from him today. That was, until his phone lit up, this time with a phone call.

Jillian.

"Excuse me, everybody," Nick apologized, standing from the table with his phone clenched in his hand. "I'll be right back."

"He won't be," Emma said when he was out of earshot. "She even called me this morning asking where he was, since he wasn't answering calls or texts."

"That's odd of him, they're usually connected at the hip."

"I hope it's not trouble in paradise," Emma added.

"I'm surprised she doesn't have location services activated," I said, thinking I was quieter than I was.

"Do people do that?" Charlotte asked, pointing to Nick arriving back at the table looking somber.

"Everything okay?" I asked before I could stop myself. *Idiot.*

He gave a weak smile and a nod. "So, you've got some news?"

Cooper took Emma's hand in his and they faced the rest of us with beaming smiles. "We've never been great with the traditional order of things. This isn't an exception."

Henry sucked in a breath and slapped the table. "Oh my God, you're having a baby!" he shouted joyfully, and jumped up from his seat. When it dawned on him what he had just blurted to a crowd of onlookers, he promptly covered his mouth and sat down. "I'm so sorry. I don't know what came over me."

Charlotte was holding back laughter as were Cooper and Emma. Nick didn't even flinch.

"Uncle Henry, start buying the books now. You'll be in charge of the library," Cooper said, confirming the news for his friend.

"Baby Peroni-Endicott will be here in September," Emma said, joyful tears in her eyes.

Cooper leaned over and gave Emma a searing kiss and the restaurant applauded. I wasn't even paying attention to the fact that the entire place got quiet when she began her announcement. That was one way to quickly disseminate news through town. Come to a busy diner to make a statement.

Henry stood again and gave Emma a sweet kiss on the top of her head. "I'm so happy for you guys." He went over to Cooper and clapped his hand on his shoulder. "This baby will be the most well read in town."

Emma laughed. "I have no doubt."

Charlotte followed suit. "I can't wait for the baby shower."

Cooper shook his head. "Charlotte, we need to get through the wedding first."

"Sure, sure, that planning is done, though. I need something new to focus on."

When I took my turn, I smiled. "I can't think of two people who will shower a baby with more love than you guys. I'm so happy for you."

When I returned to my seat, Nick was still there, unmoving and looking dazed, staring in his lap. His phone was on the table beside him, blowing up with messages. When I returned to my seat across from him, I gently kicked his leg, jolting him out of the fog he was in.

I cocked my head to the side, and mouthed *Say something* to him. Shaking his head, he plastered on a fake smile. "I'm so happy for you guys. I just wish Jillian was here for the news too. I know she'll be disappointed she missed it. I'm sure she'll call you with congratulations later."

Who was this? There wasn't a smart-ass comment. No *Uncle Nick is going to be his or her favorite,* or anything that would show that he was genuinely happy. He just looked like he was going through the motions. I didn't know if it was a combination of the phone calls and baby news, or if he was just in a funk. Whatever it was, it was noticed by everyone at the table.

Charlotte tapped him on the arm. "You okay?"

He gave her a weak smile. "Sorry, I'm distracted. I'm crazy busy today."

"Are you sure? Do you want to go outside to talk?" she offered, and I was so glad that he had her to confide in. Not that the guys wouldn't listen, but there was something about having that best girl friend to talk things through with. "I just have a lot on my mind," he said. "Jillian and I have been talking about me spending time in Barreton instead of her coming here all the time."

"Oh, Nick. Are you sure? That's a lot on you, and between work and . . ." She paused.

I know she wanted to include *and us,* but she wouldn't add to the guilt trip that he was already feeling.

"No, actually, I'm not sure about anything anymore," he said, giving me the briefest of glances. "I hate to do this but I'm going to bounce." Emma looked on with tears in her eyes. "Guys, seriously, I'm so happy for you," Nick said, getting up from the table and walking out, not looking behind him to see the deflated expressions on his friends' faces.

20

In the three weeks that had passed since the "diner debacle," as I was calling it in my head, I hadn't seen Nick except in passing. If I was getting a ride into town, I'd wave to him if I saw him drive past, or if he was on my street, he'd shovel but not stick around for me to come out to chat. At the bakery, where he spent almost as much time as I did, we were on opposite schedules. It was avoidance at its finest.

When it came to the bakery, everything was done via Post-it. I was an early bird, in by four-thirty or five, and he'd come by long after I left in the early afternoon. He was helping with the arrangement of the tables in the teaching area, but if we ever happened to be there at the same time, he popped out the back door when I came in through the front. The most interaction I got was a bright yellow stickie on a chair saying:

This place is great. I'm proud of you.

The ladies saw him daily, which made me feel good, because him avoiding me was one thing. Him avoiding them because of me—well, I couldn't live with that.

We still talked via text and email, but never about anything other than the bakery or one of the friends or ladies. If Jillian was with him, he would pretend that he didn't see me, and head in the other direction. Much like I had done at the beginning of my visit. Jillian, of course, always saw me and gave me a big-toothed smile that said, *I won, you lost*.

I wouldn't deny that it hurt. A lot. But I was rolling with it, because I had enough going on without focusing on Nick and what, or whom, he was doing. The ladies and I had been filming videos—about two or three a week—and uploading one a week. And the bakery was coming along fast. We'd be ready to open in about a month, which was crazy, but necessary—we were growing out of Mancini's kitchen with the videos.

But then one night, about a week ago, when I couldn't take it anymore, I had a spur-of-the-moment idea to put everything I was feeling in an email and send it.

Nick,

You're being a real shit. Ignoring me when we see each other? Avoiding me in such a small town? What is wrong with you? Who are you? Where is the guy I met last year? The one who would talk to me endlessly about anything and everything? Even when we were naked on the leather seats of your truck you were still chatty.

Where is that conversationalist now? When we *have* things to talk about? I appreciate your help with the bakery and

Golden Girls, I really do. But I thought we were supposed to be friends? Friends do not behave this way.

There isn't anything we can do now to change the past but if we want to move forward in any kind of way you need to be an adult.

We can only go forward and decide what kind of future there is.

P

When it went un-replied to, I vowed not to do it again. Not to put myself out there for him to ignore.

The whole situation was ridiculous, not only because we were adults, but because I was falling right back into the same rut I was in before—the weird plateau of wondering if we were friends, or if that had fallen by the wayside too. Why was I wasting energy trying to be friends with someone who would never fully be my friend in return? So, I put the friendship part of our relationship on a shelf and focused only on what he could offer me as a small-town busi-nessman. Which, I had to admit, he had a knack for.

The business emails that Nick and I sent to each other were clear-cut. They were professional and to-the-point, and always in-cluded either Mancini, Emma, or Cooper so as not to give Jillian any possible reason to come at him for it. Like the one we ex-changed yesterday.

From: Parker Adams <parkeradamsnotthefamily@gmail.com>
To: Nick Arthur <nick@ArthurLandscaping.com>
CC: Suzanne Mancini <queenmancini@aol.com>
Subject: Signage

Hey Nick,

Can you give us the name of your contact in Barreton for the flyers and sign? Mancini mentioned that you had a guy.

Thanks,
Parker

From: Nick Arthur <nick@ArthurLandscaping.com>
To: Parker Adams <parkeradamsnotthefamily@gmail.com>
CC: Suzanne Mancini <queenmancini@aol.com>
Subject: Re: Signage

Sure. I'll call him and handle.

From: Parker Adams <parkeradamsnotthefamily@gmail.com>
To: Nick Arthur <nick@ArthurLandscaping.com>
CC: Suzanne Mancini <queenmancini@aol.com>
Subject: Re: Signage

Perfect. Thanks.

Everything was civil but totally professional. There were no salutations or personal greetings.

It's like I had never seen him naked.

* * *

"Parker, this is very exciting," Mancini said, coming over to stand beside me as I stared out of the side window into Charlotte's shop.

One of the biggest changes that both of our businesses were undergoing were the windows we were installing to lead out into the hallway. Each space would have full windows inserted on the wall that ran parallel to the hall so each business had more display space, but also so Charlotte and I could dorkily wave to each other when I was in the bakery and she was in the flower shop.

"Would you have ever guessed that you'd be next door to your best friend like this?" Mancini asked, placing her arm over my shoulder and giving me a slight squeeze. The shops were side by side, and I'd be able to wave to her whenever I was inside. It felt like we were ten-year-old Parker and Charlotte again.

"I will answer honestly and say hell no. I wasn't even sure how often I would be seeing her when she first moved here, because Hope Lake got its claws into Charlotte and she hasn't ventured back into the city since. I have to admit, this is the happiest I've ever seen her."

"Well, I think it's a combination of things. Returning and spending time with her family certainly helps, and Henry, of course. But, Parker, you being here has given her a new light too. Sure, she's reconnected with Emma and her childhood friends, but you're the only person here besides her father and Gigi who knew her while she was growing up. I think she's feeling like everything in her life puzzle is finally being pieced together properly."

"I'm glad I get to see her in her element. I always thought New

York Charlotte was who she was supposed to be, until I saw her here."

Mancini smiled, and we both waved from across the way to Charlotte, who was balancing her phone on her shoulder as she inserted some sort of white snowball–looking flower into a hand-wrapped bouquet.

"She's certainly busy," I remarked, seeing the stacks of yellow slips beside her.

"You're right, but I hear she's hiring someone else. The high school had a couple people interested in horticulture at the technical school, and she said she'd speak with them to see if any of them would like to work with her."

"You know everything. I swear, something doesn't happen in this place without being run by you first."

"Psssh," she chided, but winked and I knew I was right. She didn't just have her finger on the pulse: she *was* the pulse of the town.

"Tell me, Yoda. What are the piles of flowers for that my friend is slaving over?"

She gave me a thin-lipped smile as if to say, *This is your test?*

"That's for the Malacari wedding tomorrow," she said confidently. "They're going to be lucky if they get through it all before the storm hits."

"My God, does it ever *not* snow here?" I said, exasperated. Since I arrived at the shop that morning, it must have snowed a foot and a half. This was insane.

"Where's the wedding?" I wondered.

"Country club. The menu is delightful."

"I reiterate, you know everything." She shrugged knowingly. The woman was a marvel.

She nudged me with her shoulder. "I know some things. More than a few, less than a bunch."

"I find that hard to believe." I threw her a glance, knowing that she knew a very important something about me and Nick.

"Okay, most things." She lowered her voice a smidge. "I know that girlfriend of Nick's is not the right fit for him."

My eyes widened in surprise. "You see it too?" I tried to hold in my response, but I was glad someone else had seen it. It wasn't just me and the jealousy I wasn't able to admit to myself.

Mancini looked at me as if to say, *Give me a break.* "Please. There is something wrong with that woman. I've seen through that two-faced little bitty since I met her. No one is that nice. Not even me."

I laughed hard. God, I loved Mancini. "Did something happen?"

She shook her head. "No, I'm just observant. When us old broads are around, people tend to drop their guard. I think they almost forget we're in the room and pay us no attention. As a result, we see it all."

I leaned in closer, knowing I was going to get a good story.

"After Nick first started bringing her around, I actually didn't mind her. She wasn't necessarily my cup of tea, but he seemed happy and you know I want my Nicholas to be happy. But then I started noticing things. I'd overhear things she'd say to him. Things like 'Oh Nicky, do you really need to hang out with Henry and Cooper again? Don't you want to hang out with me instead?' or 'Nicky, you're the nicest person, but do you really need to shovel everyone's snow? I don't want you to get sick.'" Mancini's impressions were spot-on.

"At first it seemed harmless, but then I realized Nick started changing. He stopped hanging out with Cooper and Henry. He stopped coming by the community center. And then it hit me, she was manipulating him to not do things he wanted to do!"

"Mancini, that is what I've been thinking since I first saw them together. Thank goodness it's not just me!"

She nodded. "I thought Nicholas was happy. But the longer he's been with her, the unhappier he's seemed. And when you came breezing back into town, well, then everything changed."

"I don't know what you mean," I lied, but we both knew it.

"You know he started coming around to visit me more, to see his friends again. They noticed it too, the change. It's not the same as it was last fall when you were cavorting around together, but I still notice a difference, and I'm not the only one who's equating it to you being here. There are moments when he seems happy again. Is there something new going on that you're not telling me, Parker?"

"Of course not. What we had last fall was clearly not meant to be. For as much as I dislike Jillian, I'm not going to engage in anything that would result in Nick cheating on her."

"Dear, I never thought he'd be a cheater. Or that you'd allow it. You're both too good for that. But I was hoping—I guess I was hoping—that you would find your way back to each other after he gave her the heave-ho. But, since she's still lingering around . . ."

"I have no idea what's going on with them."

"Jillian is here and wreaking havoc like the rotten tomato she is."

"That's an oddly specific vegetable to choose. Am I missing something?"

She turned and clapped her hands. "Emma told Cooper, who told Henry, who told Charlotte, who told me that for the first time Jillian dropped her mask the other day and flipped in the grocery store about you. When she did, her whole head turned bright red like a tomato. It took almost a half hour for her to go back to scary pale."

I took a step back. "Wait, what? Why was she mad about me? I haven't even seen him!" I argued, feeling my blood boiling to the point where I too would look like a tomato.

"Emma overheard her saying that she thinks that he has secret accounts that he follows you from. Something about the snippity Snapchat. I guess she went through his history and found *a lot* of Parker searches saved on the Google. Add in the video that you two made being all over social media—well, let's say all of it got her to explode."

"She saw the video earlier. He promised her he wouldn't hang out with me one-on-one anymore and he hasn't. What's the issue now?"

Mancini took my hand. "Honey, you're so blind to it. Your video was a screaming advertisement for a hopeful romantic. Two people with enough chemistry to make a boring cooking lesson into a sensation! People keep commenting about how you two should be more than friends. That the chemistry is palpable through the screen. They're right. You're magnetic together."

"That's ridiculous." Although I'd been actively avoiding any comments on that video so I had no idea what people were saying, I still wanted to touch base with him, to tell him that I was sorry for causing problems even when I was actively trying to *not* cause problems. "Nick and I are—*were*—friends. There's nothing more there to exploit."

She frowned. "If you say so, dear."

* * *

The following Saturday, I was supposed to meet with Mancini, Clara, Viola, and Gigi to tour the bakery and make a checklist of who was handling what before we were ready to roll. The television that would hang on the wall and air the videos hadn't arrived yet. Nick promised that the second it showed up, he'd mount it. The chairs had nicks and needed to be replaced by the manufacturer, and the valances that would hang over the large window were the wrong size. Nothing was traumatic but it was still a pain that we had to fix silly mistakes.

Since it had snowed again, the ladies were running a few minutes late. It was difficult to safely navigate Gigi's scooter over the snowy sidewalks. Mancini had texted me that they would be behind by at least an hour, so I was taken aback when I heard the door's overhead bell ding.

"Hey," Nick said, carrying a stack of file folders in his hands. He placed them on the countertop and looked around the room. "I had some free time and wanted to stop in to see if you needed any help."

I smiled tentatively. "Kind offer. I'm surprised you're here. What's in the folders?"

Nick grinned slowly, and opened the folder on top of the stack. "Grand-opening ideas. I contacted the *Hope Lake Journal*, but I also got the Barreton and Mount Hazel papers too. The local newswoman is going to come out for a quick interview and spotlight. Also," he said, scanning my face, "why would you be surprised I'm here? I've been here every day." He set the first folder aside.

"Wow, that's awesome, thanks. I'm sure the ladies will be thrilled to be on television," I said, hoping that it would put focus on them and not on my involvement. As if he read the worry on my face, he pulled up the second folder. "And sure, you've been here every day, but never at the same time as me. I got the feeling that we were back to—"

"Parker, I've just been trying to make it easier on the both of us. Sometimes I think it's better if there isn't a constant reminder of *us*. I didn't know if it would affect your creativity to see me every day, and I certainly didn't want to contribute to that. I just wanted to make sure you had some space."

I can't argue with that.

I kept my eyes down and nodded. "I get it. I just wish you conveyed that. My default is always to think the worst. Tell me more about the paper."

"I know you don't want to be the center of attention but, Parker, it'll ultimately help if people know you're involved. So, I'd like you to rethink it."

I knew his argument was valid. I just needed to accept that me being in the mix would help.

I sighed. "Okay, just something small and secondary to the big story, which is them."

"Deal," he concurred, moving on to another folder filled with names and emails.

"What's this?"

"Mailing list," he said, pushing the top sheet toward me. "I started compiling it. You'd be surprised how many people want to keep up with the goings-on here. Everyone in town knows these ladies, and they're thrilled you're doing this. You're going to have a great turnout for the grand opening."

"Speaking of, you're coming, right?"

"Nothing will keep me away," he insisted, smiling. I turned, not wanting my face to show him how much I missed seeing him around.

I almost said, *Are you sure about that? What about the pint-sized brunette you always have following you around?* but I kept that comment to myself. *As long as he's happy* was the mantra I kept repeating to myself.

As if the Golden Girls knew I needed saving, in they came.

"Parker, this looks fantastic. I love the French feel to it. Very chic, very swag, very tight. I like it," Gigi exclaimed, taking a turn around the shop. She expertly maneuvered around the white wrought iron tables and chairs with her scooter.

As expected, we'd made quick work of remodeling the space

into something that worked as both a bakery and a classroom. It had been surprisingly easy, what with the mountains of free time I had. Still, I needed to get the ladies' opinions on the finishing touches. I couldn't wait for them to see what I'd been working on.

"What's this?" Mancini asked as I met her in front of my favorite place in the shop: the wall behind the pastry shelving.

I exchanged a smile with Nick. I looped my arm in hers and explained what I'd done to surprise them. "I have two surprises. First, there's this shop I know in Brooklyn. They do all these printed keepsakes, and I was thinking that your recipes would look great on a tea towel. I was thinking I would get you one for each of your kids, and we can have some here to use too. The towels would be printed in the recipes' original handwriting, so it would be really an amazing gift."

Everyone was silent and Mancini teared up and pulled me into a hug.

"I love this idea. Please tell me how to reach them and I'll order for the kids. I'd like one for myself too."

"Already ordered, for all of you. My gift for going on this crazy adventure with me. But that's not all. The shop that we got the towels from had a bunch of other options that I didn't know about. One of which was wallpaper." I motioned the group over to the featured wall, which was covered in custom wallpaper.

"Parker, this is amazing." Mancini's voice wobbled, and when she pulled me in for another hug, her tears spilled down her cheeks.

On the wall, under a sign that said RECIPES FROM THE BAKED NANAS, were five individual panels of wallpaper, each separated by a wide gray stripe. Their original recipes were written on the wall in their ancestors' handwriting, just like I'd promised for the tea towels. Below each panel was a picture of the recipe's creator and a note indicating which of the Nanas they were related to.

"I guess you like it?" I asked the group, all of whom were in varying stages of disbelief. "I knew it would be perfect. It wasn't hard, or expensive, so don't give me any lip," I teased, and one by one they each gave me a hug in thanks.

"You and Nick sure make an incredible pair," Viola gushed. I refused to look at Nick, who quickly made an exit after the comment.

"You ready for the rest?"

The Baked Nanas had helped me create the menu, a tentative schedule for the shop, and four more YouTube videos all prior to today. This place was a living, breathing extension of them, and I hoped people would understand and appreciate that.

"Overall, I think that we're almost done. Just a few finishing touches here and there, depending on what you guys would like to see."

"Parker, you did an amazing job. Truly," Mancini said.

The ladies began prattling on about the chalkboard menu design, another Nick idea, and how clear and simple it was. I, unfortunately, was distracted.

"He's coming for dinner tonight, you know," Mancini offered up without me asking.

"Oh, that's good. I hope you have fun," I said lightly.

"Are you doing anything for dinner? You should stop over and eat. Charlotte and Henry, Gigi, Emma and Cooper are coming too."

"Everyone is?" I asked, a part of me a little upset that I was only just told, which was silly because I knew I always had a standing invite.

She nodded. "It just came up when I saw Henry at the store earlier this morning. He texted Nick, who texted Cooper and then Emma. I knew I would be seeing you, so I said I would ask you when we came by too. It's stuffed shells night, and we could use some dessert if you're up to it."

Mancini was the only one who knew that I was baking every

free moment I had at the house. The process was coming along, and while I wasn't back to my old super-creative self, I was getting better and had even managed to invent some new things. Still, I didn't think anything was store-ready yet.

I still needed to find my contribution to the shop. The ladies could handle a lot of it—the specials and the classics—but the daily staples fell to me until we found someone else to take over.

"I made some cupcakes this morning. I'll bring those," I said, stepping over to where my laptop was set up. I turned toward her and the others.

"Honest opinion time, what do you think?"

On the screen were six different logos that I'd been playing with: three options for The Baked Nanas channel, and three for the shop. With the latter moving forward like gangbusters, we needed to lock it in and get the sign ordered as soon as possible.

"Numbers one and five," Mancini said quickly, the rest nodding in agreement.

"I like the simplicity of them and how they match each other," Clara offered.

"You're right. They look like they belong together," Viola agreed.

"You've got a great eye for detail, I'll tell you that. Those are my favorites as well. Should we go ahead and order, then?"

Mancini nodded but asked, "Who are we ordering from?"

"Nick's contact. He put me in touch with someone at Barreton University who will print flyers and order forms for you. They're also going to get a website together, because while I'm okay with some coding, I'm not great with adding a shopping cart feature, and that's all that you'll need for taking online orders."

I paused when they looked at me nervously. Mancini mouthed the word *online* to Gigi and they both paled. Then it dawned on me what their fear was.

"Relax. It's not as hard as it sounds, and besides, I'll be here for a while helping out until you are comfortable."

Mancini glommed onto my comment before I could reel it back in. "Oh, you're staying awhile. How long is that, exactly? Through to Emma's wedding at least, right? After that? Forever?" She added the last bit with a giggle.

"You're funny. I don't have a set plan. I guess that's the joys of having the life of a shiftless layabout." I sighed dramatically.

"Yes, the first thing that comes to mind when I think of Parker Adams is shiftless layabout," Gigi said, rolling her eyes at me. "You're doing more in a day than most people do in a week. Between filming and editing and uploading the videos, getting this bakery together, plus trying to get your own bake on— Parker, you're a woman of many talents. I just wish you'd take some *you* time."

I smiled and leaned down to give her a gentle hug. "I know it may not seem like it, but I'm getting just as much out of this as you."

Mancini interrupted. "Like what, dear? I'm curious, because to us, it seems like you're just a genuinely kind person who's donating a ton of time and money to a bunch of old ladies and getting nothing in return."

I frowned. "First of all, you're not old. So stop it. Second of all, I am! You're helping me help myself with the recipes. If I didn't have your old family recipes to work on, I wouldn't be testing and baking nearly as much as I am. Besides that"—I paused, taking the printouts of one and five from the green folder—"you're teaching me a lot."

They didn't look like they believed me.

"For example, Mancini, I'm jealous of your tenacity. I wish I had that for myself or had you to look up to when I was younger. You're a very grab-the-bull-by-the-horns type of lady, and I love it."

She preened. "You're right there, but it took time. My husband passed away almost thirty years ago, but when he was still alive and my kids were still at home, I wasn't this audacious and outspoken. It took years to build up my confidence after my honey died. Suddenly, I was a single mom with four kiddos. When that happens, you tend to grow a thick skin quickly, and over time—well, the experience turned me into the woman you see here today."

"Well, I'm not happy about the journey that you had to take to become this person, but I'm damn glad that I met you." I pulled her into a hug. "I'm also grateful for the tips you've given me on my macarons," I said, turning to Viola. "I'm hoping with your tips, I'll be able to perfect my new salted caramel desserts."

"You will, it just takes time."

"Gigi, you're one of the smartest and funniest people I know. The way that Charlotte always talked about you made me want to meet you so badly. I had always hoped that you'd adopt me as another granddaughter, because you're genuinely amazing."

Gigi wiped a tear away, smiling. "You are my family, Parker."

"And while you might not have taught me anything about baking," I said, laughing when she pretended to be offended, "I've never met a more willing taste-tester, and for that I'm grateful."

"Listen here, I can make a mean microwavable mug cake. They come in a box and they're delicious," she said, playfully slapping Mancini when she pretended to put her finger in her mouth to gag herself.

I shared with the rest what they had shared with me, and what I had learned from them. Before I was finished, they were all a bit blubbery and so was I.

"We're grateful to have met you too, Parker," Mancini said with a hiccup. "Now, let's get moving. Clara, Vi, and Gigi have to run but I'll stay back and meet the oven guy and the painters for the teaching space. After that, girls, we just need chairs delivered and then we can finish decorating, which is my favorite part next to the baking."

We said goodbye to the others, and I couldn't scrub the smile from my face.

"This is going to be awesome. I'm so excited for you guys."

"For us," Mancini corrected, pulling me again into her side. She planted a kiss to my hand, and we stood side by side looking at the bakery case that had been installed that morning.

"Just think, Parker. Very soon, that case will be full of delicious goodies."

"I sure hope so."

"Be confident in yourself. I believe in us—this is a group effort. Besides, I don't just say that to everyone or anyone. They have to earn it. You did and I'm proud of you."

"Thanks, Mancini."

"Now, tell me what else is going on in that amazing head of yours. I know something is bothering you."

I ripped off the metaphorical Band-Aid. "I'm going to pass on dinner tonight." She began to interrupt but I stopped her. "Thanks for inviting me, but I really don't want to make it awkward with everything going on. It's clear Nick is avoiding me, and I'm not going to insert myself into his life and make things more difficult for him and Jillian."

"But he was here and things looked okay?" she said, hopeful. "I know it's awkward, but don't miss out because of her."

"I just can't. It's not because of her or him. It's for my own self-preservation. I'm tired of feeling like crap. I have to get over it and move on . . . with everything," I said, admitting to myself what I had been avoiding.

She mumbled something that sounded like "Well, I'm not okay with that," but when I asked her to repeat it, she just sang, "I understand. If you change your mind, dinner is at seven."

No one was making moving on easy. That included me.

21

The following day I wasn't in the best of moods and things were going south, fast.

"What do you mean he's not here?" I asked Mancini, who for the first time since I had met her looked dejected.

"He hasn't returned my calls. The student who was doing the work for us at the college said everything is ready, the website included, but that Nick hasn't come or contacted him. The kid said he'll meet me halfway so I don't have to drive all the way to Barreton to get the flyers. But I'd have to leave now because he has something to get to."

"I can't believe he would do this. Right before we open, no less. He promised he would be here with everything," I said, furious. Nick and I had things squared away. The plan was simple. Nick was going to pick up any last-minute supplies, like the grand-opening flag sign, a project he said he'd handle, while me and the Golden Girls put all the finishing touches on the bakery.

But then he decided to throw a grenade in it and not show up. Or return a phone call or a text. He wasn't even ignoring just me this time. He was ignoring everyone.

"Don't call him anymore. I'll go to Barreton and you stay here. Maybe Charlotte can come over when she's done with whatever that giant flowery thing is," I said, waving behind me to my friend across the hall, who looked like ivy was devouring her.

Mancini was pacing and looking more nervous than I had ever seen her. "You can't go!" she shouted, clearly aggravated. "You have to stay to work with the ladies on how to arrange everything in the cases. That's not my forte. It's faster if I run and you stay and get everything done that you can. I just hope he's okay. I'll stop by his house to check on the way back."

"You're right, you're right," I said, with a combination of nodding and shaking my head. Nick was fine—I was sure of it in my gut. But he wouldn't be once I got ahold of him.

"Be careful. It's cold and the roads are wet," I said, pulling her in for a hug. "We got this."

"You're damn right we do. I'm so proud of you, Parker. You're like one of my own and I love you." With a kind smile, she left the shop, the chime signaling her departure.

I stood for a moment, relishing her words. I loved them too. This town as well. Charlotte wasn't kidding when she'd said it grew on you like moss. It blanketed around you until you couldn't tell where you stopped and the town started.

I stepped to the counter and moved our little No Cell Phones sign to the side. I read over my checklist for what absolutely had to get done by the time we opened. The bakery wouldn't open until noon for the first week, until we worked out the kinks, and after that we'd run from eleven to five. Which were great store hours, considering that it was supposed to be a part-time operation. Then two evenings a week we'd be open for classes. If in the future the class side of things picked up, and had more eager teachers, we'd see what we could swing.

We'd promised Cooper, and the council, that we would revisit the business hours in the summer when tourism picked up, but for now, in the dead of winter, this was more than enough. I didn't want these women straining themselves.

The lights were on, the tables and chairs were ready, and the décor was spot-on. It was the perfect combination of boutique French pâtisserie and small-town America. The highlight, though, were the recipe walls. I loved them, and they made for a great conversation starter. A few people who had come in for local press coverage had asked what the funny measurements meant, and the Nanas were always delighted to explain it. It added that final touch that said this belonged to them.

"Okay," I said, a bit weepy at the final product. I took a deep breath and I began running down the list.

Cupcakes
☑ Vanilla
☑ Chocolate
☑ Éclair
☑ Cannoli
☑ ~~Banana~~

I crossed the last one off but cursed myself for being petty. Just because it was Nick's favorite didn't mean I had to take it off the menu. Other people, myself included, loved a good banana cupcake, and mine were damn good.

I reluctantly erased the cross-out. I'd leave the banana cupcakes on there, but only if Nick had the gall to show his face after screwing us over today. I was pissed at myself for spending so much time on that recipe—especially considering how hard it was to perfect.

I returned to my checklist to review the staples that each of the Nanas wanted to recur on the menu.

Classics
- ☑ Clara's Apple Cake
- ☑ Viola's Carrot Cake
- ☑ Suzanne's Chocolate Cake
- ☑ Pauline's Red Velvet Cake
- ☑ Gigi's Hummingbird Cake

Checklist done, I walked to the back section of the bakery to straighten a photo of all the ladies and me that Nick had taken. We'd posed for it after filming our first YouTube video, and we were surrounded by equipment, both baking and technical for the shoot, and we looked deliriously happy. He had had it framed and dropped it off one morning when I was on my way out.

The biggest question that was pressing on me for an answer lately was whether or not I was going to stay here or eventually head back to Brooklyn. I wasn't as attached to New York as Charlotte once was. Maybe because I had spent my entire life there and could afford to travel back and forth whenever I wanted.

And if I stayed, was Hope Lake big enough for me and Nick (and Jillian)? I didn't want to make it more awkward for everyone. It was clear that Jillian wasn't going anywhere, but between them, Henry and Charlotte, and Cooper and Emma, they were a group of three couples. I was a single. I didn't want me being here to add to the awkwardness. It wasn't fair to Nick or Jillian. Or me, for that matter.

A clatter in the back broke me out of my thoughts. Walking

over, I found Viola and Clara hiding something behind one of the shelves.

"Ladies, what's up?" I asked, startling them. It was funny to watch them scurry about trying to hide whatever they were working on.

"Parker, nice to see you," Clara blurted.

"How's it going up front?" Viola said, looking anywhere but at me.

"What's on the shelf, ladies?" I asked, cutting right to the chase.

They looked defeated, but also excited to show me what it was. "Nick's not the only one who's quick with a camera," Viola explained, reaching behind a speaker to pull out a wrapped present.

"What's this?" I asked, taking it from her.

"Open it." She smiled. "We could wait for Gigi and Mancini if you want. They know we were going to give this to you."

"As long as they're not going to be upset that I'm looking at it now," I said, and then I immediately started tearing into it.

I let the paper fall to the floor at my feet. "Well," I breathed. It wasn't what I expected. "This is nice."

It was a framed photo of Nick and me to match the one Nick had done of the ladies. Looking at it, I knew the moment it captured. My head was tipped toward his, almost leaning on his shoulder. If I didn't know better, you'd have thought we were a couple, because we looked serene, happy, and dare I say a little bit in love.

"It's from the same day he took our photo," Viola exclaimed. "We thought it was a nice moment between you both."

The ladies seemed so happy with themselves that I didn't have the heart to tell them that while lovely, this gift would cause a ton of problems for both me and Nick.

"We thought we could hang it by our photo," Clara said, pointing to a spot in the hall where it would fit perfectly among the other photos that we had hung up.

I smiled. "I think it's lovely. But maybe we should ask Nick first," I said, placing it on one of the tables.

If they realized that it bothered me, they didn't let on.

"Now, if you'll excuse me, I just want to check out a couple things back here to make sure we're all ready to go."

The ladies left me in the back of the shop, the photo on the table mocking me.

I ignored it and toured the space.

The studio was ready to go with a large television and a pretty sweet audio/visual setup that was a not-so-anonymous donation from Mayor Endicott, with the understanding that if anyone asked where it came from, I was to answer "Santa."

I wandered into the kitchen. The refrigerators were piled high with treats that we'd spent exhaustive hours making and freezing for the first few days, just until we saw what we liked and what we had to cut back on.

"You should be proud of yourself," Charlotte said from the doorway. "This looks amazing. I'm so happy you're my neighbor."

I winked. "I'm pretty damn proud of this. I won't lie, this was a lot of fun, C," I said, stretching my arms overhead.

She took a moment to scan my face. "You looked like you were enjoying yourself, but you don't have that sparkle that you did yesterday."

I flattened my lips. I wanted to say, *Nick, Nick is the problem!* But I wouldn't say that, because while Charlotte was my city BFF, she had her town BFFs, and Nick was one of them. When I left to go home, she'd still be here, with him, doing best-friend things.

I wasn't jealous at all.

"Is it the mojo?" she asked.

A perfect excuse, even though it was almost back. "You're

right. It's not one hundred percent, but it's close. I've got recipes, ideas."

"Well, whatever happens, I'm glad that you did this and if for no other reason, that it gave you a bit of an anchor to Hope Lake. You have no choice but to come back and visit often."

Just then a customer walked into Charlotte's shop, so she gave me a hug before running back down the hall.

Visit, definitely.

Stay for good? I was moving up the list of possibilities, but I wouldn't be telling anyone that just yet. Not until I figured out if it was what I really wanted.

When I was about to leave for the evening, after trying to reach Nick one more time, I put up the bat signal for the Uber driver and decided to wait out front to enjoy the balmy thirty-degree heat wave we were experiencing. I hoped that the weather stayed this way until we opened. At least it wasn't snowing.

I had just stepped onto the sidewalk and was locking the front door when a rough hand on my arm yanked me back. "What the fu—" I began to say, but stopped short when I saw the troop of children clamoring to enter the building next door, where they held music classes.

"Hi, everybody!" I said sweetly before turning to face a harried-looking Jillian. Her normally sleek bob was wayward and curly. Her eyes were smudged with mascara and her face was red and blotchy.

"Jillian, are you okay?" I asked, concerned that something really bad had happened to her. "I can call—"

"Oh, cut the shit, Parker," she sneered, and a couple jogging by sucked in a shocked breath. "We both know you can stuff that faux concern right up your rear end. I'm tired of pretending."

Someone is ready to finally show her true colors. Where were the Golden Girls and their spy network when I needed them?

"Well, that makes two of us," I deadpanned, crossing my arms. "To what do I owe the pleasure, Jillian?"

"You know, you think you're so slick with the cool, bitchy New Yorker vibe, but I had you pegged from day one. I know about you and Nick and I can't believe he fell for someone like you!"

I took a step forward, hoping to intimidate her by the fact that I had at least four inches on her. "Listen here, you want to talk about someone like me?"

She was pacing now, looking like a caged tiger. A disheveled caged tiger, and I was lunch. There wasn't a crowd gathering, but there were definitely people starting to pop out of the shops to watch. She couldn't have picked a worse time to do this. I was tempted to ask her to come into the bakery just so we weren't right out front of the shop, but I didn't want her to taint it.

"I've put in a lot of work with Nick . . ." she started, mumbling.

I sighed. I could handle this conversation one of two ways—stand toe to toe with her and put her in her place, or just concede. She was his girlfriend, after all, and I was . . . someone he chose to be friends with when it suited him. I didn't need this drama, so I chose the latter.

"Can I ask you why you're here? What could you possibly want from me?"

She stopped pacing and looked at me, as if truly pondering her answer. Maybe I was going to get something real from her.

"Come on, Parker, cut the crap. To land and keep a guy like Nick, it's what has to be done. Don't judge me. I put in all this time and energy and then you just stroll into town—"

"What is it that you want? For me to avoid him? Stop talking to him altogether? If that's the case, you could have saved yourself a trip on Nick's Uber account. We have a business relationship, nothing more. If you don't believe me, ask him."

She sneered. "That's it. I did, and you know what I got? Pushback from him about you. What the hell is it about you that is so special that everyone fawns over you? I see you for who you really are—you're the kind of woman who goes after another woman's man."

My hands balled into fists. It would be so easy to just catfight in the middle of town, but what would that accomplish?

Relieve a lot of pent-up frustration?

I took a deep breath and when I opened my eyes, Jillian was no longer looking enraged but sad. "I would never, ever try to pull Nick away from you," I said. "That's not how I operate. I don't care if you believe me or not. I have nothing more to say to you, Jillian."

When I moved past her to walk toward the bookshop where Henry worked, she caught my arm again, not letting go this time. "I don't believe you. I think you're trying to lure him away and I'm going to prove it. I can't wait to get him away from you. I've nearly got him convinced to move to Barreton with me."

My stomach sank. Leave Hope Lake and all these people? That was so not Nick. "If that's what makes him happy, then I'm glad. Now let go of my arm."

"'Makes him happy,'" she mimicked me. "Let me tell you something. I know about you and him last year. He didn't tell me everything, but I figured it out. I read your little email to him. You were stupid for letting him go because he'll do anything to make me happy. Anything, even if that means leaving this place behind."

I looked at her ugliness and frowned. "You'd do that, Jillian? You'd manipulate him into leaving his home? All his friends and his business behind? Why would you be so cruel?"

She shrugged. *Shrugged.* As if nothing I said made any impression on her. "What is your game here, Jillian? Why are you so damn miserable?"

"Look, Parker, not that I have to explain myself to you, but I've been through a lot, and when I met Nick and saw how desperate he was for a connection, I knew that if I was going to be stuck in small-town Pennsylvania, I should at least be stuck here with someone like him. So I'll be damned if Baker Barbie comes into town and undoes all the hard work I've put in. Do you know how excruciating it is to deal with Nick and his stupid childhood friends?" She rolled her eyes. "And don't even get me started on the old people in this town."

Now she'd crossed a line. You could talk shit about me, you could talk shit about Nick, but you could *not ever* talk shit about my friends or the Golden Girls. But before I could say anything, someone approached.

"Jillian?" came a voice from the side of my building. Nick was standing in almost the same spot we'd been in the day he'd given me a piggyback ride from the car. "Jillian," he said, more forceful this time.

For a split second, she had a deer-in-headlights look, but the mask was up in a second. "Nicky!" she called, and danced toward him, arms outstretched. She leaned in to give him a hug and a kiss, but he sidestepped her, almost causing her to fall in the snow piled along the sidewalk leading to the alley.

"I heard everything," he said, not looking at her. "I can't believe you."

The rest happened very quickly. Jillian turned back to me and stormed forward. Nick tried grabbing her but slipped, and before Jillian could reach me, Mancini came out of thin air and stepped in between us.

"Stand down, turn around, and get in the Uber and go back to Barreton," Mancini said in a tone that I had never heard from her before and hoped I would never hear again. It was deep, raspy, and terrifying.

"Listen here, I don't have to listen to the likes of you," Jillian said, and I was convinced in that moment that she did have a death wish.

"Jillian, I think it's time for you to go," Nick said, turning to the waiting driver to give him directions. "Can you send her to 13 Andrew Lane?" My stomach sank. He wasn't sending her to Barreton— instead, she was going to his house.

Jillian slid into the backseat of the Uber looking smug when she heard where she was going, and I wanted to slap the smirk right off of her face. When they pulled away, Mancini turned to Nick.

"What are you doing, dear?" she asked, taking his hands in hers. "You don't owe that woman any more of your precious time."

He nodded, keeping his eyes fixed on the ground. "I have a lot to say. I've been up in the woods behind Emma's parents' house just thinking all day. I must have missed a hundred calls from her, Parker, you—everyone was trying to find me."

I stayed silent, not wanting to interject my two cents into the situation and make him feel worse than he clearly already did. He looked exhausted. I wondered if he had seen Jillian's true colors before this, or if he was torn up about other things.

"Parker, I'm sorry—" he offered, but I stopped him with a raised hand.

"You take care of what you have to, Nick. Mancini will take me."

"Thanks. I'll see you soon."

He shuffled away, and within a minute, we heard the rumble of his truck. I wondered how I didn't hear him pull up when Jillian and I were yelling at each other. I guess we were that loud.

"Okay, Mancini, you ready to roll?" I asked.

For once, Mancini didn't say much on the drive. I think we

were both shell-shocked by what we'd witnessed. And if I was being honest, I was a little disappointed that Nick had her brought to his house. I would've sent her packing that minute.

When we got to the lake house, Mancini reached over and squeezed my hand. "Get some rest, Parker. It's going to be a long day."

* * *

"This is going to be friggin' amazing," I said, fighting back a yawn. What was the old adage, *I'll sleep when I'm dead*? I was feeling it today, especially after the showdown with Jillian the day before. No one had heard from Nick since it happened. Before I fell asleep last night, Charlotte and Emma conference-called me to get the scoop. Apparently, Nick had called Henry and Cooper on the way to his house, saying he had to cancel their guys' night again, but this time because he had witnessed Jillian attack me. Needless to say, Charlotte and Emma's mama-bear instincts rose. The call had started with Emma saying, "I'll bring the shovel and the rope," and Charlotte finishing with "When are we burying the body?" Man, I loved them. After giving them the play-by-play, I stayed up half the night thinking about it.

Rolling into the bakery with only a couple hours of sleep was something I did back in my twenties. Not at my age.

But now, looking at the bakery from the street with a sense of pride, I realized it was all worth it.

No, the nice weather hadn't held out for us. Yes, there was snow on the ground and, yes, it was colder than the Arctic, but people were still lined up and ready to go and so was I.

The sign was an old-school number with THE BAKED NANAS printed on in all its black-and-white glory. People were snapping photos and remarking how it looked similar to the one that used to hang on the old bakery Hope Lake had back in the sixties. It was intentional, since the ladies said they all met in that decade.

The ladies were ready inside, sporting their new black-and-white aprons with the logo embroidered on the front. Simple chalk signs hung inside displaying what the classic daily specials were.

The handwritten-recipe wallpaper was front and center, and it made for a perfect picture with the ladies in front of it.

They each had a role to play once the doors opened, and they were as eager as ever to get started.

"Okay, Viola, you're on the register because you're the most familiar with it, but make sure you eventually show Mancini and the rest how to use it so they can learn it too." Viola nodded with a smile.

"Mancini, you're meeting and greeting because—well, that's what you wanted to do, and I can't seem to say no to you."

"I'm hard to say no to, dear. I know this, I love this, and I will teach you how to be me someday."

"That's a lesson I'm eager to take." She pulled me into a hug.

"Okay, girls. Let's make some magic," Mancini singsonged with excitement.

We hurried everyone outside for the ribbon cutting.

"Emma, do you want a photo of all the ladies in front of the store?" I asked, ushering her and Cooper over to the storefront to get the ribbon-cutting picture for the paper. I waved to the other senior ladies to come out and line up. They were there strictly for moral support, and I was grateful they'd agreed to schmooze the crowd as well.

Donned in their winter's finest, they made sure you could see their aprons, and the logo, before smiling widely for the cameraman from the paper.

"Excuse me, but you need to be in this too!" Emma shouted, and Charlotte pushed me toward the group. I stayed off to the side, making sure that the Golden Girls were front and center.

"Here," Emma said, handing me a giant pair of shiny brass scissors.

I looked around, thinking maybe Nick would show up in time for this. In time to see his friends and the people who adored him accomplish something amazing, but he was still nowhere to be found. He was as much a part of The Baked Nanas as the rest of us were. But, when it was clear he wasn't going to make it, I forced myself to shift my attention to where it should have been all along: the people there to support us. They were going to be my focus, not him disappointing me.

I walked over to Mancini, handing her and Clara the scissors. "Ladies, it's all you."

The others gathered around, each smiling brightly for the camera. As they cut the giant red ribbon together, encouraged by the cheering crowd before them, it swirled to the ground, the red ribbon a stark contrast to the snowy pavement.

With that, the doors were open for business.

* * *

That night, when I didn't think I could possibly stand up for a moment longer, I wondered how I'd worked the hours I did for so many years back in the city. I was on my feet for twelve hours a day. Today was half that but I was twice as exhausted. It was another check in the "Parker needs to get some exercise" column.

I took the longest bath I could, draining all of the hot water out of the tank. Epsom salts replaced my trusty bath bombs and provided some relief to my aching bones, but the aches I felt elsewhere weren't so quick to melt away in the warm water.

The ladies were who I was the most excited and worried for. They were riding the energy rush from earlier, but were they okay now? Feeling the same soreness that I was?

I decided to give them a break tonight and check on them first thing in the morning, before I opened the bakery with Clara.

As I drifted off in the warm, salty water, I could have sworn I heard a truck rumbling over gravel, but decided I surely must have imagined it. No one would be visiting now. It was probably someone turning around in the driveway on their way back into the heart of town.

And then a little *what if* presented itself. The rumble sounded like Nick's truck. I checked my phone and didn't see any messages from him. There was no way he would pull a no-show for the grand opening and then have the audacity to show up here.

Then I heard a little *rap, rap, rap* at the door and I sat bolt upright in the tub, sloshing water over the sides. "Shit," I grumbled and angrily stood, wincing when my muscles revolted against me. "This is not happening."

Was it too much to ask to enjoy a bath in silence?

I grabbed my fluffy white robe hanging from the bathroom door and twisted my long blond hair up in a towel before I stormed out of the bathroom, wishing I had the knife from Nick's last impromptu visit with me. It probably was a good thing that I didn't have it.

Carefully, I marched determinedly down the stairs. I was angry, of course, but cautious enough that in my haste I didn't slip thanks to wet feet. The last thing I needed was to beg Nick to take me to the emergency room for a broken ass.

At the door, I took a deep breath before swinging it open. Nick was there looking a bit worse for wear. He looked exhausted, with bloodshot eyes and some shadows under them.

"Nick," I breathed over the whistling wind that zipped through the porch. It was positively freezing, and being in the doorway wet and barely dressed was not how I wanted to end this night.

He turned quicker than I expected. When he saw me, he smiled, but it faded almost as soon as it lit up his face. "What are you doing here?" I asked.

He held up something long and wide and wrapped in white paper, but didn't say anything.

I was freezing, my hair was soaked, and I was still dripping from the bath, the droplets icing over on my legs. "It's too cold." I pulled the robe tighter around me and backed away from the door, leaving it open.

Once he got to the door, he stayed on the porch, the package hanging limply at his side. "Nick, I'm not kidding, either come in or leave," I said through chattering teeth.

I walked into the kitchen, wishing I'd put on socks because the hardwood was cold on my bare feet. Once there, I put on the coffee, even though I knew it would be a mistake at this hour and likely keep me awake long after he left. I dug around in the pantry for something hearty to warm me up and settled on oatmeal.

When Nick came in through the kitchen's swinging door, he stuck close to the wall, almost as if he was going to bolt. He set the package on the counter and returned to the wall, looking even worse.

"Why are you here?" I asked, not in any mood to mince words. "I'm tired, physically exhausted, and I have a headache, so if you're here for another round of you telling me that you want to be friends, then go screw off." I paused for a breath, but then I realized I had more to say to him. "You let me down. And more than that, what about the Golden Girls? They dote on you for years, and the one day they have a big moment, you're nowhere to be seen. How do you think that made them feel?"

When I turned, he had moved to the island to sit on one of the stools. He was playing with the edge of the paper from the package. I hadn't even heard him move the chair to sit. His head was resting on his other hand, his fingers twisted in his brown hair, which stood up on all ends wildly. It looked like he hadn't brushed it in days.

"Nick?" I asked again, annoyed but also worried that he wasn't answering or looking at me.

I took a deep breath and went to him, placing my hand on his shoulder. His hand slid up and rested on top of mine. His skin was shockingly cold, and I wondered how long he'd been outside waiting for me.

"They're for you," he said quietly, pushing flowers toward me. I could see the blooms peeking out of the haphazardly wrapped bouquet. Carefully, I unwrapped them and held in the gasp that nearly escaped me. They were . . . ugly, and while I recognized the paper lining from Charlotte's Late Bloomers, these were clearly *not* done by my friend.

"What are these for?" I asked, irked that Charlotte didn't tell me he was coming with flowers. Unless she didn't know. That might explain the poorly done bouquet.

"They're to say I'm sorry, because I don't know if you'd believe the words if I said them to you again." His voice was strained and gravelly in a way that made me think he was yelling before he got here.

"Why are you apologizing this time, Nick?" I wasn't trying to be aggressive or overtly mean, but how many times was I expected to go through this song and dance with him?

"About being MIA. About letting you down. About letting that woman into everyone's lives. About everything," he said, smothering a hiccup with his hand.

When he looked up, I took a step back. "Nick," I gasped. His eyes were so bloodshot that he looked like he'd been swimming with his eyes open in a too-chlorinated pool for hours. "What happened?"

"Jillian," he said. And by his tone, I understood that WWIII had happened over the last two days in little Hope Lake, Pennsylvania. "I was so wrong about her. I heard what she said to you, Parker, and I saw her. Really saw her, for the first time yesterday. I had no idea . . ." He was all over the place.

"Nick, why don't you start from the beginning."

He let out a sigh. "I'm not stupid. I'm sure you think that I am for falling for what she was selling, but I did see *some* things. Some cracks in the façade, but—"

"You didn't want to believe it?" I asked, knowing what it was like to defend someone who you knew in your heart wasn't a great person. Insert all my ex-boyfriends.

He shook his head. "I didn't. I thought maybe it was just in my head. She wasn't really bad," he sighed. "I met her the week of Thanksgiving."

I gave him a nod to continue.

"We don't need to rehash what happened between us, but I was in a pretty shitty place. I was at HLBC having a beer, trying to figure out what to do about you, and she approached me all doe-eyed and the epitome of sweetness. She said all the right things and laughed at all the right times. It was just easy. And with how hard it was for the two of us to get on the same page, I guess I just . . ."

"Took the easy road and gave up on us," I finished for him. I should have been upset with him, but at least I was getting honesty.

"So I . . . I decided to go all in with her. She was here. You weren't, and when you were, we were hiding, and that bothered me more than I ever admitted. Looking back, what I did was a real shit thing. To both of you, actually. I bailed on you because it was getting hard and I used her as a rebound to try to get over you."

He took a deep breath. "She was never like that around me. Moody and aggressive is the opposite of her personality, or at least I thought so. Did I know she manipulated me with her doe eyes to get what she wanted? Yes, but she was always so sweet."

I felt the heaviness seeping into my bones. I was exhausted, and as much as I wanted to hear this, I was losing my spark. "Nick, I understand that you need a friend right now, but I needed you today too. Friends are there for each other."

"I know that," he said, the contrition evident in his voice.

"Okay, then why didn't you show up or do anything you promised you would? If not for me, then for the Golden Girls?"

I was angry we were depending on him, and he bailed on us all.

"I didn't want to miss it. Believe me, I wanted to be there, but Jillian went nuts when she realized I brought her back to my house to end things. Like, actually nuts. She threw all of my shit around my house. It's trashed. She trashed my place because of you. My feelings for you. She said they ruined us from the start. She insisted that we would have never worked because I was still hung up on you."

I sucked in a breath. "She trashed your place?" I said, trying to ignore the rest of what he said.

They

Broke

Up

"So, you're saying your house is trashed and she went nuts because of me. I don't understand, Nick."

"Remember the email you sent me a while ago? Where you

called me out for avoiding you and mentioned that you saw me naked?"

Mental note: Don't write angry emails. Guess the same rules for drinking and texting applied to emailing. I nodded.

"She had her suspicions about us, but when she saw that it was like the nail in the coffin. She grilled me for hours about what happened between you and me. And I might have admitted some things that I shouldn't have."

My eyes widened, my heart sped up, and though I was cold and wet from the tub, I was feeling warm all over.

"Like what, Nick?" I kept repeating his name, more for myself than for him. I was forcing myself to remember that I was mad, that this was Nick, the person who was at the root of my hurt feelings.

"The fact is that when I met her, I was pretty much getting over you. And that you being here was bringing everything back up. Let's not even start on when that video of us went up."

I cringed at my contribution to his misery. "I'm sorry. I shouldn't have uploaded it."

"No, it was fine. Remember that day at the diner when Emma said she was pregnant? I was so happy and yet I was so hurt that they didn't include Jillian in the announcement. I was so mad that they couldn't wait. Parker, do you know how angry at myself I am for being mad at Emma and Cooper? I can never get that moment back. Now I realize that I was an ass for putting her before them. Always. Lost part of my friends, and I let the Golden Girls down because of her. Because I wanted to prove that I could have this normal, easy relationship. Now that I think about it, I don't think I did it because I loved her. I was doing it to prove I could. Prove I could sacrifice."

With that last sentence, everything fell into place.

"Do you not think you've sacrificed in previous relationships?" I asked, hoping to coax it out of him.

"Parker, I resented you for a while. For not putting us first. For keeping us a secret. It was easy to blame you for the downfall of our relationship, if that's what you want to call it. But then at the same time, I knew I wasn't willing to sacrifice, either. I always wanted you to come to Hope Lake. I was more hesitant to pick up and come to New York. I did a couple times, but I wanted you here. I was being selfish. So I was mad at myself for not trying harder. For not sacrificing."

"So with Jillian, you tried to do everything you felt you didn't do with me." Wow, I was not expecting this.

"Fuck, I'm so stupid."

Part of me wanted to agree, but I couldn't be so cruel. He was obviously beaten up over this, and as a friend, I needed to help him as best I could.

"Nick, what did she have to say? I mean, why was she playing all these games with you?"

"It *was* all a game to her. When she finally stopped screaming, she said she had been using me to get back at an ex of hers who had moved on and was engaged. It wasn't even for sex, because that ended weeks ago, which was probably another problem between us. She was dangling the life I wanted in front of me, making me think that she would be a part of it, and all she did was toss my hopes into a blender and hit puree. I think she was just very unhappy with her life. I have no answers. I don't want to ever see her again, but I still have so many questions. Why me?"

Nick was at a place where I wasn't sure that I was qualified as a friend to help him dig out from. Henry, Emma, or Cooper were probably more equipped to deal with this level of melancholy. They were his friend longer and knew his ups and downs. While I wanted nothing more than to help him, I was worried that I'd only make things worse.

"Nick, can I call someone for you? Maybe one of the guys can come get you and you can fix up your place a bit?" I offered, reaching for my cell phone, which was near his hand.

He shook his head. "I have to talk to you. No one else understands me like you do. I honestly thought we had a connection and then—"

"What? We went through this already. You gave up. I'm not going to apologize for something I had nothing to do with. I can admit I might not have communicated my feelings for you clearly, but you gave up. That is on you."

He choked out a laugh. "I misread things. It's hard to read your intentions when you're always avoiding seeing my friends. I mean you hid in a closet so you wouldn't run into Henry. How was I supposed to read that?"

"You're mad because I hid in the closet when Henry came over?"

He was referring to the night that I ventured to Hope Lake as a surprise. I rented a car after I made sure that I had the morning shift at D&V covered. My plan was to stay over and maybe talk about what we were doing, but Henry knocked on the door looking for sugar and I panicked and ran naked upstairs, leaving Nick to explain to his friend why there were women's clothes strewn about his living room. "I barely got out of there without flashing him! Is that what you wanted?"

"No!" he roared, tugging at his hair. "I just wish that you didn't take off. Or make me lie to my friends about who I was seeing because you didn't want anyone in town to know about us."

"I didn't ask you to lie to anyone, Nick. I just said that we should keep things between us until we knew where it was going. I didn't want anyone, especially Charlotte, getting their hopes up that we were going to be rounding off their little sextet. And I'm glad we didn't tell them, because look where we are. No matter how much responsibility I am willing to take in this, you need to own up to the fact that you didn't give me the opportunity to communicate with you because you gave up. You walked away to find the 'easier' route. Don't you dare blame that on me."

Nick slid off the stool and stepped to the wall, taken aback by my words. He toyed with the wrinkled paper from the flowers.

"Don't be mad at Charlotte for the flowers. I begged her to make something and she wouldn't. I think she thought they were for Jillian, not you. That's why they look so sad. I did it myself."

"Nick, I'm not sure what you hoped would happen by coming here. It's not just me you disappointed, but Mancini, Clara—the lot of them. They were counting on you. I don't want to add insult to injury, but you've got to settle things up with them first. Me—well, I guess we'll just have to try to work our way back to being friends someday."

I wanted to believe what I said. I needed him to believe too, because even after everything, I still wanted to have him in my life somehow. It just had to be on terms that we could both agree on.

"Parker," he said quietly, and when he looked up, I felt a rush of emotions toward him. None of which was something that we could discuss tonight. I was too tired, and he was too emotionally and physically drained from everything that had already happened.

But when he looked at me, at all of me, I felt something else that I wanted to drown with the hot coffee. He eyed the knot in my robe. The exposed skin above my breasts, the towel that covered my hair.

He stepped forward, slowly at first and then more determined. He stopped just before he reached me. "Nick," I whispered, again saying his name to remind myself that I was mad at him.

"Parker, what will it take for you to forgive me?" He sounded so pained that I wanted to hug him and say that everything was okay, but it wasn't. He wasn't, and I didn't want to be his rebound.

Still, we were only a few inches apart, and seeing him this close made my heart skip. Not from the rush of old feelings but from new ones. Sympathy, anger, and a little bit of lust rolled in. All of them, plus sheer exhaustion, made me rise up and ruffle his hair. "We'll talk another day," I promised.

I reached up and kissed him on the cheek, my lips lingering a bit longer than normal. Nick's chest was rising and falling with shuddering breaths, and when I glanced up at him, his eyes were darker than I had seen them in months.

Hungry.

Slowly he leaned down, and I was certain that he was going to capture my lips, but instead he brushed his cheek against mine and dropped a solitary kiss near the birthmark behind my ear.

My hands slid up and my fingers gripped his biceps, curling themselves into his shirt. "Nick," I whispered, and dragged my lips across his cheek.

His hands moved lower until they rested at my waist.

"Parker."

I turned the last few inches until my lips grazed his. It was just a touch. A slight push of our lips together. Our eyes were open, wide, and in shock over what we were chasing.

It was innocent—the words, the hair ruffle, a simple kiss on the cheek—but it reminded me of that first night we were together on the Fourth of July.

"You're in a bad place right now," I said, still leaning the slightest bit closer.

"You're right. You're always right, and it's driving me crazy that you're in that robe, and that I have to leave," he said, leaning in until I could feel his warm breath on my cheek.

He placed a tiny kiss just on my jaw. A spot where he once pointed out I had the tiniest birthmark that I never knew about. Whenever we got together, he would kiss that spot just before leaving. I melted into him just enough that his hand rested on the bathrobe knot.

It could have been so easy to pull it open, but what would that have accomplished? "I won't be the rebound," I said honestly, placing my hand over his on the knot.

He blew out a long breath. "Rebounds are second choices. That's never, ever been you," he whispered, and placed one more kiss behind my ear. His hand left the knot of my robe, and I so wished when he backed up that he would tug it open.

But I knew Nick too well to know that he wouldn't push the issue. Not tonight. Maybe not ever again, but whatever happened, I knew the ball was now in my court.

I just needed to know if I was going to take the shot or let the clock run out.

22

"Thanks for tuning in to *The Baked Nanas*. I'm Mrs. Mancini." The video ended with their ridiculous, and yet popular, sign-off. "Don't forget, go get baked with your Nana!"

I smiled, watching Mancini in her element. She was the one whom I had been the most worried about on-camera, given her predilections for swearing at inappropriate moments and her uncanny ability to go off script with everything, including the recipes. Her favorite measurements were a pinch of this and a shake of that.

"Cut!" Nick yelled from the corner of the bakery. We had decided to film the last two episodes at the bakery, in the classroom kitchen. It had been a week since the grand opening, and we wanted to get some videos done before the weekend. It was easier now that the equipment was rigged up and we had so much more space than in Mancini's kitchen.

"Nick." Mancini nodded, and instead of pulling him into a hug, she simply breezed by him. A move that everyone, including him, noticed.

"I deserve that," he said, and took a seat in front of the smart board we had bought with Cooper's generous donation.

"What are you doing here?" Clara asked just as curtly. I was surprised they were sticking to their guns. From what I understood, they rarely got mad at him, and when they did, they'd stay annoyed for less than a day. As soon as the dimples came out, he'd be forgiven.

"I stopped in because I knew today was key lime pie day. It's not every day that you can get this. It's a treat! And, Mancini, you do make the best," he said in an effort to suck up to her.

She preened momentarily before dropping the mask back over her face. "We missed you on opening day, you know."

We missed you. It wasn't an accusatory *Where were you?* or *How could you?* Having spoken to them, I knew that they felt deeply let down that one of their biggest cheerleaders hadn't shown up.

"I'm so sorry. I really am and I'm mad at myself for missing it. I heard it was amazing."

"It was," Clara interrupted. "You would have known that if you were here, like you promised."

"I know, and I deserve the cold shoulders. It's why I came. I was hoping you guys would hear me out."

Mancini looked on with sadness. For a moment, I thought she was tearing up, but she turned when he asked to speak. They all loved Nick, that was clear, but Mancini seemed to really go out of her way for him.

"You guys stay here, I'll sit out front in case someone comes in," I offered, nodding when Nick mouthed *Thank you.*

"Sweetheart, I think you need to hear this as much as we do,"

Mancini insisted, tugging me by the hand to sit beside her. "The bell will ring if someone comes in the door."

Once seated, they waited with their hands folded on the tables.

Nick began, "You have to know how sorry I am. There aren't enough words to tell you how badly I feel for missing everything. If I could turn back time and make it, I would in a heartbeat."

"Nick, what happened? We know you and Jillian broke up, but no one heard from you for days," Clara said, and her anger was replaced by worry.

Nick rubbed his hand over his face. "We did break up, but she refused to leave until Monday afternoon, and by then it was too late. Let's say Jillian decided that the best way to react to our breakup was to throw everything she could at my walls and windows. I needed to make a dent in the wreckage."

The ladies gasped, looking scandalized. Mancini and Gigi looked like they wanted to drive to Barreton and kick Jillian's ass.

Wait in line, ladies.

"Most of the fighting is immaterial to this apology. Just know that I am so sorry and I'm at your disposal for whatever you need, whenever you need it."

The ladies remained quiet until Mancini pushed her stool back and stood. "You know we love you, Nick."

He nodded, looking a bit green. He must have thought this was going to end poorly for him.

"You really did disappoint us. I'm not sure what's worse, the hurt or the disappointment, but whichever it is, know that under all of it, we still love you and want to see you happy. You weren't happy, not really, and I think seeing you that way hurt all of us."

"You're right. I think I wanted to be happy so much that I forced myself to believe that I was," he said, looking defeated.

Mancini walked over to him and rested her hands on his shoulders. "Nick, stop beating yourself up over it. We know now that this was out of your control. We'll get over it."

"I think I am over it already," Clara said, smiling kindly at Nick. "You did something stupid. We don't give up on people for doing that. We wouldn't have anyone left if it was a one-strike system."

Viola nodded. "I think the main takeaway is that you should always listen to us and no one else. We're clearly the wisest."

Nick laughed. "You certainly are."

One by one they gave him a hug. While I didn't know if this would be the end of Nick's apologies to each of them, I knew it was at least a start in the right direction.

"I'll still be coming by later to shovel, Clara," he said, earning another smile, this one accompanied by a squeeze of Nick's cheek with her bony fingers.

"Parker, we'll man the front of the house while you work on the video edits and chat with Nicky," Gigi said, and took off through the door into the bakery.

"Oh, no, that's not necessary. I'm sure he's busy, and I can do the editing later."

Mancini put her hands on my shoulders, forcing me to stay in the seat. "We just told Nick to listen to us—you should totally do the same. We are wise."

There was no sense in arguing. If they wanted us to talk, we would have to talk. When they left the classroom, they made sure to close the door on the way out.

"Hey," he said, and began twirling the mic cord between his fingers. "That was a good video, huh? Everything is going to be okay?"

I nodded, not entirely sure what he was referring to—the video or us. "Yeah, it's definitely going better and growing faster than we thought. I mean, we figured people would think they're funny, but most of the comments are legitimate questions about the recipes and how to manage when you can't read your own great-whoever's recipes."

"Have you thought about airing *The Baked Nanas* videos in the bakery?" Nick asked, and immediately tried to backtrack. "Sorry, I shouldn't have said anything. I know you know what you're doing here with the no cell phone policy, and everyone chilling out."

"No, no, what are you thinking? New videos or old ones?" I asked, pulling up the note app on my iPhone.

"I think both. Maybe you can even have a suggestion box or something. It would help everyone, including the Nanas. Live comments from the peanut gallery, I guess you could call it. There's a way for people to ask for stuff on YouTube but not in person. I think that may go a long way," he explained.

"Also a great idea. I'm not totally sold on a television here except for airing the videos. I'm thinking we can have them air in the hallways of the building as well. Maybe a slide show or something of the businesses, and then still shots of the loft apartments upstairs."

"Yeah, Charlotte could have something, and the restaurant."

"You're on a roll. Have anything else?" I asked, watching his face light up at the thought of giving more suggestions.

"A couple," he said with a smile. "Can I play with your site?"

I nodded. "What are you thinking?"

He rubbed his neck. "I know you want the focus to be the Nanas, but I think people need to fully understand what you're doing here and how you're behind it." I gave him a face. He chuckled. "I know, I know—*it's not about me, it's about them*—and that's wonderful and noble and I love it, but I think pushing the fact that you're behind this will only elevate it. I know you're not hiding it, but you're also not full-blown making an announcement with skywriting or anything."

"I see what you're saying. I can do that, I think," I said, and he looked forlorn. "I mean, unless you really want to go nuts. The less I have to worry about the better. My mind has been going in a hundred different directions from everything coming up between the bakery and the videos. If I had one less thing to worry about, Nick, that would be super helpful. Thanks."

Grateful, I reached up and kissed him on the cheek. We hadn't discussed the kiss from the other night, and this felt like we were heading down that path again.

As if reading my mind, Nick stepped forward and whispered, "Parker."

The word was simple, full of longing, and I didn't know how to respond. This was public, something we weren't used to. We'd avoided the scrutiny and the gossip before.

I glanced up at his darkening eyes and smiled. "Nick." He took a tentative step closer and repeated my name with more longing, more need.

Closing the short distance, I stood in front of him and pulled his hands so I held them in mine.

"Nick, I'd like you to kiss me now," I said simply. If he needed an invitation, there it was.

He smiled, dimples and all, and leaned in to firmly capture my lips.

At the same time the front door chimed.

"Oh, sorry!" Emma said, covering her eyes with one hand and her belly with the other. "Baby and I didn't see anything we weren't supposed to, but if we did, we'd be asking what the H-E-double-hockey-sticks is going on here and why didn't we know about it?"

We separated, knowing that we'd been busted.

Turning to her, I smiled. "Hey, Ems. What's up? How are you feeling? Want a snack?" I rambled it all quickly, but it did nothing to thwart her curiosity.

She looked between Nick and me repeatedly before calling for Mancini to join us.

"I've been summoned," she said, coming into the studio from the bakery, and it reminded me of the first day that I met her. She appeared out of nowhere.

"Emma, looks like you interrupted something back here?" Mancini asked, searching for some gossip. She crossed her arms over her chest.

"I daresay that I don't know. Tell me, Mancini. What did I walk in on?" she answered, smiling when she looked at Nick's reddening face.

"Nothing," I said flatly. "I gave Nick a kiss on the cheek and Emma is interpreting it as something *more*."

Mancini's eyes widened, and her mouth made a perfect O. "I see. Well, I must say if there was something going on here, I would certainly approve of and encourage it."

"You're both nuts. We're friends, right, Nick?" I said, bumping him in the arm with my hand.

Nick was looking down, much as he had that night at my house when he came to apologize.

I swallowed, thinking that this was going to backfire, but if I was going to get into a better place with Nick, I needed to square up with our friends. Come clean.

"Although, he's single now and I'm single, so, who knows?" As soon as I said it, both Emma and Mancini smiled widely and were suddenly giddy like teenagers sharing secrets.

Nick didn't say anything, but I could see the hint of a smile.

* * *

A week later, after I finished going over the schedule for the bakery and the upcoming YouTube shows for the ladies, I sat in the bakery kitchen staring at the recipes that I was toying with.

Things were *finally* up to the old D&V standards, but I felt I had more to give. What, I didn't know, but it was a lingering feeling.

The recipes were laid out in the style that my old D&V menu was: simply stated on plain crisp-white cardstock with black typeset lettering. One side featured pricing for single servings of cupcakes, pies, cakes, cheesecake, brownies, and cookies, and the other side listed the same items but in whole sizes. The longer I stared at the menu, the more I wished I could just create something *more,* for lack of a better word.

Charlotte thought that was my problem. That I spent all this time trying to re-create something that was over and done with. I shook my head. Sometimes simple was best.

At midnight, I made another pot of coffee and started in on a new poster board. The recipe order was rearranged, and I had two new ideas planted on it: bananas Foster and pumpkin caramel cupcakes. Neither was reinventing the wheel, but both were delicious. Mancini's secret ingredient for the caramel, pink Himalayan sea salt, was brilliant, and I was eager for everyone to try it.

"Another win," I said, and began putting together and mixing up the ingredients for the cupcakes I was experimenting with.

When I woke the next morning, I was still sitting at the counter and had a strip of caramel down my cheek.

I made breakfast, packed up the cupcakes, and after the world's quickest shower, I requested Uber to come pick me up.

"Oh, you're kidding. I'm so late already," I whined into the air.

According to the app, the Uber driver was out of commission thanks to a nasty head cold.

I paced the kitchen, holding my phone tightly. I could call it off, ring Mancini and have her fill in for me. It was my morning to open, but I had no way of getting there. Unless . . .

Shooting off a quick text, I waited for a response. He texted back that he'd be ten minutes. And sure enough, Nick was soon at my doorstep with a cup of coffee and a smile.

"Thanks, but you didn't have to do that," I said, taking the proffered cup. "I just appreciate the ride."

"Are you ready?"

"Just a second." I handed him the coffee and went to get the boxes of cupcakes for the bakery.

"Okay, all set." He took a deep inhale when we got into the truck.

"Those smell unbelievable. What are they?" he asked, hungrily eyeing the boxes on the backseat.

"Something I was trying out for the shop, and maybe for YouTube, who knows? You had a great suggestion the other day about the comments—finding out what people want? Well, I made up two recipes according to the comments that I received on the D and V blog ages ago. I can't remember why I never baked these before, but I made them to try out at the bakery today. We'll see how it goes."

"Do I smell banana?" he said, licking his lips. "Parker, tell me there's banana in there."

I smiled. "You'll have to wait until we open to see."

He groaned and playfully slapped the steering wheel. "I'll buy them all if you'd let me. Hell, I'll eat them all right now."

"I hope you feel that way after you try them," I said.

Since I still didn't trust myself around him, I turned and faced the window, watching the trees whip by on the way to the bakery. We didn't discuss the kiss. Or kissing again. Or what would happen if and when we did kiss again, because I think we both knew damn well what would.

I was torn between wanting to move that along and savoring this little dance we had. Nick and I had jumped into the first relationship after a hot minute. Why was I in such a rush to repeat that?

23

A little over a month after the opening, I was enjoying a burst of creativity and inspiration on my end, and the bakery had a steady stream of customers. I had hoped that once the good spring weather broke, we'd see a real uptick in the shop and the classes.

"Parker, anything to tell us?" Charlotte asked, taking a sip of her tea.

Emma and Charlotte had met me at the 81 to grab some lunch while Mancini and Viola relieved me at the bakery. "Oh, yes. The business is booming. Emma, I have to thank you for the coverage in the paper. Really well done. It's brought in a ton of people."

"That's not what we meant, and you know it. What's going on with you and Nick?" Emma asked, dipping another french fry into the ketchup.

I rolled my eyes. "You guys, I told you nothing is going on. We're friends."

"Yes, but do you find him attractive?" Charlotte asked, raising an eyebrow at me. "Like, horizontally attractive."

"Where's your creativity, Charlotte? I could find him vertically attractive too." As soon as the words left my mouth, my cheeks flared with heat. "You guys, I'm not kidding. There's nothing going on now with Nick. He just got out of a relationship."

Emma's hand that clutched her hamburger hovered right in front of her mouth. "What did you say?"

I repeated the sentence. "Nothing is going on with Nick."

"Now. Charlotte, did you hear that slip? *Now*. Nothing is going on . . . but adding the *now* makes me think—"

"—that something was going on before. Oh my God! When were you sleeping with Nick?" Charlotte shouted. Literally shouted in the 81 so that the entire restaurant turned to look at us.

I slid down, trying to escape under the table, but Emma put her foot there to stop me. "You get up here right now and explain yourself, Parker Adams."

"This is why this town has no secrets. You guys put shit on blast in the middle of the diner and expect it to stay locked down. My God, you're all nuts!"

No matter how much deflection I threw at them this time, it didn't work. They were sharks in the water, and I was the chum.

I sighed. "What was the question?" I asked, stalling.

"Did you, or did you not, have relations with Nicholas Arthur?" Emma asked.

"This doesn't leave this table," I insisted, pointing a finger at the two of them.

When they said yes, I nodded. It was an honest, affirmative answer. It wasn't specific, and it didn't explain when or how many times, even though I had a feeling those questions were next.

"Charlotte, you look like you've seen a ghost," Emma said, poking her with her butter knife.

"That's who you meant when you said it had been a while. Oh my God. I can't believe you banged Nick."

She looked at me . . . proudly? She had a smile on her face, and her eyes were watery as if she was about to shed a tear over my sex life. It wouldn't be the first time.

"Yes, I was referring to Nick."

If I kept my answers simple, I wouldn't get caught up in a lie, or accidentally divulge too much information. After all, I hadn't told Nick that I was spilling the proverbial beans about us.

"Wait, wait. Wait," Charlotte said, and began ticking off her fingers.

"You're saying Nick was the last person you slept with, right?"

I nodded. "And?"

"The last time you were here was the Fourth of July. That's *more* than three months ago like you told me. So, you either . . ."

Charlotte's lips curled in as she fought back a grin. "You bitch! You were here and didn't tell me! I'm so annoyed and yet so proud that you ventured into Hope Lake for a booty call!"

I winced. The term rankled me, mainly because it was how Nick thought I saw what we shared together. One long-distance booty call. When it was anything but.

"I swear, if any of this leaves the table, I'll kick your ass, Charlotte. Twice because Emma is pregnant and I can't kick hers."

They both crossed their hearts.

"Fine. We hooked up after the fireworks on the Fourth of July last year. You guys all left us, and we went drinking. Well, one thing led to another, and we had sex in his truck—you can say we made our own fireworks."

"Oh."

"My."

"God."

They each said the words with their hands over their mouths.

"And then at the lake. It was pretty close to where I'm renting, now that I think about it. Oh, and again on the way to Gigi's house since I was staying with her. She doesn't know about it but Mancini does. She was looking out the window and I think she might have seen Nick's butt through the windshield."

"You've tainted Mancini with your sexual prowess! You should be both ashamed and high-fived for your efforts."

"I think we can all agree that she wasn't tainted by anything that we did. Nick and I exchanged numbers and honestly, I didn't think he'd call. I didn't know if I would either, but then two days later, I got a text. It was sweet, and I'm not going to share it, but it made me rethink what I thought about him initially.

"After a few more days, he appeared at D and V just as I was closing up. He stayed in the apartment until the weekend, and then after that, we would either meet here or he came to the city a few times. That lasted until November."

Emma's hand covered her mouth. "Jillian."

I nodded. "Yep. It was a lot of miscommunication by both of us. Eye roll, I know. He met her and that was it for me. I wasn't in the best mood back then, if you recall, Charlotte. It was right around when The Confectionary was closing in on the D and V deal."

Charlotte gasped. "Parker Adams, tell me that you didn't sell D and V . . . to be with Nick?"

I leveled her with a disbelieving look. "No, you know me better than that," I answered honestly. "I did it for me. He just missed out on hearing that I suddenly had a lot more free time on my hands and that we could see each other more because of it."

"So if he had not been a wuss, you two could still be together?" Charlotte's eyes were practically bugging out of their sockets.

"I don't know. I can't answer that honestly. But I'm glad things happened the way they did. I needed to come here and spend time with you two and the Golden Girls. I needed this for me."

"Like an adult," Emma said without a hint of sarcasm. "What?" she asked as Charlotte looked at her in shock. "I've done stupid shit to escape before. People need to put more focus on their mental health and well-being. If selling your business for a bazillion dollars is what gets your mind right, go for it."

"Thanks," I said sincerely. "It helped, and FYI it wasn't a bazillion. But I won't lie, it *was* great to forget about it all. It brought up a lot of self-evaluating questions, like maybe it was me that had too much change going on, and I handled that horribly or something like that."

They both nodded this time. "I can't believe it," Emma said, smiling at me in a way that said, *I'm planning your wedding next.*

"Slow your roll, homeslice. You're putting the cart before the horse."

"Fine, fine," she relented.

"Did Nick fill you in on the demise of his relationship with Jillian? On the *why* of the whole thing?" I asked.

Both of them nodded again. "He came over and told us," Emma said.

"He seems okay, though, right? I mean, you've talked to him. He's totally over her, right?" I asked.

"Totally. I'm not sure he was ever really that sold on *her* in the first place. I think it was the *idea* of her."

"Good. That makes me feel a bit more on solid footing with him."

"We're all going out to eat tonight with the guys," I reminded them. "If either of you spill this, I'll definitely kick Charlotte's ass."

"Twice," they said, and promised not to utter a word.

* * *

I should have known they couldn't keep their lips zipped. The moment we got to Casey's for pizza, both Henry and Cooper gave me wry, knowing smiles.

"I'm going to kill you," I whispered to Charlotte, who laughed and ignored my threat by giving me the finger.

"You know the rule. Significant others do not count in the secrets department."

"Who else is coming?" I asked, wondering why they'd seated us at a table that fit ten people.

"The Golden Girls. They're looking forward to a night out on the town. They've been working hard and deserve it," said Emma.

"Gigi was going to come but she was tired, so I'm bringing her dinner home later," Charlotte explained. "Oh, here they come now," she said, pointing toward the door.

In they walked—Mancini, Clara, Pauline, and Viola—and we held our glasses up in celebration.

"To you, the Golden Girls of Hope Lake. Cheers."

"Where's our drinks?" Mancini asked primly. "Don't you know it's bad luck to give a toast when not everyone has a drink in hand?" She winked. The entire table laughed, and Henry waved over a waiter to take their orders.

When Nick arrived a few minutes later, I felt a shift. The entire table looked at him, and then turned to look at me. Everyone, including the Golden Girls, was smiling knowingly.

"Do I have something in my teeth?" he asked self-consciously. "Or toilet paper on my shoe?"

I shook my head. "No, nothing like that at all. Our friends are just looking for a dog-and-pony show, and we're going to give it to them." Before I lost the nerve, I turned to look at Nick. I took his head between my hands and planted a kiss on him that made my toes curl.

The table erupted in cheers, claps, hoots, and hollers. All of it directed at the two of us, and I couldn't be bothered listening to it.

Instead, I deepened the kiss, leaning into him.

"Parker," he finally whispered as we pulled away.

Out of the corner of my eye, I could see them all staring, waiting for us to separate before attacking us with questions that I wasn't sure I knew how to answer yet.

"What was that for?" he asked, leaning into my ear to whisper so that no one could hear him. Once again, he placed the lightest brush of his lips against the small birthmark by my ear.

"I was proving a point." I smiled, giving him one final kiss, but this time the urge to prove something was gone. This was more me quenching a need than giving them something to wag their tongues about. I hoped that by giving them a spectacle, I would validate that yes, there is or was or will be something between Nick and me, something that I wasn't embarrassed about or hiding. It was all laid out in the open for everyone to see.

"Well, anytime you want to prove that point, let me know. I'll always be game, Parker."

24

Thanks for the ride home. I know it's well out of your way," I said, walking side by side with Nick after dinner. He was parked at the very back of the Casey's Pub parking lot under a flickering bulb, which reminded me of the last time we were in this very spot.

And what it led to.

Would it again?

Admittedly, I was counting on him to make a move. Throughout the course of the night, sitting next to each other was both wonderful and torturous, because each time his hand migrated over to my leg, I smiled, and everyone saw it.

Not that it mattered. The cat was out of the bag.

Once we were ensconced in the truck, we sat silently, waiting for it to warm up. My hands were tucked beneath my legs, enjoying the heated seats against my cold fingertips.

Nick locked the doors and flipped on the wipers to get rid of the snow from the light flurry that had fallen while we were inside.

Turning to me, he smiled. The kind that lit you up from the inside, and I wondered how I ever thought I was going to resist him.

"We're not going home yet," he said with a wry smile. "I was promised cupcakes. I plan on getting *some*."

"Oh yeah?" I said, reaching over to tug on his collar.

It wasn't the beer, or the adrenaline, or even the memory of the last time we'd been here together. It was the current running between us that I wanted to capture.

"Parker, this wasn't the *some* I was referring to," he whispered, looking down at my lips.

I licked the lower one, pulling it between my teeth. "We *could* go to the bakery, but you should know I saved two cupcakes at my house."

I leaned over the center console, keeping my eyes locked on his.

"What are you waiting for?" he teased, kissing me soundly.

The windows were already fogging up as my hands reached into his hair, tugging at the soft curls at his neck.

We tried to inch closer together, but just as I was about to capture his lips again, a loud *tap, tap, tap* rang out against the driver's-side window. It was followed by a flashlight shining inside.

Nick slid his window down. "Chief Birdy," he said, his voice a singsong. "What brings you out this late tonight?"

I ducked my head, burying it into his shoulder and hoping that Birdy wouldn't know it was me.

"Ms. Adams, nice to see you're, uh, enjoying your stay in Hope Lake."

Birdy lowered the flashlight and grinned. "You go on somewhere private, now. I don't think anyone needs another viewing of this one's behind," he said, pointing to Nick.

I could hear his laughter the whole trip back to his patrol car.

Nick shouted out the window, "Sorry, Birdy!"

"Do I want to know?" I asked, placing my hand against my fore-head.

"Probably not."

* * *

The ride to my house was quick. I kept my hands to myself the entire time, though they were twisting in my lap anxiously. But the second Nick pulled onto the gravel lane of my lake house driveway, a spot where I knew we were safe from other cars, prying eyes, and patrolling police cars, I vaulted myself onto his lap.

"Whoa, whoa," he said, laughing as he pushed the truck into park.

My lips found his, slanting over them. Every single time I kissed him, I felt wild.

Nick pushed his lips against mine more firmly, his hands running over my shoulders and into my hair before using the belt loops on my jeans to tug me closer to him.

My hand reached down between the driver's seat and the door, trying to find the release that would send him back into a reclined position. "Wait, wait, we can get into the house," he urged, but I found the lever and pulled it, sending him backward as a response.

"Consider the great outdoors foreplay," I said, grinding myself against him.

Nick's eyes rolled back, his mouth fell open, and he didn't complain or stop me when I yanked open his flannel shirt, sending buttons pinging off the windows of his truck. "Oops," I said, lowering my lips to his chest. "Cold?"

He shook his head, laughing slightly when I got to his rib cage with my lips. "Parker," he said weakly, sucking in his lower lip when I ground down on him again.

"Foreplay, remember?" I took both of Nick's hands and moved

them behind the seat's headrest. "Stay," I instructed, pointing to him with my index finger.

Nick nodded, his eyes dark and stormy as he watched me remove my coat first, tossing it aside onto my seat. Then came my sweater, which left me in only a thin white shirt and my bra.

Nick's hands were fisted together behind the headrest, and judging by the strain on his face, I knew that he was itching to touch me.

"I don't know what it is about your truck," I whispered, pulling my shirt over my head. Nick's eyes didn't leave mine, which was unexpected, considering what I was doing.

Shifting my hips, I let myself relax into him. Feeling him beneath me, seeing the want in his eyes. "Parker," he choked, moving his hands quickly to my hips. "You've got to stop moving."

His teeth were gritted, his eyes were unfocused, and his breathing was labored. "Why?" I asked innocently, slowly rolling my hips over him again.

"Parker." His voice was barely audible, and I knew if I kept it up, we would both let go in the truck like two horny teenagers.

"It's okay, just feel." I shifted once more. Nick's hands were digging into my hips, guiding me to a pace that was going to send him over.

My hands were on my breasts, his eyes now glued to them as he panted through his orgasm.

My own rumbled through me when his hands reached up, settling over mine. I slumped back, accidentally beeping the horn when my back hit the wheel.

"I can't believe we're doing this," he said, rubbing his hands over his eyes. "I haven't done this in . . . forever."

"Well, I can tell you I'd never done this before I met you," I said honestly. When he looked at me disbelievingly, I explained. "I grew up in the city. No one I dated had a car. We only had the subway, and last I checked, humping on the train was frowned upon."

He laughed and sat up awkwardly. "Seems I have a bit of a mess on my hands."

"Come on, we're about to have a bigger mess. I've got a sturdy island and a cupcake with your name on it."

"What about extra frosting?"

"I like how you think, Nick."

25

It was the beginning of April, and while the snow was still threatening to pile up again, there was finally a light at the end of the tunnel.

"The lake is defrosting. For now, at least," I explained, wondering if we would fish in the spring or swim in the lake again like we had last summer.

Nick and I were officially unofficial. We were as inseparable as we could be, considering how busy we were, but when we were together, we were *together*.

Neither one of us was interested in putting a label on it. Part of me thought that was potentially a problem, considering we weren't great at being undefined, but this was different. We weren't hiding anymore, and the constant togetherness filled me with hope of what Nick and I would be in the future.

"I'm thinking that maybe we spend a couple weeks in the city soon," said Nick. "You can show me around your neck of the woods and maybe, I don't know, we'll see what happens there."

I looked up, confused. "Where is this coming from?"

He looked worried. "Bad idea?"

I shook my head. "No, no, I'm just . . . This is the first I've heard of this."

He shrugged. "I've been thinking about it for a while now."

"Nick, what are you saying?"

He smiled. "I'm saying that although I was hoping that you would want to stay here, I'm willing to come with you to New York too."

My hope ballooned up. It wasn't something that I ever thought he would consider, and it wasn't something I ever thought I would want. His whole life was spent here. He loved this town and to think that he'd leave it for me—well, I didn't have many words for that.

I sat him down before I sat down myself, facing him on a stool in the bakery. It was quiet, still too early to open, but there were people in the hall going to Charlotte's or going to work at The Vault.

"Nick, I love that you want to spend time there. I'd love that. But I love how you are here too. And honestly, I really love it here."

Four loves in one statement. If he didn't get the hint, I'd have to spell it out in cupcakes. In fact, maybe I would.

"I think that our place is here for now," I continued. "Or maybe we'll be snowbirds like the old folks do. We'll spend the fall and winter in New York, wishing it was warm like Florida, and then the rest of the year here."

"You'd do that?" he asked hopefully.

"Sure, why not? I mean, Viola isn't busy in the winter, and neither are you. We both would be here for the summer months since that's when your business is busy. And hopefully the bakery. I can still find someone else to help with the bakery schedule and whatever while I'm in New York, and if something happens, we can be here in two hours."

"Why does this all seem so simple and yet so perfect?" he asked, pulling me in for a kiss.

"I think because it is. I'd need to see if I can find somewhere permanent to live here."

"I've been thinking about selling the house. Henry and Charlotte want something of their own."

"Maybe then you and I look for something too. I hear that my lake house may be up for sale. I'd love to get my hands on that. When we're in the city, we'll probably need a bigger apartment since I lived in a shoe box with Charlotte."

"Are we really doing this?" he asked, standing and pulling me into a hug.

"Well, I think we are. What do you think? Are we crazy?"

"If we are, there's no one I'd rather be crazy with than you."

epilogue

Turns out, being snowbirds wasn't all it was cracked up to be. You actually needed to be in a warm place during the cold months of the year for it to work. And after spending an unseasonably cold week in April in New York, we realized that we both were happier in Hope Lake.

I was still keeping my city apartment for the time being, although I was now considering using it as an Airbnb at the advice of my finance guy.

Which meant I needed a full-time place to live. So when, true to town gossip, my Airbnb was put up for sale, I decided to buy it—and Nick wanted in too. While we weren't super traditional, having something like property connect us seemed fitting. It gave a permanence and a definition to our relationship that we didn't have before.

Nick and Henry decided to sell their shared house as is, instead of taking the time and money to renovate it, and Nick was fully moved into the lake house a week after we signed the paperwork. Even though it was a big next step, neither one of us was in a rush to add engagement and wedding talk into the mix. We were perfectly content being Parker and Nick. If it ain't broke . . .

"What are you up to?" Nick asked, sidling up to me at the counter. The marble was covered in neat stacks of paperwork. One was for recipes that we were working on, another was recipes we were making for the week, and a third was a pile of résumés from chefs who wanted to come to teach a class.

With the amount of interest we'd received both from young people and older folks, we had to develop a schedule that worked for everyone.

"Do you want to see the sketch for Emma's cupcakes?" I asked, giving him a quick kiss on the cheek.

I leaned back against him as he put his arms around my waist. "She didn't want something that screamed 'baby shower' since this is both her wedding and baby party rolled into one."

"That has to be challenging," he said, and he couldn't have been more right.

"*Challenging* is the nice way to put it. She's pregnant and driving me nuts with her demands, but I adore her and will do whatever I have to so that she's happy."

"I love that you love her. It means a lot to me that you've fit so seamlessly into the dynamic."

I smiled. "They're easy people to get along with. Even when they're hormonal and pregnant."

"Can you believe the wedding is in a month?" he said, pointing to the calendar on the wall. July twenty-third was circled with a big green heart, and Charlotte had scribbled *C & E* inside it. She had that moony look about her as well, and Nick mentioned that it was only a matter of time before Henry popped the question to her.

Nick and I were thankfully on the same page of the book titled *Marriage Isn't Something That We're Desperate For.*

"These look great," he said, tracing his finger over the drawing of a tower of cupcakes.

"They're all different flavors. It's basically a little bit of everything that Emma's been craving this whole pregnancy, plus a couple thrown in for Cooper."

"Banana?" Nick asked hopefully. He frowned when I shook my head. "I only make those for you," I insisted, pulling up the note cards for today's show.

"What time are you guys recording?" he asked, sliding his hands underneath my apron.

I swatted him away with a pink spatula. "Charlotte is next door and can see you trying to get some."

He shrugged. "Like they don't know what goes on in the back room. Here's a hint—it's the same thing that goes on when Henry visits her back room."

Nick rubbed his nose against the back of my neck, placing a gentle kiss there. "How much time do you have before the video?"

The bakery wasn't open, so I didn't need to worry about a customer coming in, but I didn't want to look thoroughly ravaged on camera either.

Listening to Nick's advice, I had begun inserting myself more and more into the productions, but never did a baking video myself. I never wanted the focus to be taken away from the ladies, but after they gave their blessing, I figured, why not?

"Mancini is supposed to be here in thirty, which means she'll be here in forty-five because she's never met an appointment time that she likes."

"I can do a lot in forty-five minutes."

"I suppose I can show you what's underneath this apron if you're good. What do you plan on baking?"

Nick nipped at my ear and tugged on the knot to release the apron. "Oops."

He picked up a blank index card and pretended to read. "I see we have all the ingredients we need: you and me."

acknowledgments

For Kimberly: If I could give you back all the patience you've shown me, I would ten-fold. Thank you for everything.

Molly Gregory and the incomparable team at Gallery: Thank you for everything, truly. You've made this the best experience possible, and I'm grateful.

For my family: Thank you for the endless patience while I toiled away on the Hope Lake series. I hope you will continue being patient while I work on something else. . . .

For the readers, bloggers, friends, and the romance community at large: You've made toeing the line between publicist and author a real treat. I can't thank you enough for the kindness, support, and all the love that you've given.

recipes

Can't make it to Hope Lake to visit The Baked Nanas?
Not to worry: you can make their recipes in your own kitchen!

I hope that you've found an overlying theme in the Hopeless Romantics book series: *Food!*

Whether it's a getting-to-know-you bite of pizza at Casey's or Mama Peroni making Emma her favorite pastina soup when she's feeling down, food is a great way to bring people together: couples, families, friends, strangers—anyone! The Baked Nanas are known for their wisdom and delightful treats, and Notte's date-night menu knows how to bring the romance.

Turn the page for some of the recipes that I love and included in *The Ingredients of You and Me*.

I'm hoping that if you make them, they too bring *your* friends and family together.

XOXO,
Nina

cucidati
(*Italian fig cookies*)

Italian fig cookies are a traditional Sicilian treat, but many other regions in Italy have their own spin on the recipe. Traditionally, they're made for Christmas, but in my family we make them for Easter as well and change up the decoration. I think many of the creatively decorated cookies that Italians make can be shared any time of year—these included!

INGREDIENTS

Filling

1 package 12-ounce (dried) figs

¾ cup raisins

1 cup chopped walnuts

zest of 1 orange

zest of ½ lemon

¼ cup orange marmalade

¼ cup honey (local is best)

2 tablespoons Galliano

1 tablespoon lemon extract

1 tablespoon cinnamon

¼ teaspoon cloves

Dough

3½ cups all-purpose flour

1 teaspoon baking powder

¼ teaspoon salt

2½ sticks unsalted butter
   (room temperature)

²/₃ cup granulated sugar

2 large eggs

1 cup shortening

1 tablespoon lemon extract

1 tablesoon vanilla extract

Icing

3 cups confectioners' sugar

1 teaspoon lemon extract

3 egg whites

(colored sprinkles if desired)

DIRECTIONS

1. Make the filling first. Using a food processor, grind figs, raisins, and walnuts until well blended. Add the rest of the ingredients and blend well. Set aside.

2. Sift flour, baking powder, and salt into a large mixing bowl. Hand-whisk in the sugar until well mixed.

3. Fold in the shortening with a pastry blender and work the mixture until it has a cornmeal-like consistency.

4. In a separate bowl, whisk together the rest of the dough ingredients.

5. Add to flour mixture. Mix by hand. Dough should be soft when finished mixing.

6. Flour surface and place dough ball on top. Roll into a large ball. When finished, wrap in plastic wrap and chill for an hour.

7. Once large ball is chilled, slice it into quarters. Cover quarters while working with one at a time. Roll out dough on floured surface. Section should be 12 inches long by 6 inches wide.

8. Take filling mixture and form a tube-like section. Place filling into the center of the dough. Fold dough over the center, and

roll the entire log a few times to "seal" where the opening was. Repeat until all dough and filling is gone.

9. Chill again for an hour.

10. Once logs are chilled, slice them into 3-inch pieces. Place on a cookie sheet and bake until golden brown (375°F for about 15 minutes).

11. Let cool while preparing icing.

12. In a chilled glass bowl, combine confectioners' sugar and extract. Add one egg white at a time by folding them into the sugar mixture until well combined. The icing should not be too runny.

13. Dip the rounded part of the cookie into the icing, place on parchment, and decorate with sprinkles (optional).

apfelkuchen
(German apple cake)

᭡

My aunt shared this recipe because I'm incapable of making an apple pie. My crust is always crumbly—and not in the good way. This is the recipe I give to anyone who shares in my inability to create a beautiful pie crust. I had a traditional one of these cakes in Berlin a couple summers ago, and I can tell you it's even more delicious there!

INGREDIENTS

5 large egg yolks

2 medium tart apples, peeled, cored, and halved

1 cup (2 sticks) plus 2 tablespoons unsalted butter, at room temperature

1¼ cups granulated sugar

2 cups all-purpose flour

2 tablespoons cornstarch

2 teaspoons cream of tartar

1 teaspoon baking powder

½ teaspoon salt

¼ cup 2% milk

confectioners' sugar, for dusting

DIRECTIONS

1. Preheat the oven to 350°F. Grease a 9-inch springform pan wrapped in a sheet of foil. Let the egg yolks stand at room temperature for 30 minutes.

2. Slice the apples into thin wedges.

3. Cream the butter and sugar until light and fluffy in a large bowl using a hand mixer. Add one egg yolk at a time, beating well after each addition. In another large bowl, sift the flour, cornstarch, cream of tartar, baking powder, and salt twice. Gradually beat into the creamed mixture on a slow setting, until well mixed. Add the milk; mix well (batter should be thick).

4. Spread the batter into the prepared pan. Gently press the apples, round side up, into the batter. Bake until a toothpick inserted into the center of the cake comes out with moist crumbs, 45 to 55 minutes. Cool on a wire rack for 10 minutes. Loosen the sides of the cake from the pan with a knife; remove the foil. Cool for 1 hour longer. Remove the rim from the pan. Dust the cake with confectioners' sugar.

hummingbird cake

Hummingbird cake is a Jamaican recipe named after their national bird. I never knew that until I watched a Food Network show about cultural desserts. It's one of my favorite cakes to make at Easter because it's fresh—and so delicious!

INGREDIENTS

For the cake:

3 cups all-purpose flour

2 cups granulated sugar

1 teaspoon baking soda

1 teaspoon salt

1½ cups canola oil

3 large eggs

1 (8-ounce) can crushed
   pineapple, drained

2 cups mashed bananas

1 cup chopped walnuts

For the frosting:

1 (8-ounce) package cream
   cheese, at room temperature

½ cup (1 stick) unsalted butter,
   at room temperature

1 pound confectioners' sugar

1 teaspoon vanilla extract

DIRECTIONS

1. Preheat the oven to 350°F.

2. Grease and flour two 9-inch cake pans.

3. To make the cake, sift together the flour, sugar, baking soda, and salt in a large bowl.

4. In a separate large bowl, combine the oil, eggs, pineapple, bananas, and walnuts.

5. Add the flour mixture and mix together by hand until well combined.

6. Pour the batter into the prepared pans. Bake for about 1 hour until a toothpick inserted comes out clean. Remove from the oven and allow to cool on wire racks (2 hours or more).

7. Prepare the frosting by blending together the cream cheese, butter, sugar, and vanilla until smooth. Evenly spread the frosting on the middle, sides, and top of the cake.

Italian wedding cookies
(*anise cookies*)

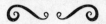

If you've ever been to an Italian bridal shower, you've surely seen the endless supply of homemade cookies from all the zias and nonnas in the room. The tables are filled with delicacies, and these are a staple! Delightful anise flavor packs a punch in every bite. You can use food coloring to change the color of the pretty standard icing so that the cookies become seasonal favorites. If anise isn't your flavor of choice, feel free to switch out the extract for another: vanilla, lemon, etc. The cookies remain delicious little treats.

INGREDIENTS

For the cookies:

⅔ cup vegetable oil

⅔ cup whole or 2% milk

2 tablespoons lemon extract

3 large eggs

½ cup plus 2 tablespoons granulated sugar

4 cups all-purpose flour

3 tablespoons baking powder

For the icing:

2 cups confectioners' sugar

1 tablespoon anise extract

whole or 2% milk (add in small amounts until desired thickness is reached)

DIRECTIONS

Cookies:

1. Preheat the oven to 375°F.

2. Combine the oil, milk, lemon extract, eggs, and sugar in a large mixing bowl. Using a hand mixer, on low speed, blend well. In a separate bowl, mix the flour and baking powder. Add the flour mixture in gradually, using your hands to create the dough. Dough shouldn't be too sticky; if it is, add more flour sparingly.

3. Shape into quarter-sized balls and place on a cookie sheet. Bake for 10 to 12 minutes or until lightly browned.

Icing:

1. Icing thickness is a preference. The thicker the icing, the better it stays on top of the cookie. Place the confectioners' sugar into a chilled bowl. Add anise extract and slowly add milk until desired thickness is reached.

2. Dip the top (rounded) part of the cookie into the icing. Allow to dry completely before storing in an airtight container to preserve freshness.

3. Icing can also be dyed with food coloring for seasonal cookies. Use less milk if using liquid food coloring. (Gel is also good.) You can also add sprinkles or decorated elements.

ciambellone
(Italian tea cake)

⁖

Each region of Italy seems to have their own version of this cake. Some use fruit and nuts, others keep it simple with just the light fruit flavor. Either way you make it, it's the perfect light dessert to enjoy with a cappuccino after a family dinner.

INGREDIENTS

1 tablespoon anise seeds (previously soaked in water for an hour and then drained)

1 cup granulated sugar

3½ cups all-purpose flour

3 tablespoons baking powder

grated orange peel (1 small orange)

3 tablespoons shortening

1 tablespoon unsalted butter, at room temperature

3 large eggs

1 cup whole milk

1 cup freshly squeezed orange juice

1 tablespoon anise extract

½ cup each of raisins, walnuts (chopped), maraschino cherries (drained)

confectioners' sugar, for dusting

DIRECTIONS

1. Preheat the oven to 375°F. Coat a 10-inch bundt or tube cake pan with nonstick cooking spray and dust with flour. Tap out any excess flour from the pan.

2. Sift the anise seeds, sugar, flour, baking powder, and orange peel in a large bowl. Mix the shortening, butter, eggs, milk, orange juice, and anise extract in a stand mixer. Combine flour mixture into milk mixture slowly.

3. Drop half of the batter in large scoopfuls equally around your cake pan. Sprinkle the nuts, cherries, and raisins, add more batter, then smooth, and tap the pan on the counter a few times to ensure there are no trapped air bubbles.

4. Bake for about 40 minutes, checking in at the 30-minute mark to rotate the pan for even coloring, and to ensure it's not baking faster than anticipated. Cake is done when a toothpick or tester inserted into the cake comes out batter-free (crumbs are fine).

5. Cool in pan for an hour or until it comes out of the pan easily.

6. Sprinkle with confectioners' sugar once cooled.